PROMISE OF HEAVEN, PROMISE OF HELL

by

SURREAL

CHIMERA

Alice – Promise of Heaven. Promise of Hell first published
in 2002 by
Chimera Publishing Ltd
PO Box 152
Waterlooville
Hants
PO8 9FS

Printed and bound in Great Britain by
Cox & Wyman Ltd, Reading.

ALICE
Promise of Heaven. Promise of Hell

Surreal

This novel is fiction – in real life practice safe sex

'Then, Alice, you have nothing to worry about. Except the punishment I am going to mete out to you in a few minutes.'

Alice scowled. Her heart missed a beat. 'What punishment?'

'The strap, Alice. The sharp shock I spoke of. And then I shall take you back to Carters where I wouldn't be surprised if Miss Lake didn't thrash you again.'

Alice's face reddened. Anger boiled. 'You've no right to beat me. You're not my father.'

'No, thankfully, but I am your legal guardian. Would you like me to terminate your education? To pull you from Carters? I'm quite entitled to do so, you know.'

'No, please, I like Carters. I've been there for years now.'

'Then you have no choice, do you Alice?'

She glared, her only possible defiance.

Barker produced the strap; a wide, lengthy barber's strop he used to sharpen his razor. 'A first for you, eh, Alice?'

She hid her emotion, not wanting him to see the fear. Voice lost, she nodded.

Richard tapped his thigh with the brute. 'I hope this will suffice to turn you back onto the straight and narrow. If you're as clever as they say you are, then you'll straighten yourself out. Now turn around and bend over. Touch your toes.'

Prologue

I met Alice Hussey about ten years ago. Retired from Holy Orders as I understood, she eked an existence in the Sussex coastal town of Worthing. Living next door at the time, I helped to make her rented accommodation comfortable.

A friendly, approachable and down to earth woman, Alice and I held many a long chat, the lady often recounting the lighter side of life. She didn't, however, divulge the more intimate aspects until a particular and somewhat embarrassing incident some months later.

Having offered to help paint the lounge, I came to question that rash nature when waking to the hottest day of the year. But never one to disappoint, I donned white T-shirt and shorts and embarked resolute on the short walk next door. Alice, bless her, offered the chance for postponement, but not wishing to appear insincere I insisted; one of my better decisions, as it transpired.

So with the temperature approaching the mid-eighties we embarked on the task with grim determination.

Alice, a lithe, sprightly and attractive fifty-one, entered the chore with unbridled enthusiasm. She even suggested tongue firmly in cheek that we might go about the task in the raw. Happy go lucky lady that she was, she could provide enough laughs without my help.

The room at its hottest and yours truly at the top of the ladder, paintbrush in hand, I heard the announcement. 'Tea up!' Mind still on the job I missed my footing and took the shortest route to the floor, my only concern for the carpet. I did succeed in containing the spillage, the dip between hips filling with *eau de nil* (yes, I do retain a dip there – well, laying down I do).

Alice didn't give a damn for the furnishings, my welfare foremost in her mind. Having checked I suffered no injury

5

she set about mopping the puddle, my remonstrations met by, 'Don't be silly. I've seen it all before. You are no different anatomically to any other man.'

What could I say? The pool of viscous light green fluid dutifully scraped away she surveyed the whites, pronouncing, 'They'll have to come off.'

'It'll dry,' I assured her.

She laughed, an infectious chortle, and asked, grinning, 'Shy about your willy, are you?'

I defended, 'I was brought up in the belief that it should remain private.'

The dispute only banter, she returned, 'You do realise that half the billions raping God's earth are male. Men with the same genitalia as you. And I as Sister Clare have tended to hundreds, if not thousands in the naked state.'

'I'm not sick, Alice,' I argued. I knew she only joked, but there hung an electricity in the air. A sensuous tension. And to be honest, the prospect of her stripping paint from my crotch did appeal.

She lifted my shirt and examined the skin beneath. 'It's penetrated. Look, your belly is green. Do you want your precious vitals tainted? I know how much they mean to the dominant male.'

'It's only emulsion. It'll peel.'

'At least let me pop next door and get you a change of clothes. You can have a wash while I'm gone.'

That I didn't argue with.

The bathtub had been ripped out pending the plumber's return. So I took advantage of the sink in the kitchen. I guessed Alice would be hooked up talking to my Pam for a half-hour, and I would have plenty of time to wash.

Standing naked at that unit I heard the door open. I froze, and then cautiously looked over a shoulder. Alice stood in the doorway, clean shirt and shorts in hand.

'Oh,' I breathed.

'Did you do that when you fell off my ladder?' she asked.

Dying of embarrassment I felt my face warm. 'No,' I answered. 'The wife did that last night with a rattan.'

'Cane, you mean?'

'Yes.' On the very eve of that hard day's toil I had beseeched my good lady wife to flog my backside with a supple rod, the subsequent marks quite outstanding, that being the primary reason for wanting to keep my pants on. I have long ceased to be abashed about the airing of genitals.

'Punished?' she enquired, raising an eyebrow, obviously amused.

I faced her, she having the strength of character not to dip her line of sight. 'No Alice, I asked her to.'

'I see.' She said no more.

An awkward silence ensued; Alice still poised in the doorway with my fresh clothes in hand.

'Do you want me to go and never darken your door again?' I enquired, suitably humbled. I could think of nothing worse than being found out by an ex-nun.

'Oh goodness gracious me,' she said absently. 'Of course not.'

'Can I have my clothes then?' The naked state wore thin.

She approached and handed them to me. 'Sorry,' she excused. 'Seeing those stripes threw me completely.'

I dressed. We sat down to a hot mug of tea. 'Alice,' I said.

'Yes?'

'Is there a big black hole around here I could crawl up and die in?'

'You're upset?'

'Mortified.'

'It's my fault. I shouldn't have walked in like that.'

'You weren't to know. If I wasn't a pervert it wouldn't have happened.'

'John! You are no pervert.'

'What, enjoying having my backside thrashed is normal?'

'For you, yes. It's the way the Almighty set your cap. If pain pleases, then why not?'

'I wish everybody held that attitude.'

'People will always look for a whipping boy.' She laughed, her face radiating bonhomie. 'What I am trying to say, is that certain ignoramus will always vilify what they don't understand, although they have the odd skeleton or two rattling in their own cupboard.

'Can you face your God when you exit this mortal sphere? That is the main question. Can you?'

'Alice, I am what I am. I am not ashamed of what I am. I just don't wish to broadcast it or alienate you.'

'John, we are brother and sister in that respect. I sympathise totally with your needs. I retain certain longings in that department, although at my age they are unlikely to be assuaged.'

Uncertain, I sought ratification. 'Are you saying you have a taste for the rod?'

'For many years,' she answered.

I experienced a murmur below as an idea struck. A sick proposal. 'Erm, Alice...'

'Yes?'

'You don't still have your nun's habit, do you?'

'And which habit do you refer to? Biting my nails? Playing dip the wick on hot sultry lonely nights? Or smoking reefers in the catacombs?'

'The one you wore.'

'Oh, that. Why do you ask?'

'To be whipped by a nun, I can think of nothing more stimulating.'

'And what would Pam have to say about that?'

'She wouldn't mind. You see, Alice, and I'm sure you'll understand, she fears for my health. She won't take me to the limit. Now a severe drubbing from a zealot, without favour to my behind, that would be something to endure.'

'And you think I could flog you without care for injury? I've warmed to you, John. I wouldn't want to hurt you.'

'Not hurt. Fulfil. You must realise what I mean.'

She smiled. 'I do. Now if I don the black and white and administer cruelty to your behind, what can I expect in return?'

'The same, Alice.'

'Do you have a habit? Because you won't fit into mine.'

'I could wear no more than a thong.'

'What makes you think I would want you to wear that much?'

'No thong, then.'

'You could always go to that fancy dress shop on Barton Street.'

'What, for a birthday suit?'

'How about a rubber diving suit?'

'Hot!'

'I joke.'

I finished my tea. 'Are you up for it, Alice?'

'Don't you find me a little old for sexual horseplay?'

'You're a fine looking woman. No, I'd rather enjoy the experience.'

'So, what would you expect?'

'Blow by blow, you mean?'

'Precisely.'

'Do you have any implements?'

'None whatsoever.'

'If I brought a cane over later, we could have a get to know each others limits rehearsal.'

'What, with the state of your bum?'

'Ah, there you have it, Alice. Would the true draconian say that?'

'Probably not. I knew a certain mother superior that didn't.'

'You'll have to tell me about that.'

'My life story, perhaps.'

'I would be fascinated.'

'You haven't heard it yet.'

So it was. Over the next few weeks Alice told me her story. I will never forget the lady, or the rigorous strokes she pounded my bum with. She lived a traumatic life in her youth. How she survived to possess such a lively and lovely nature I will never know. Sister Clare, however, existed for only a short period of a turbulent life. As that unfolded I understood the pretence.

This is her story.

Chapter One

Alice Rose entered the world in Southport, Lancashire.
The daughter of Edith and Reginald Hussey she was soon
placed beneath the ecclesiastical umbrella of the Catholic
domain. For those first few impressionable years her
mother and grandparents raised Alice, the father away in
North Africa doing his bit for king and country.

Demobbed after the war, Reginald returned to a daughter
that barely knew him, though the delicate and bonny young
girl soon warmed to him. A love affair quickly ensued,
one that would last until his premature death ten years
later.

With the shortage of male labour, Reg soon found work
as a factory hand. A conscientious employee, hard
working and loyal, he rose rapidly through the ranks. By
1951 he enjoyed the rewarding position of General
Manager.

The young Alice, apple of Reg's eye, wallowed in the
financial security that offered. Having passed her eleven
plus with ease, she entered as a boarder, the sanctum of
The Carter Academy for Girls at Stoke on Trent; a private
school that possessed a formidable reputation for
scholastic results.

Although the faculty participated, as did most in those
days, in corporal punishment as both discipline and a
deterrent, Alice avoided all confrontation. A model pupil
she applied herself with determination. Her father urged
her to do well, and Alice relentlessly pursued top grades.

By 1956 she had toppled the Academy's record for
examination passes. Alice looked to the future and the
prospect of her finals.

Then that year disaster struck. Her parents travelled to
Blackpool for a long weekend, Alice staying at the boarding

school. That memorable two days were terminated by one of the most violent storms in history. Reg, determined to be back home in time to prepare a report for the following Monday, ran the gauntlet of torrential rain and blinding lightning.

The evening sky as black as night, the headlights on his car inadequate, he left the road on a tight bend and rolled the vehicle into the River Douglas. Initially unconscious, he and Edith both perished by drowning.

Alice awoke to a prod from the housemother. 'Miss Trimble. What is it?'

'The headmistress wants to see you in her office, Alice. Just slip a dressing gown on and I'll escort you over there.'

Puzzled, wondering why, desperately trying to think of what she could have done wrong, Alice followed the portly figure of Trimble into the night and across a courtyard to the head's office.

There she found a concerned Miss Lake and an ashen-faced Uncle Richard. Her stomach lurched. She realised there could only be one reason for the relative to be there.

'Alice.' Miss Lake greeted her with a weak smile. 'Please sit down. Your uncle has something to tell you. Grave news, I'm afraid.'

'It's father, isn't it?' she surmised, desperately hoping it wouldn't be.

Richard wrung his hands. A small, balding man dressed in tweed sports jacket and dark trousers he avoided eye contact, the round wire glasses he wore reflecting the artificial light. 'I'm sorry, Alice. I'm so sorry. There's no easy way of saying this. Your mother and father were both killed in a car accident this evening.'

Her world disintegrated. 'No,' she whispered. 'Tell me it isn't true. Not both of them, surely.' Tears welled. She felt sick. Numb. All meaning evaporated. Nothing made sense.

She studied her hands, fingernails drawing blood from the palms. Strangely, she felt no pain. 'What happened,

Uncle Richard?' she asked, dismissing the surroundings as a bad dream. 'How did they die?' She would wake in a minute and feel ecstatic. The horror would fade and she would be doubly grateful, at least until lunchtime.

'You remember the storm earlier this evening?'

Alice nodded.

'They were heading home from Blackpool in that. According to the police the conditions were a nightmare. My brother-in-law lost control on a tight bend. Visibility would have been close to zero at the time. The car rolled and plunged into the river. It was an hour or so, they think, before anybody noticed. Of course, by then it was all too late.'

'Where are they now?'

'In the mortuary.'

'Have you seen them?'

'Yes. Formal identification was necessary.'

'They're not mangled, are they?'

'No, Alice. They look as if they're asleep.'

'I want to see them; say my goodbyes.'

'Maybe I could sort something out in a day or two. I'll have to think about it. I'm not sure you should. You're young. Impressionable. Perhaps it would be better if you remembered them as they were.'

'No, Uncle Richard, I want to visit them.'

'Your uncle is right, Alice,' Miss Lake concurred.

Her heart rent and wishes seemingly denied, Alice reared. 'They are my parents and I fucking well want to see them! Why won't you fucking listen to me?'

'Alice!' rebuked Lake. 'That is quite enough of that foul language.'

'Is it? Well, Miss Stagnant Pool, I happen to feel like swearing. Life's a fucking shit! A bloody sodding shit! You work like a slave and all you get is pissed on by that prick up on high!'

Lake leapt up and slammed a cane on the desk. 'Enough!' she yelled. 'How dare you swear and insult the Almighty?' She glared at Alice, the girl's defiance as black as the storm that killed her parents. Lake shook her head, fire abating. 'I know, Alice, this is a terrible time for you. I understand how you must feel. But please, that sort of attitude will not change matters. You must face the future with courage.'

Richard Barker added his unwanted advice. 'I think you should apologise, Alice.'

'Should I, uncle? Should I care? I mean, what's life got for me now? What will you do if I refuse? Beat me with that cane? Thrash me until I do? Do you honestly think I'll feel it? Do you honestly believe I give a fuck?'

'Alice, you are now my responsibility. I won't have you swearing. I won't stand for you profaning. You are not doing justice to your father's memory. He was very proud of you. You can serve him best by being a model student.'

'He's dead! Mother's dead! And I might as well be dead.'

'I expected tears, Alice. But there are none. All I see before me is a hysterical child. I thought you had more gumption. Now, I have matters to discuss with Miss Lake, so if you wouldn't mind waiting outside.'

'Miss Trimble will stay with you, Alice,' assured Lake.

Wordless, tearless, Alice left.

'Will you be leaving Alice with us?' the headmistress enquired.

'I don't know. It all depends on the will. If my brother-in-law has left sufficient funds for her future then I don't see a problem. However, if he hasn't, then I'll have to think again. You see, Reg did well in life. I was not so fortunate. I have little in the way of funds. I must admit, I never considered taking my niece on full time. But I assure you, I will do my best by her.'

'That outburst is most unlike her. She shows enormous potential. A highly intelligent and tenacious young woman. She is no age to suffer such a loss. Removing her from Carters I think would only serve to hurt her further.'

'As I said, it all depends on whether sufficient funds have been allocated.'

'And if they are not, what then?'

'I don't honestly know.'

'It might be worth looking into the possibility of gaining a grant. If not a council one, then maybe a private backer. She's worth the investment. We expect her to do well in her finals. She has mentioned she would like to go on and study sociology at degree level. Carters offer excellent college facilities. We may not have the fame or resources of Oxford or Cambridge, but with Alice's capabilities I'm sure she could secure that qualification.'

'Thank you for your time and concern, Miss Lake. If I could leave Alice in your capable hands for the time being I would be grateful. There is much to be sorted. I'll notify you of the funeral date.'

'Alice's fees are paid until the end of term. That is in six weeks. There will be no problem until then.'

Richard Barker left that office. Alice sat emotionless staring into space, Miss Trimble unsure how to console her.

'I'm going now, Alice,' Barker informed her.

'Thanks for coming, uncle.'

'That's okay. I'll ring Miss Lake when I've sorted out the funeral. Perhaps you could get a taxi down.'

'To say my goodbyes, you mean.'

'Yes.'

'What funeral directors will you use?'

'The best, Alice; Goodman and Goodman.'

'In Southport?'

'Yes.'

'Mother and father will be kept there until the funeral, yes?'

'That's usual.'

'What will you do with my house?'

'I don't know. I haven't read the will yet.'

'Father lodged that with his solicitor, didn't he?'

'I believe so.'

'Let me know, uncle. Let me know if I have lost my home as well.'

'You'll always have a home, Alice. Mine.'

'You're too kind.'

On that note Richard departed.

'He seems a very nice man, Alice,' remarked Trimble.

'He does, doesn't he,' came the girl's sole comment.

Two days later Richard received a phone call. 'Mr Barker? This is Teresa Lake, headmistress at Carter's Academy.'

'Yes, Miss Lake. What can I do for you?'

'I'm afraid Alice has gone missing. She went to her dormitory at the usual time last night. She was there at the midnight check, but missing this morning at breakfast. I've called the police and they are checking the train station, etcetera. She left no note and took no clothes that we know of.'

'The stubborn little… I think I might know where she's bound. I'll ring you back if I'm right. Apart from absconding in the middle of the night, how is she coping?'

'Much the same as you saw. She's rude, awkward, and refuses to apply herself. But she'll get over it in time, I'm sure. We must be patient.'

'Lack of application I can understand, but not rudeness. She'll have to be pulled up sharply if that continues.'

'In the years Alice has been with us I have never had to reprimand her. I rather hope I can leave that record unblemished.'

'And for running away? Do you intend to let that go unpunished?'

'That will depend on the reason.'

'Whatever that may be, Miss Lake, it is extremely remiss of her to run off without a word to anyone.'

'I agree. But the softly, softly approach may yield more beneficial results.'

'Of course I will leave that entirely up to you. I know what I would have received in my day, and I would not have cared to sit for some time after.'

'That of course is always an option. In fact, the school rules would normally invoke such punishment. However, I feel I must consider the circumstances carefully.'

'The circumstances have nothing to do with her attitude. Running off, rude, awkward and plain idle. She's wayward and needs pulling up sharply. If she gets away with this then what's to stop her repeating the episode, or worse? Surely I don't need to point out how adolescents rear at authority. The cane keeps them in their place. It is the only treatment they respond to. I won't tell you how to do your job, Miss Lake. Far be it for me to know better, but I *will* hold you responsible for her future behaviour.'

'There is something in what you say, Mr Barker. I will decide when Alice returns.' The headmistress replaced the receiver, deep in thought. If she overlooked the girl's misdemeanour she might give the wrong impression. She also had to consider the rest of her pupils. If she let Alice off with a lecture, then the other girls might see it as favouritism, or even weakness.

Richard Barker drove to Goodman and Goodman's parlour. Leaving the car parked outside he went in.

'Ah, Mr Barker,' greeted Goodman senior. 'To what do I owe the pleasure?'

Typically curt, Barker enquired, 'Have you had a visitor this morning? A pretty girl by the name of Alice. About five foot nine. Slim. Red auburn hair. Green eyes. Most likely dressed in a school uniform; green blazer and skirt.'

'Ah, the late Mr and Mrs Hussey's daughter. Yes, she sits with them at this very minute.'

'I'd like to speak with her.'

'She's in the chapel of rest.'

Goodman showed Richard Barker through.

'Alice, what the devil do you think you're doing?' he demanded. 'Running off without a word. Everybody's worried sick. Miss Lake was so concerned she called the police. You, young lady, are in a lot of trouble.'

Alice looked up, eyes red, tears staining her face. 'It's my right, uncle. You wouldn't even talk about my seeing them, let alone condone it. So, I took it upon myself. They're burying them next week. It would have been too late if I'd waited for you.'

Richard stared at Goodman, pale blue eyes cold, challenging. The man took the hint and left.

'It doesn't end here, you know. I can't have you running off without a by your leave whenever the fancy takes you. You have a responsibility. You're old enough, for goodness sake. You should know better.'

'Do whatever you will, uncle. At least I've seen my parents now. That you can't take from me.'

'I'm not looking to take anything from you, my girl. All I ask is for you to listen to your elders and betters.'

'So, I'm listening. What now?'

'I'll take you home.'

'And?'

'That will depend entirely on what you have to say for yourself.'

'You mean, if I fall to my knees, confess my sins, you'll forgive me?'

'That's no more than I would expect from you. Don't forget you also are a Roman Catholic. You may have swept it under the carpet because it doesn't suit, but you may find you're in for a rude awakening. I am proud of my faith, Alice. Your insolence and ridicule will not solve anything. You just make matters worse.'

Barker drove the girl home in silence. Leading her into the house, the living room a shrine to the Catholic Church, he demanded, a harsh edge to his tone, 'Well? I'm waiting.'

She shrugged. 'I'm sorry, uncle. Is that what you want to hear?'

Indignation simmered. 'No Alice, that is not what I want to hear. You were wrong to flout my wishes. You were blatantly disobedient. You bordered on gross misconduct, absconding. What shall I do with you? That is the question.'

'I dare say you'll come up with something.'

'You have an acid tongue. Why don't you like me, Alice? What have I done to make you hate me?'

'I don't know you, uncle. How can I like or dislike? Although you only live a couple of miles from us you rarely visit. And when you do it's because you want something.'

'What are you suggesting? That I'm a scrounger? That I used my brother-in-law because he had money? How dare you? How dare you say such a thing? I loved my sister and she me. We didn't live out of each other's pockets. We had our own lives to lead.'

'Really? Why did I hear father say that he only ever saw you when you wanted to borrow something, usually money? Which you never paid back.'

'That's a downright lie! Insolent puppy! Oh, how Reg used to crow about you. My daughter this and my daughter that. Butter wouldn't melt in your mouth. True, I never really got to know you, and having the chance now, I don't know if I want to.

'So far you have proved to be foul-mouthed, undependable, irresponsible and a liar. Perhaps a short, sharp, painful shock is what's required.'

'I wondered when you'd get around to that. Father always said you were a bully, and that you suggested I should be beaten for ridiculously minor things.'

'Eavesdrop a lot, did you? Listen at doors? You always were a snot-nosed troublemaker.'

'And now you're lumbered with me.'

'Oh no, I'm not. Either your inheritance pays for you to stay at Carters, or I place you in the care of a suitable boarder. Either way I shall have as little to do with you as possible.'

'So much for looking after me. I shall stay at Carters, have no fear of that. Father left me a trust fund. And I know he did. He told me so.'

'Then, Alice, you have nothing to worry about. Except the punishment I am going to mete out to you in a few minutes.'

Alice scowled. Her heart missed a beat. 'What punishment?'

'The strap, Alice. The sharp shock I spoke of. And then I shall take you back to Carters where I wouldn't be surprised if Miss Lake didn't thrash you again.'

Alice's face reddened. Anger boiled. 'You've no right to beat me. You're not my father.'

'No, thankfully, but I am your legal guardian. Would you like me to terminate your education? To pull you from

Carters? I'm quite entitled to do so, you know.'

'No, please, I like Carters. I've been there for years now.'

'Then you have no choice, do you Alice?'

She glared, her only possible defiance.

Barker produced the strap; a wide, lengthy barber's strop he used to sharpen his razor. 'A first for you, eh, Alice?'

She hid her emotion, not wanting him to see the fear. Voice lost, she nodded.

Richard tapped his thigh with the brute. 'I hope this will suffice to turn you back onto the straight and narrow. If you're as clever as they say you are, then you'll straighten yourself out. Now turn around and bend over. Touch your toes.'

Reluctant, the girl obeyed. Barker admired the offering before lifting the pleated skirt and laying it over her back. Beneath he noted white sheer panties stretched over toned buttocks, partially see-through, the shadowy division visible.

A sharp intake of breath in order, having not been with a woman in years, Richard ogled those scantily covered cheeks. Alice waited with no idea of what to expect. She had only seen the tearstained faces return after a session with the headmistress. Teeth clenched, she waited apprehensively.

She caught the movement of his lower body and filled her lungs, holding that air in anticipation. Her uncle, intent on making an impression, raised the strop shoulder high. Determined she would reel to the consequence, he powered the leather through an arc, the parting of air dramatic. The strop slapped noisily, wrapping to her hip, an incendiary left in its wake.

Horror gripped as fire filled her rump, the jolt to her mind disturbing. Her stomach contracted, seemed to climb her throat, bile burning the windpipe, adding to the discomfort. Tenacious, the pain refused to subside. Insufferable it lingered, her cheeks ignited.

Richard, raised on corporal punishment and religious fervour, genuinely believed in 'spare the rod and you spoil

19

the child'. In his mind unruly behaviour, no matter what the reason, should be met with inflexible discipline. He levied a second to her stinging nates.

The crack resounding, Alice reared, hands gripping that traumatised flesh. Back arched, chest out, she hopped from foot to foot, pretty countenance fraught.

Firm of purpose, Richard barked, 'Back over, Alice!'

Rubbing burning haunches until the last second, she grudgingly obliged.

'Lift your skirt, girl. And if you don't stay down this time I'll strap you on the bare backside.'

Those words affected. Pulling the skirt up she felt a pleasant sensation below. A tingling, electric feeling deep in her groin. She had no time to analyse before that thick strop welted her behind for the third time. She sucked air, her lungs in spasm.

How many would he give her? How many times must she endure the punishing crack of leather on backside? Never beaten before, she found the trial harrowing, to say the least.

A fourth slapped noisily. A horde of scorpions injected their venom. Alice gripped her ankles ferociously, knuckles white, the cumulative pain unbearable.

Not only the violence galled. The act of offering her inadequately covered bottom humiliated. Bending the way she was obliged to, humbled. Having to take the beating at all, riled.

She reeled to another solid slap, the knot in her chest tightening. *One more*, she thought. *And that's all I'm prepared to take*.

That one soon visited, Alice's lower bottom scarlet, stinging, cheeks hot and burning. She rose, hands automatically tending the hurt.

'What did I tell you not two minutes ago?' Richard fumed.

'That's it,' the girl announced. 'You're not hitting me any more. You're not my father, and as far as I'm concerned you'll never take his place.'

'What would you prefer, Alice? Me as your guardian,

or the streets?'

She scowled. 'What do you mean?'

'If I refuse to look after you then where would you go? That would mean no home. No Carters. No degree. You'd be forced to mix with the scum of the gutter. That would do a lot for your airs and graces, wouldn't it?'

Alice paled.

'Hadn't thought of that, had you? So the choice is yours. Either you bend back over or we're finished.'

Bottom lip pouting, she considered the threat.

'I'm waiting, Alice…'

'How many?' she asked, prolonging the agony.

'As many as I care to give you. And the more you antagonise me the worse it will be.'

Face furious, she lifted her skirt and doubled over again.

'Pants off.'

'Pardon?'

'I told you, my girl, that if you rose during punishment I would discipline you on the bare behind. Now, pants off.'

She straightened, face red with anger, hot with embarrassment. 'You can't be serious. You can't expect me to bare all to you, can you?'

'I don't only expect, Alice, I insist.'

Unable to look him in the eye, the demand degrading, she placed her hands beneath her skirt and pulled her panties down. The skirt lifted, she bent, Barker scrutinising the damage. Her lower bottom flushed; fine welts flourished where the strop had struck.

Trembling slightly he reached out and lay a palm to that offended rump, the girl flinching to the cool comfort. Alice disgusted by the touch, he stroked, mentally denying the pleasure he gained. Although brought up in a loving, caring environment where a cuddle never went amiss, she knew Richard's approach to be wrong.

But she said nothing for fear of angering him further. He ceased and she knew pain to be imminent.

The smack violent, noisy, she whimpered with the severity, the pain sickening. Before she could draw breath

21

Richard hit her again. Unable to cope, her threshold low, she sobbed, the air leaving her lungs in spasmodic gasps.

Her uncle treated that anguished conclusion with further hostility, he of the mind that her suffering be just.

She took a round dozen before rebelling. Unable to cope, her buttocks too sore to contemplate, she again straightened. Hoping soul-felt pleas might affect her uncle's rigid demeanour, she begged. 'Please, Uncle Richard, it's too much. You're really hurting me. I'll be black and blue.'

'Too much?' The reply mortified. 'Too much? Who do you think you are to tell me it's too much? And as for hurting, it is supposed to hurt. The strap is meant to chasten. Perhaps you'll think twice before running wild again.

'And as for being black and blue, you exaggerate. You're young; your bottom is well able to withstand. No, it is your inability to take your comeuppance.' Richard sneered, ridiculing. 'Look at important Alice Hussey. I'm too good to be spanked, even if I do deserve it. Well, miss goody two shoes, I've got news for you. Unless you do exactly what you're told you'll get the same again, except worse.'

'But you're finished now, aren't you?' she asked hopeful.

'Oh no, Alice. Not by a long chalk. My doctrine preaches that humiliation should be a substantial part of the punishment. Lest we forget ourselves and place too high an emphasis on our insignificant lives. Pain is to remind us of our immortality.

'So how better to humble yourself than to stand naked before me? Then to accept without complaint any penance I decide upon. You do that, Alice, and I may begin to believe you are truly repentant.'

'Naked?' Her mouth fell open. 'You want me to take my clothes off? You're mad! You've remained unmarried too long.'

'You evil-minded tramp!' Barker's hand struck her face before she could react. 'You will learn subservience. And you will accept your place before you leave this house.

Now, take your clothes off.'

'No!' Defiant, she challenged her uncle.

'Very well, you leave me no choice. Get out.'

'Go back to Carters, you mean?'

'I don't care, Alice. I wash my hands of you.'

She gently rubbed her stinging behind, puzzled. 'Just like that?'

He nodded, and picking up the daily paper, began to read.

'What happens when school finishes for the summer holidays?'

'You seem so sure of yourself, you tell me.'

'My fees run out then, don't they?'

'Yes, Alice, they do.' He raised an eyebrow and held her with a fixed gaze. 'You could always get a job, I suppose. Maybe even sell yourself on the streets. You have the assets and the looks. Although prostitution does tend to age a person prematurely. Of course, your education would go straight down the toilet. No finals.'

'I could get myself a part-time job and a flat in Stoke.'

'Yes, Alice, you could even grow wings and fly.'

'What's that supposed to mean?'

'For a flat you would need references and a deposit. The hours a girl of your age would have to work to pay for fees, rent, electricity, gas, rates, clothing, books, food would be extensive to say the least. I take it you don't need sleep?'

'Have I burned my bridges with you?'

'Not at all, Alice. I am a devotee of the Almighty. Compassion is part of my creed. All you have to do is say you are sorry for your outburst and we will put it behind us.'

'You still intend to make me take my clothes off though, and beat me further?'

'Alice, I have no intentions of making you strip.'

'No?' She breathed a sigh of relief.

'No. You will do that voluntarily. And you will subject yourself to another session with the strap.'

'Compassion? That's a joke, isn't it?'

Richard licked his lips. 'I didn't expect to end up looking after you, Alice. I didn't beget you. I haven't had the pleasure of your growing up. Seeing you blossom. You expect to continue your education at my expense. You expect me to furnish you with all you need. You, Alice, expect.

'I will, naturally. Without complaint. Is that not compassion? All I ask in return is that you show me due reverence and some civility. That you accept my guidance. That you accept being in the wrong. That you don't know it all.

'You think I punish you for my own benefit? You have a temper, Alice. You have an arrogance. If you are to meet with success in life you have to learn to accept when you are wrong, and the appropriate punishment.'

Richard made some obscure sense. Guilt descended. 'I'm sorry, uncle.'

'Sense at last.'

'I'll take the punishment.'

'That is very magnanimous of you.'

Embarrassed, she asked, 'Are you going to watch me take my clothes off?'

'You find that demeaning?'

Her face coloured. She loosened the tie about her throat, and then she about-faced and began unfastening the buttons of her blouse.

'Face me, Alice.' Richard adjusted his spectacles. 'Don't you know it's rude to turn your back on someone?'

Indignant she obeyed, the top four buttons loose. Trembling she persevered, finally pulling the blouse apart and removing it from her shoulders.

Richard considered the lacy white brassiere she wore. 'Is that underwear standard uniform?' he asked, abrupt.

'I'm not at school, am I?' Alice retorted, some fight retained.

'No, but you are in uniform.'

'Mother bought it for me.'

'I don't care who bought it for you. It's not something a girl like you should be wearing. There's only one reason

I can see why you choose to do so. Is it the boys in the local village? Or do you have one closer to home?'

Control short-lived, she refuted his allegation. 'I don't have a boyfriend. Up until two days ago all I cared about was my work.'

'So why cavort in a fancy brassiere like that?'

'I'm not cavorting. As I said, mother bought it for me. And that's why I wore it.'

'You won't be wearing it any more, Alice. Place it on the sideboard. I shall burn it later. Now, just then you said that all you cared about was your work. Which implies you don't any more.'

Undoing the garment and holding the cups to her breasts, she sought a diplomatic reply. 'I will again. Soon, I promise. When I've got over the loss.'

'That sounds more like the Alice Hussey I've heard so much about. I expect you to apply yourself. If you don't, then I will take the necessary action to change your attitude. Do I make myself clear?'

'Yes, uncle.'

'The skirt, take it off.'

Flustered, awkward, Alice lowered the bra, Richard Barker the first man to behold her so. The shape and consistency of her breasts captivated, her uncle concealing his disquiet well. The flesh sleek, strained to an almost swollen bearing. They rose and fell to her anxious gulps for air. Nipples set high on prominent areola, those teats through fear, stimulus or cold, expanded. She laid the bra on the sideboard, a delicate jostle initiated. Self-conscious she bent to lower the pleated skirt. Well endowed, those breasts hung, enticing. Tender, they embraced her ribs, barely giving to gravity. Richard did not take his eyes off her.

Legs clamped together, forearms guarding those youthful breasts, Alice asked, 'What now?'

Suppressing his agitation he replied, 'We resume your punishment, of course.'

'You want me bent over again?'

'Of course. But before you do, tell me how you feel.'

'Feel? I feel frightened, of course.'

'Humiliated?'

'Yes, very.'

'Strange, isn't it? Remove the pretence and the creature flounders. Clothes maketh woman. But they don't, do they? They merely serve as a disguise. They camouflage the identity. Dressed, you are Alice Hussey, impertinent adolescent. Naked, you are nothing.

'There you are in God's given covering and you feel insecure. You don't know which bit to hide. But why should you try to conceal your breasts? Why aren't you proud to stand before me? After all, your body is a divine gift.

'So, tell me how you feel, and why.'

'Isn't the strap punishment enough?' Alice asked. 'Why do you want me to describe my feelings?'

'It isn't a punishment, Alice. I'm interested. I want to know you better.'

'How would you feel if you were stood naked before me?'

'You don't answer a question with a question. But as you ask, it wouldn't bother me at all. I'm proud of my body. Why shouldn't I be?'

'I'm proud of my body as well, but it doesn't mean I want to exhibit it. To be honest, I feel very self-conscious – very uncomfortable.'

'You feel vulnerable?'

'Yes.'

'Embarrassed?'

'Yes.'

'Good. Bend over.' Richard rose from the stool.

Alice doubled again, that reddened sphere thrust out, stretched. Richard swung the strop, sensitive flesh abruptly halting its flight. The slap disconcerting, Alice experienced a visitation from hell. She yelped as the import unleashed an unbearable furore, her backside torched.

No time to recuperate. The hard leather ripped into her haunches, the fire all consuming, abominable, extreme. A strangled expletive rent the air, not missed by the strap-wielding devil.

Barker levied one to her loins, a downward swing that devastated the lower back, extricating a howl of anguish, the girl distraught.

Compassion far from his thoughts, Barker aimed the next a lot lower, raking her upper thighs, Alice believing herself branded.

Tears flowing she grappled with the impulse to run, to escape her uncle's vehemence and flee. But she had to dress; she couldn't run naked through the streets. There again, what choice did she have? To all intents and purposes she was alone in the world. Parental protection taken from her, no one to turn to, that brutal uncle was the only family she had in the world. And even he would turn his back if she didn't bend to his will.

Face flushed, sweat beading on his forehead, Richard pounded those scarlet dunes. He would continue to do so until he noted the requisite deference. Alice sobbed, choked, the all-consuming fire in her bottom beyond anything she could have imagined.

Alice lost count, not that that was ever her intention. Richard, on the other hand, knew exactly how many times that broad leather cannoned into supple cheeks. Eager he witnessed every shudder of buttocks, every shimmer of flesh and the continuous shiver of breasts.

Eighteen murderous strokes he applied, her behind, loins and thighs provoked to the deepest scarlet. Barker backed off. He returned to the stool, Alice waiting on his word.

'Can I expect obedience in the future?' he asked.

'Yes sir,' Alice replied without thought.

'I do hope so. Very well, you may dress.'

He watched her do that also, Alice temporarily forgetting about the bra. As she moved to regain it he shook his head, lips pursed. She withdrew the hand without argument and slid on the blouse.

'Have you money for the journey?' Barker enquired.

'It's a return ticket,' she sniffed, her eyes bloodshot, red-rimmed.

'Then after I have rung Miss Lake I shall drive you to

the station. If I were you I'd spend the journey praying. Beseeching the good Lord that your headmistress won't cane you.'

Richard made the call and fulfilled his promise. Alice fidgeted as the train rattled along the tracks, so aware of that lack of support. Jacket buttoned for fear of her blouse's transparency, she sweltered. No matter how she sat her bottom cried for comfort.

She dwelt on the rough handout, concluding that she was best out of her uncle's way. His integrity she had always doubted, but after that episode she also questioned the man's sanity.

Her thoughts eventually fell to that interesting sensation that occurred when the ogre had threatened to strap her on the bare behind. Why? The actual beating proved awful, something she cared not to repeat. Perhaps it could have been the suggestion, the act of unveiling her very private rump to almost a stranger. Alice concluded that might be the case.

Once her inheritance came through she would be self-sufficient. She would finish her education at Carters and dispense with her uncle's guardianship. She would be her own woman.

Alice switched at Manchester and caught the four o'clock to Kidsgrove. Carters lay only a short walk from there. At five p.m. she entered the grounds of the Academy.

Miss Trimble was the first to spot her trudging the gravel drive. She almost ran to the young redhead. 'Alice! Thank goodness you are all right. Where have you been, you mischievous girl?'

'To see my parents, miss. I just had to.'

'Oh, you poor thing. You do know the police have been searching the countryside for you, don't you? They were even talking about dragging the lake.'

'My uncle rang the headmistress at lunchtime. She knew where I was.'

'Oh, well this all happened this morning. I don't think Miss Lake is best pleased. Best you go and see her straight off.'

Alice ran up the stairs, her stomach a swarm of butterflies. God, what if Stagnant Pool did cane her? What with her bum beaten to the colour of a Victoria plum already.

She knocked and waited, the vibrant voice of Lake reaching her ears some half a minute later. Alice, hesitant, worried, opened the door and entered.

'Alice, so nice of you to finally make yourself available. Tell me, are you sure you have time for we humble pedagogues? Note, I use the word pedagogue. Do you understand the explicit meaning, Alice?'

'No, miss.'

'There is a dictionary on the shelf. Look it up.'

Alice readily found the definition.

'Well, read it out to me.'

'Schoolteacher, miss.'

'That is the archaic use. Read me the usual one.'

'Strict or pedantic teacher.'

'Exactly. A side you have been shrewd enough to avoid in the past. I thought a lot of you, Alice. You demonstrated such enormous potential. I accept your recent loss. I have compassion for your feelings. I was prepared to turn a blind eye to your lack of interest, which I readily contribute to the shock you have suffered.'

She paused for thought; Alice remained motionless before the desk, hands behind her back. 'But running off without a thought for anyone but yourself I find difficult to forgive. A simple note left on your pillow would have at least saved us the worry, and the police their time.

'Alice, I understand why you did it. Under the same circumstances I would have probably acted similarly. However, had I absconded as you did, then I would have expected to reap the penalty on my return.

'I have thought about little else since your uncle rang me to say you were safe. The decision I have made did not come easily. Maybe if I hadn't had to involve the local constabulary then I could have tended toward leniency.'

Alice's stomach turned over. She knew what was

coming. How the hell could she face that?

'You will understand, Alice, that if it were any other pupil I would have to punish them. I cannot be seen to offer favouritism. I think you realise where this conversation is heading.'

'Yes, miss.'

'And how do you feel about that?'

'Frightened, miss,' Alice admitted. 'But I accept I deserve it.'

'I shall leave it until Saturday when most of the girls have gone home for the weekend. Also, it will give you time to dwell on your error. If I don't discipline you and do it with some severity, then how can I expect others to adhere to the rules?'

'I understand, Miss Lake. And thank you for being so candid and understanding. May I ask what I have to prepare myself for?'

'For the cane, Alice. I will administer twelve strokes. You will wear your P.E. kit for the punishment. So, Saturday at three o'clock I will deal with you in the gymnasium.

'Until then please try to stay out of trouble. Apply yourself to your studies. You have a future if you can put this unpleasant business behind you.'

'Yes, miss, thank you.'

Grateful for the postponement but not for the sentence, Alice headed directly for the dormitory and hopefully a bit of peace and quiet, but unfortunately her best friend, Kate Howell, spotted her.

'Alice! Where the hell have you been? Old Stagnant Pool is doing her conkers. You're in the shit and no messing.'

'I've just seen her, Kate,' Alice said ruefully.

'And what did she say? Or should I ask, do? Can you sit down, Ali?'

'The simple answer to that is, with care.'

'She whacked you?' Kate asked, wide-eyed.

'No, I get that on Saturday afternoon in the gym.'

'So why can't you sit on your botty?'

'Because my uncle beat me with a strap.'

'Really?' Kate pursed her lips. 'How many, Ali?'

'I didn't count. I can tell you though, my backside feels as if it's been roasted.'

'Can I see?'

'Oh, you really are a bloodthirsty barbarian, aren't you?'

'Yes. Can I see? Oh please, Ali.'

'Oh, all right. I'll show you in the dorm.'

Kate, a spirited plump brunette, indulged in other's punishments. She possessed a macabre interest in the marks left by cane, slipper or strap. The girl in her proved a jolly and worthwhile companion, if not a touch eccentric.

By her bed Alice lowered her panties and lifted her skirt, and Kate immediately inspected the offended rump.

'Oh, wow! He *did* whack you, didn't he? Your bum is all mottled and there are dozens of thin welts all over your arse, Ali. Gosh, he even flogged your thighs. I bet that hurt.'

'It all hurt, Kate. Seen enough, or should I lay on the bed while you get the magnifying glass?'

'What's Stagnant Pool got lined up for you on Saturday, then?' she persisted, impervious to the dig.

'A dozen of the cane on my blue knicks.'

'Oh, Ali! You've never been whipped with the rod before, have you?'

Alice shook her head.

'The knicks won't help. They're just for decency's sake. She'll pull them up tight. Most of the material will disappear between the cheeks. So, Ali, you virtually get it on the bare.'

'You got it last term, didn't you? You remember, for drinking cider.'

Kate laughed. 'Yes, I had a hangover at the time. I don't know which end hurt the most, my bum or my head.'

'So Kate, did it hurt much?'

'That will depend somewhat on the rod she uses. If she whacks you with the regulation cane then it will sting like hell. But if she decides to use that knobbly thrasher on you, then you'll find it almost impossible to suffer twelve.

In fact, we would be able to hook our hockey sticks on the welts.'

'Thanks, Kate,' Alice said contritely, 'you know how to cheer a person up.'

'I expect it will be the regulation cane, Ali. It's a whippy bugger. It wraps around the haunch and slashes to the hip. Chill your bum beforehand. I've heard it reduces the sting.'

'And how would you suggest I do that?'

'Cooky's refrigerator.'

'What, just stick my bum in there and hope nobody notices?'

'She finishes early on Saturday. Oh Ali, I do wish I could be here to comfort you after. Your poor, poor botty. Whipped twice in one week.'

'Well, Kate, I'm going to try to not think about it. Until Saturday, that is.'

Try as she might, Alice couldn't switch off. The forthcoming flogging numbed. Each and every minute of every day she thought about it. At night she woke in a cold sweat; the nightmare receding; the memory crystal clear. No pain in dreams, but there would be on Saturday.

Kate didn't help. Alice suspected that her friend relished the prospect and would have purchased a ringside seat if she could have. She fair gushed possibilities.

'Imagine, Ali, that gorgeous physics teach, Mr Trueman, giving you a sound thrashing. Skirt up. Knickers tight in the cleft of your bum. All that private flesh on display. Ooh, what a thought!'

'It may be all that private flesh in your case, Kate, but I can assure you my bum isn't that big.'

'Are you saying mine is?'

'Let's just say Mr Trueman couldn't miss the target.'

'Ooh, you cat!'

'And you aren't, I suppose.'

'What do you mean?'

'You keep going on about my sentence. I've got enough on my plate without you forever reminding me.'

32

Kate's face fell. Large brown eyes softened, and appearing suitably chastened, she offered, 'I'm sorry, Alice. I didn't stop to think. Have you heard when the funeral is?'

'Next Tuesday. Who knows, I might even be able to sit again by then.'

'Stagnant Pool should have let you off with a lecture. I think it's rotten her caning you. Especially with a dozen…'

'Kate!'

'Oh, sorry, I sometimes think my mouth isn't connected to my brain.'

'What brain?'

'That's what Miss Whinstone said.'

'Tell me, Katy, why are you so bloody intrigued by corporal punishment? Whenever anybody gets whacked you're always first on the scene. Come to that, I do believe that you've been whipped more than anyone I know.'

'Aah.'

'Aah what?'

'Promise you won't tell anyone. Not a word. Not a whisper. Not even to your best friend.'

'You are my best friend, idiot!'

'Am I? That's nice. Cross your heart and hope to die.'

'Okay, cross my heart and hope to die. Now *aah* what?'

'I like it, Ali.'

'You like it? How can you possibly like it, Kate? It hurts.'

'Oh, it does to begin with. The first couple, they shock. But after that it sort of glows. It goes right to my, um, you know.' Kate placed two fingers furtively in her lap and pushed towards her groin.

'The first couple? How many do you get, for goodness sake?'

'As many as I can without jeopardising my scholarship.'

Alice shook her head in disbelief. 'So tell me, Katy, the last time, how many and what for?'

Kate shrugged. The sincere expression twitched. Those large brown eyes twinkled. She grinned. That became a wide beam and she began giggling. 'I upset Mr Trueman…'

'Now there's a surprise,' interrupted Alice.

'He really despises profanities. So when I knew he was within earshot I cussed. I used the Lord's name in vain and then I added Christ's for good measure.'

'And he whapped you for it?'

'And how. Twelve with the slipper. Oh Ali, how my backside burned. It was absolute heaven.'

'Twelve with the slipper? That was a lot for a couple of profanities, wasn't it?'

'It was my fifth offence.'

'You're mad. When will it be the sixth?'

'It won't. I don't want to push my luck. I'll have to dream up some other minor violation.'

'I'm surprised he didn't despatch you to Stagnant. I mean, he is a man, so he shouldn't really be whacking you at all.'

'I had the choice, Ali. By him or by Stagnant. I chose him, of course. He said it would be kept entirely between he and me.'

'I bet he did. So was it on the skirt or the knicks?'

'The knicks.'

'And in private?'

'Of course.'

'That's wrong, Katy, and you should know that. He shouldn't be getting an eyeful of your scantily clad hindquarters. If Stagnant found out she'd go mad.'

'Well she won't find out, because I'm not going to tell her.'

'Just be careful.'

'Want a ciggy?' Katy offered Alice a Woodbine.

'After another thrashing, are you?'

'There's no one about.'

'You can, but leave me out of it. Twelve is enough to face, I don't want any additions.'

'I won't be caught.' The dizzy Kate lit the cigarette and puffed away at it.

'So you get a sexual kick out of being flogged?'

Kate nodded.

'There's a name for that, isn't there?'

'Yes, masochism.'

'I was thinking of insanity, actually.'

'I suppose somebody who didn't understand would think that.'

'So Katy, make me understand.' Alice reflected on that strange occurrence with her uncle.

The girl continued to puff while she sought a way to explain her complexity. 'I think it's to do with sensitivity. Or maybe it's hormones. All I know is that just dreaming about it makes me go all randy. It's me being submissive and being subdued. Being punished and not being able to do anything about it.

'The more whacks I'm sentenced to the more randy I feel. And when I'm told to raise my skirt and bend over! The mere thought of my nearly bare botty being exposed just throws me into heaven.

'What I'd really like is some masterful man to make me strip completely. And then to tie me down. And then to whip my bum until I can't take any more, and then some. That's what really turns me on.' Kate winked at Alice. 'As you said, insane. What turns you on, Ali?'

Alice lay back on the bed. She placed her hands behind her head and examined the ceiling. 'What you said about a strange man seeing you in the buff. Or having to reveal your nether region. That does.' She glanced at the girl. 'When my uncle thrashed me he threatened to whack me on my bare bottom. Which, incidentally, he did eventually...'

'Ooh, you lucky beast.'

'That's a matter of opinion. Anyway, I had this funny feeling down below. Just like a minor electric shock, it was. To be honest, it was nice.'

Serious, Kate asked, 'Have you ever had an orgasm, Ali?'

'No, I'm still a virgin, Kate.'

'Oh, I don't believe you. You've never masturbated?'

Horror-struck, Alice felt the tide of embarrassment wash over her. 'You mustn't do that, Kate. That's defying the Almighty's scripture. That's almost blasphemy.'

'You are naïve, Ali,' Kate scoffed. 'It's a perfectly natural thing to do. You get randy, you relieve it.' She held an index finger up. 'Just one of those, that's all it takes. You don't have to wait for marriage to find out what it's like. That feeling you had, that was a prelim to orgasm. Now you know what you're missing. Imagine that, only a hundred times stronger.'

'I don't think I could stand it,' Alice said pensively.

'You don't stand, idiot, you lay down. Then you writhe with passion as the feeling gets stronger. You close your eyes and think about what you would like done to you. Then this terrific pins and needles hits you in the groin and, oh Jesus, it's *wonderful*.'

'And you use your finger to do that?'

Katy nodded, grinning.

'Eugh! I hope you wash it after.'

Kate leant forward and whispered, 'I read this book, Ali. A dirty book. This man licked the woman there. Can you imagine that? Having a tongue up you?'

'Katy! I've never heard anything so disgusting in all my life. It's bad enough putting up with you know what in there, let alone a tongue. How revolting!'

'Oh, I don't know, Ali. I shall say to my boyfriend, when I get one, lick my fanny. You'll do it if you really love me.'

'And if he says, *eugh?*'

'Nothing ventured, nothing gained.' Kate lit another cigarette. 'Sure you won't have one?'

'Alice obviously has a lot more sense than you, Kate Howell.'

The girls leapt to their feet to face Miss Oliver, the physical education mistress. Kate froze with hand inches from her face, cigarette burning, a trail of blue smoke rising to the ceiling.

'Why are you in the dormitory, anyway?' the young and attractive teacher enquired.

'That's my fault, miss,' offered Alice. 'I've just got back and needed to change. Kate came up to keep me company.'

36

'You've seen Miss Lake, I take it?'

'Yes, miss.'

'Kate Howell, you are in uniform and on school grounds. What the devil do you think you are doing smoking?'

Kate lifted an eyebrow. 'I like it, miss.'

'And do you like the cane on your backside as well?' Both restrained spontaneous giggles with difficulty, but Oliver noticed the twist of lips. 'So you think it funny, do you?'

'No, miss,' they replied as one.

'Kate, go to the gymnasium and fetch my slipper and cane. We'll find out just how funny you think a lesson will be.' The girl broke into a trot and headed for the door. 'And put that cigarette out, Howell.'

'Yes, miss.'

'So, where have you been, Alice?'

'I went to see my parents, miss.'

'I thought they were...'

'Dead, miss. They are. I wanted to say goodbye.'

'I see. Then why didn't you ask?'

'I did. Permission was refused. I'm too young. The sight would freak me out.'

'And did it?'

'No. I feel better for it.'

'Good. What did Miss Lake have to say about you running off without a word?'

'She wasn't happy.'

'Kate probably isn't the best company to keep if you want to stay out of trouble. I've lost count of the amount of times I've had to reprimand her. She's a difficult girl to comprehend and impossible to get through to.'

'She has a heart of gold, miss.'

'I'm sure she does. I just wish she would toe the line.'

'She's a scatterbrain, miss.'

Oliver laughed. 'Yes, you're probably right.'

Breathless, Kate trotted back in. 'One cane and one slipper, miss.'

'Being keen somehow takes the edge off punishing you, Howell. Can't you pretend to be even slightly upset?'

'Oh I am, miss.' She held out her hands. 'I'm shaking, look.'

'Somehow I think that is to do with running rather than fear. Oh well, let's get it done with. Bend over, Howell, and lift your skirt.'

Kate went over without hesitation, skirt flicked up. Alice, in a suitable position, watched as Oliver selected the slipper, a size nine plimsoll. Whether deliberate or not Kate's knickers stretched over her ample rump, the majority of the material claimed by the cleft.

Oliver had a reputation for applying absolute stingers. She raised the slipper and brought it down in an arc, the heavy tread colliding with Kate's left cheek, the movement of flesh considerable.

A slight adjustment to stance and she whacked the right buttock, the crack of rubber on flesh echoing about the empty dormitory. Alice winced for her.

Again the left cheek, already colouring. Finally the right.

'Stand up, Howell.' Oliver tapped her thigh, waiting. Kate straightened, grimacing. 'Well, Howell, was that to your liking?'

'No, miss.' Kate pouted. 'It really stung, miss.'

Oliver beckoned to Alice. 'You Alice, bend please.'

'But miss, what have I done?' the girl protested.

'I can hardly punish Kate for smirking and not you, now can I?'

'No, miss.' Alice took the dreaded position.

'Skirt, Alice.'

She flicked it up over her back.

'Goodness gracious, Alice, look at the state of your bottom. Did Miss Lake do that?'

'My uncle, miss,' Alice disclosed quietly. 'He wasn't best pleased with me. He gave me the strap.'

'Then you're excused this time, Alice. I'm sure Kate won't object. Will you, Howell?'

'No miss – definitely not, miss.'

'The cane then, Howell,' the teacher went on. 'Resume your position. You can watch, Alice. Maybe it will help deter further misadventure.'

'I'm sure it will, miss.'

Kate bent, scarlet cheeks proffered. Alice followed the flight of rod. It's slap and wrap, poor Kate's bottom quivering. Alice noted the discoloration of the first as that flexible brute homed in on another portion of partly exposed buttock. The sharp smack and Kate's whimper informed her the girl suffered.

A third cut wickedly, the thwack louder than ever. Kate's knuckles whitened.

The fourth whipped low, the connection of thigh and buttock reeling to the slice.

Oliver altered position slightly; her next incendiary aimed at the upper cheeks. That cut close to the coccyx, the discomfort evident by the girl's anguished squeal.

The last one, thought Alice as Oliver cut her there again. But the woman aligned the rod to the lower half and deftly struck for the seventh time.

Thick red stripes adorned the girl's backside, reaching almost to the far hip. Merciless the rod returned, cracking loud on stinging flesh, executing its manic dance, a violent scorch in its wake.

Kate made no attempt at complaint, nor did she try to rise. She remained doubled, her copious cheeks etched in carmine. Oliver delivered one last cracker, the rod biting deep into the lower buttocks, Kate's cry moving.

'You may rise, Howell, but if I catch you smoking again I'll double that punishment. Oh, and I'll have your cigarettes, as well.' Kate handed the pack over. 'Now both of you, downstairs; tea will be served shortly.'

'Well, Katy, did it glow?' Alice asked. 'Was it orgasmic? Are you all randy now?'

The girl pursed her lips and winked at Alice. 'I've never been so wet after a whacking. That last one! What a fire that ignited. My bum is still blazing. Oliver can certainly lay it on. I might just buy myself another ten Woodbines next week.'

'I thought you were suffering. You squealed. Your knuckles were white.'

'Acting. I have to make it look like it hurts. If I don't,

39

they'll tumble me and I'll end up getting boring lines or something.'

'Kate.'

'Yes?'

'Can I borrow your bum this weekend?'

'If I could take your whipping for you, I would.'

'I know. You're a terrific mate.'

Saturday came all too rapidly. The night before she had said her goodbyes, relieved in one way to see the back of Kate, and sorry in another. She was disburdened of the girl's continuous exuberance but missed her soul mate.

Virtually on her own, she counted the hours and then the minutes to that onerous meeting with Lake. Her bottom clear of marks, she knew there would be no reprieve forthcoming.

Was she regretful? No, Alice had foreseen the possibility and decided the disappearing act worth the consequences. A few minutes of acute pain, several hours of discomfort, a price she had been willing to pay. That, however, didn't ease the fear of facing the rod, a contretemps that turned her legs to jelly.

Having witnessed those nine strokes delivered with vigour to poor Kate's behind didn't help. The fire of the strap still fresh in her mind, she cringed at the effectiveness of the rattan.

At a quarter to three, so as not to be late, she changed into her P.E. kit. The jitters gripping her body, she strode the length of the corridor that connected the changing room to the gymnasium, and opened the door.

Five to three and no Miss Lake. Could it be she had forgotten? Such possibilities run through the optimistic mind. The large hall cool, she shivered. That set her body trembling, and nerves took over.

One minute to three, Alice extremely hopeful, when the door adjoining the gym to the main building opened. Her heart falling through her belly she caught sight of Lake, rod in hand.

'Ah, Alice, waiting and ready, I note. Very good. Get it

done with, eh?' She closed the gap between them. 'It's a great pity I have to resort to this. If there were any other option I would choose it. You understand that? However, the rules of the Academy leave me no alternative. Going absent without leave is punishable by the cane.'

Alice nodded. 'Yes, Miss Lake. I fully understand.'

'Good. Bend over please and pull your panties up as tight as they will go.'

Alice hitched those navy knickers up, the material pulling into buttock cleft and vagina alike. She bent, her arms hanging, eyes fixed on that lethal wand. Nearly three feet of pliable vine, three eighths thick it held the promise of excruciating pain.

'Legs apart, Alice. Fingers gripping ankles, please.'

She placed those limbs two feet apart and wrapped trembling digits about slim ankles.

'Excellent,' Lake appraised. 'You are in many ways a delightful girl, Alice. It's a shame I have to mark such a sweet bottom purely because of a wilful owner. You are intelligent, Alice. You possess enormous potential. You are also a very attractive young lady. The world will be your oyster if you learn to curb your excesses.'

The rod tapped taut cheeks several times then left, only to return with frightening speed, the air rent, a shrill whistle heralding misery. The cane struck, the slap resounding. It wrapped, briefly taking the shape of her haunches, the rod springing wildly. A traumatic scorch ripped through her buttocks, the pain jolting her mind. Her gullet contracted, refusing the intake of breath she laboured for. Impulsively she gouged those ankles, fingers clawing at the scant flesh.

Was it more agonising than the strap? In a way, yes, and in a way, no. The strap provided a broad impact, a sizeable portion of flesh stung. The cane concentrated all its energies into a narrow strip. It seemed to delve, to penetrate deep. It was like having ten inches of her skin crushed in a vice.

The smart lingering, the immediate furore receding, she at last sucked in that gulp of air, rapidly expelling it as the

41

cane bit backside again. Teeth clenched, her face twisted in torment, she begged the ire to pass and waited, as did Lake before inflicting the third.

The panties barely concealing anything, stretched and forced into the cleft, that shapely bottom reeled to the slash, the rattan ripping into the more substantial lower cheeks. Hot embers re-ignited, she grunted to release the awful knot in her chest.

Nine to go, Alice contemplated. How could Kate indulge in torture like this? How could anyone want to be flogged? The sting hung, lingered, embers that refused to die.

Three livid stripes stood proud on her bottom, traversing three quarters of her rump, terminating shy of the farthest hip. Alice heard the swish and tensed, that rod whipping mid-cheek, the blast of hot agony excruciating. Perspiration dotting her flushed countenance she whimpered, the correction whittling away at her mental defences.

Lake had made a decision. Although she had informed Richard Barker of her preference toward compassion, she could not let the matter go without punishment. An agonised deliberation followed. Her final resolve to inflict corporal punishment so as not to show favour, and hopefully to bring Alice to heel. The cane she used with force, the intent that Alice wouldn't wish to repeat the episode. Although she rued those scarlet tramlines adorning the pupil's bottom, she accepted they were necessary. She added a fifth, the echo bouncing from the far wall. Alice bit her lower lip, a mist obscuring her sight as brine filled emerald pools.

Another ten seconds tantalised before the rattan, driven with zest, tested her resolve further. Halfway and poor Alice felt her arse branded. She sniffed as tears wetted her face.

Lake leant to stroke that battered haunch before switching sides. Her fingers consoled, caressed, almost petted the damage. They kissed that tormented flesh, engaging welts from back to thigh. Alice frowned. The touch pleasant, the interlude welcome, she said nothing.

Perhaps the examination was part of the ritual, a brief respite from the harrowing discipline.

Lake inserted those fingers in the elastic of her knickers to expedite their descent. She drew them over discoloured cheeks then lowered them to the girl's knees. She offered no explanation, Alice determining the act as punishment.

Alice was to discover that Lake was ambidextrous with the cane, the delivery just as acute and equally testing.

Those soft and once sleek flanks shuddered to the renewed assault, a slice of hell instilled. A yelp finally escaped the stalwart girl, a gurgle following.

Unperturbed, Lake duly revisited, the switch flaying, the consequence atrocious. For the eighth time the crack of brutal rod on sensitive butt reverberated about the hall, Alice's hands releasing her ankles and clawing pointlessly at thin air.

Nine followed in due course, the punishment drawn out, Alice's suffering prolonged. 'Nooo…' left her parted lips. Breathing rapid, perspiration wetted her face to mix with the tears. Moisture collected between her breasts and between her legs.

Ten whipped alongside its predecessor, doubling the intolerable burn. Two left, she thought, relieved. Never, ever again.

Eleven lambasted tensed thighs, an explosion of atrocious hurt. The tears flowed faster.

Lake concentrated on those marked haunches before delivering the final and most unendurable cut of all. The cane fair shrieked to its target, flogging those hindquarters two inches below where the crease expired. Ripples of trounced flesh leapt from the impact, as did Alice. Rising, she threw her hands to tend the inferno, the panties falling to her ankles, nearly tripping her over. Sobbing, she gasped as that hurt clung, a red-hot limpet.

'I trust, Alice, that it won't be necessary to cane you ever again?' Lake enquired unnecessarily, and unable to speak or assuage the smart, Alice nodded. 'The rest of the weekend is yours. But do not go anywhere without telling someone.'

Swallowing, rubbing her nose with the back of her hand, Alice mumbled, 'Yes, miss.'

Lake left Alice to come to terms with the chastisement. The girl limped back to the changing rooms, knickers in hand. Each step a trial, she dreaded the touch of clothing. Lifting her shirt over her head she stood naked, dwelling on what had occurred.

Her life had taken a disastrous downturn, some of it her own fault she would readily admit. The barbarity meted out in return staggered, years of good behaviour ignored. She felt the damage. Welts burgeoned, stood proud, her rump smothered.

Breath shuddering she let the frustration go, sobbing her heart out. Alice refrained from sitting. That would have proved too much.

Chapter Two

With full permission, Alice left Carters early Tuesday morning to attend her parents' funeral. The cortège left from her uncle's, something Alice wasn't best pleased about.

The turnout respectable, Alice managed to chat with a few familiar faces. There were neighbours, family friends and work associates in attendance. The cortège left at midday, a procession of cars and taxis following. Her parents were to be buried at Our Lady and Saint Joseph's Church, in Southport.

Suitably attired in grey blouse and black skirt, Alice witnessed the lowering of coffins into the double grave with fortitude. The occasion became a blur in later years; to the extent she could remember very little.

Back at her uncle's house, he asked to speak with her in private, and apprehensively she followed him to the kitchen.

His mood unreadable he stunned her with the news. 'Well, Alice, it would appear your family is not as well off as you may have thought.'

The girl frowned. 'What are you trying to say, uncle?'

'I've spoken at length with your father's solicitor. As executor of the will I have to inform you that after settlement of debts there is very little left.'

'What about the house? And what about my trust fund?'

'The house is mortgaged to the hilt,' he told her. 'Once sold it will settle that and that only. Your parents' savings just about cover other debts. And your trust. Yes, Alice, you do have a trust fund. But not available until you are twenty-one. Reg obviously doubted your maturity as well.

'So you have until the end of term, and then you will have to say goodbye to Carters. At this point I have some good news, however. I have found you a backer. A man of enormous integrity. He is willing to fund your continued education if you agree to two dictates. Firstly, you finish your education at Heptonstall Manor, a Catholic inspired private faculty. With, I might add, one of the best reputations in the north of England. Secondly, you agree to work for him for a period of two years upon completion of your degree. I personally think a Catholic based education will do you the world of good; iron out a few creases in that arrogant head of yours.'

'Who is this man?' she asked.

'That will be revealed in due course. Do you accept?'

'I don't have much choice, do I?'

'Not unless you have some nest egg I don't know about.'

She shook her head, her heart sinking.

'Then as far as I can see, you have no choice.'

'All this upset will ruin my chances. I'll end up with nothing.'

'Defeated!' he snapped. 'You haven't even seen Heptonstall yet, let alone given them a chance. Because Alice Hussey can't have her own way, she gives up. To be frank, I quite expected this reaction. It reinforces my belief that you are spoilt rotten.'

'Oh, think what you will, uncle. You don't like me and that's an end to it. Perhaps I would be better off trying to get a job.'

'Then be my guest, Alice. We've been down that road. Take to the streets if you wish. That'll do a lot for your future.'

She really did have no choice. Richard called her only bluff. At least at Heptonstall she stood some chance of pursuing her examinations. 'You win,' she said quietly. 'I'll go.'

'Oh, and one more thing, Alice.'

'Yes, uncle?'

'Did the cane hurt very much?'

'How do you know about that?'

'Miss Lake discussed your case with me. I think she

saw reason in the end, don't you?'

'You mean you persuaded her?'

'But of course.' He smiled thinly. 'So remember, Alice, my influence is never far away. Behave yourself at Heptonstall or be prepared for the consequences.'

Alive travelled back to Carters a disenchanted young lady. She would have to say goodbye to her friends, especially to Kate. She would miss the equality and fair-minded staff. She had heard rumours about Heptonstall and didn't relish the prospect one little bit.

Kate sought her out within minutes of returning. 'Ali! How did it go?'

'It went and I'm glad to see the back of it.'

'That bad?'

'It's done with. Time to put it in the past.'

'I didn't like to ask yesterday in case you thought me bloodthirsty,' Kate went on. 'The whacking?'

'I wondered when you'd get around to that.'

'Well?'

'I've still got the marks. Want to have a look?'

'What, after four days you're still striped? Wow! That must have been some thrashing.'

'It was,' Alice reflected bitterly. 'Believe me, it was.'

'She laid into you?'

'With a vengeance.'

'Ouch!'

'You can say that again.'

'Ouch!'

'And there's something else, Kate.'

'What?'

'Stagnant gave me half with my knicks pulled up, as you said. Then she stroked me before pulling them down and giving me the other half.'

'Stroked you?' Kate's eyes sparkled mischievously. 'Stroked you where?'

'My bum.'

'She obviously likes you then.'

'How do you mean?'

47

'I've heard, nothing definite, just rumour, that Stagnant's a bit... you know.'

'No, I don't know.'

'She's never married, has she?'

'God! You don't mean?'

Kate nodded.

'God! I feel sick.'

'Look on the bright side, Ali; if she fancies you she's not going to whip you unless she has to. And you did get a break between strokes.' Kate grinned. 'To be honest, I wouldn't mind. I think I'd quite like that.'

'Reprobate!' Alice's expression changed as she prepared to impart her other news. 'Kate...'

'Yes Ali?'

'I'm going to have to say goodbye at the end of term.'

'Why, for heaven's sake?'

'My parents left no money,' Alice explained. 'There's nothing in the kitty to pay my fees. My uncle is transferring me to Heptonstall Manor.'

'Where's that, for Christ's sake?'

'In the middle of nowhere.'

'Oh, Ali, I shall miss you so much. Perhaps if I had a word with father he might fund your last years.'

'Don't you dare, Kate. I'm not a charity. Anyway, you know he wouldn't.'

'He might.'

'Get your head out of the clouds, Kate. I'm off to Heptonstall.'

Kate placed her head to one side, and grinning asked, 'Can I see those welts now?'

'In the toilets.'

With some pride Alice showed off her wounds.

'Oh Ali, Stagnant *did* whip you, didn't she?' Kate gasped. 'I bet that really stung. Are you going to tell me about it?'

'What, the school or the whacking?'

'Both.'

'Apparently my uncle has found me a backer. Someone who will pay my fees until I gain my examination passes.

48

There are two provisos, though. Firstly, I have to finish at Heptonstall. Secondly, I have to work for this mysterious man for two years afterwards.'

'Is Heptonstall cheaper than here, then?' Kate asked.

'I really don't know. I have heard, though, that it is a hard school. That they want results and they don't care how they get them.'

'Discipline, you mean?'

'That I don't know for sure. Maybe they have excellent teaching staff. Maybe they have means we can't even dream about. All I know is I'm worried.'

'So this man may be sending you because he knows you will have a better chance there?'

Alice shrugged.

'So, what have you got to do when you work for him?'

Again Alice shrugged.

'Suspicious or what?'

'It's only right I pay him back.'

'What about university?'

'I don't know.'

'A right rum do.'

'I'll have to suck it and see.'

'You've five weeks, Ali. Five weeks to engrave your name indelibly on Carters' history. Otherwise you'll be just another came and went. What you going to do?'

'Carters have engraved their mark indelibly on my backside, Kate. I've no intention of a rerun.'

'It didn't glow then?'

'I think you were having me on, Katy Howell. It was a terrible experience. Nobody could enjoy that. Absolutely nobody.'

'I do. Would I deliberately get myself caned if I didn't like it?'

'I don't know that you do, Kate. I mean, it could be you just push your luck too much, and then won't admit how much it hurts.'

'I'll do you a deal. I'll provoke the Mad Hatter if you do.'

'And why would I want to do that?'

'To see me get whacked on purpose, and to start the Alice Hussey Memorial Plaque.'

'You make it sound like I'm going to die.'

'Your name will appear in the punishment records over and over.' Kate grinned. 'Right next to mine. You'll never be forgotten.'

'And what if Heptonstall want a reference?'

'They'll know you're not frightened of a whacking. Go on, Ali. I'll even instruct you on how to enjoy it. I'll share every fantasy of mine. We could go into the hall of orgasmic records. I'll even let you whack me as well.'

'Oh, that really tips the balance. You seem to forget, Kate, with me it's torture. Why the devil would I want to condemn myself to five weeks of hell?'

'To toughen your bum up for Heptonstall? To get back at that vicious uncle of yours? You know, show him you don't give a damn. For all you know, Ali, he might have sold you into white slavery. It is bondage of a sort. Talking of which, that doesn't turn you on, does it?'

'What, slavery?'

'No idiot, being tied up.'

'Never tried it.'

Kate leant to her ear. 'Can you imagine it, Ali? All naked, ropes restricting every movement. Digging into sensitive and private bits and pieces. Vulnerable. A person could do anything they wanted once you were bound and gagged.'

Alice shook her head. 'Can't say the thought does a lot for me,' she said. 'You really are some reprobate, aren't you, Kate?'

'I could give you an orgasm like that, Ali,' her friend went on. 'Your very first.'

Shocked, Alice walked away.

'Oh come on, Ali,' called Kate, chasing after her. 'If you don't want to, you don't want to. Still friends?'

'I didn't say I don't want to, Kate. I need time to think.'

'Oh, touched a spot, did it?'

'You really think you could teach me to enjoy physical punishment?' Alice asked cautiously.

'I could try. Why, had a change of heart?'

'I was thinking if I could learn to enjoy it like you are supposed to, then it might help me get through my final years.'

'And get back at a few.'

'Yes, Katy, and get back at a few.'

'The old disused stables,' Kate pressed. 'Tonight. When everybody else is in the recreation room. I'll arrange a special session for you.'

'That sounds ominous.'

'Oh no, Ali. Believe me, it'll be fun all the way.'

'And you put off upsetting Attila the Hun for a few days.'

'Until you're prepared.' Kate laughed. 'I look forward to seeing the Mad Hatter's expression when miss prim and proper Hussey finally puts a foot wrong.'

'I'm not so sure I will.'

Katy wasn't present at Religious Instruction, the last half-hour period of the day. The pious Miss Valentine noted the absence and enquired if anybody knew where she might be. Alice threw up a hand.

'Yes, Alice?'

'It's that time, ma'am,' she said. 'The crimson tide. I think she went directly to the loo.'

Miss Valentine, extremely shy about bodily functions, immediately coloured. Alice surmised correctly she wouldn't probe any deeper. In fact Kate had disappeared on a quest. All Alice knew was it had something to do with the evening arrangements. Kate's idea of an introduction to the intrigues of masochism.

At a quarter to seven the pair crept inconspicuously away from the main building and down to the stables. Although no longer used they had been kept in reasonable order. Apart from the individual horseboxes the group of buildings contained a tack room devoid of leather, and a small barn minus hay.

'You do realise this is out of bounds, Kate?' reminded Alice.

51

'So? This is the start of your rebellious age, Ali. Curtailing to rules is out. All caution you throw to the wind.'

'So what have you arranged for me?'

'I'm not going to spoil the surprise. You just wait and see.'

'I'm not sure about this, Kate. Perhaps it would be best if I just toed the line. Do what my uncle says. Work hard and keep my head down.'

'And you'll spend the rest of your life under his thumb. If you don't stick up for yourself he'll do just what he pleases.'

'Only until I'm twenty odd. Then I can go where I want, when I want.'

'That's years of servitude. Years of bending. Yes, bending most likely. Bending over, Ali, all the time you're under that pig's jurisdiction. If you rebel now and show him you don't give a damn, he'll think it pointless beating you. Uncle Richard will back off. He'll disappear back under his rock. Anyway, how do you know it will end at twenty odd? How do you know there won't be other deals, ones you can't refuse? It might go on until you're of no further sexual interest. Until you're an old maid past your prime.'

'What do you mean, of sexual interest?' Alice asked, alarmed.

'Why else would a stranger offer to pay your fees?' Kate said bluntly. 'You told me to get my head out of the clouds. If you think it's for any other reason than sexual interest, then you're the one with the head in the nimbus.'

'He might have kicked me out on the streets instead,' Alice countered defensively.

'No, he won't. He's done a deal. You don't think it's solely for your good, do you? I bet he's getting something out of it. He won't want to pull out, to lose face. No, Ali, he'll remove his interfering nose from your business, especially if you cause him a bundle of trouble.'

'You think so?'

'I know so. The only retribution he knows is a flogging.

52

If you show him that doesn't bother you he'll have to give up.'

'How long before he does, Katy? How many whippings will I have to suffer before he finally throws in the towel?'

'What does it matter if you learn to enjoy them like me?'

'Oh, I'll give it a try, Kate,' Alice said resolutely. 'No promises, mind you.'

'That's my girl.'

'So, are you going to tell me what you have arranged?'

'No need. He's here now.'

'Who is?'

'Robert, the victualler's son from the village. An old and trusted acquaintance of mine.'

Alice threw her hands up in despair. 'Oh, Katy!' she shrieked. 'What have you gone and done?'

'He's twenty-two, handsome, strong, got a dick the size of a python and a hand that can make your botty sing a dozen different tunes.'

As Alice turned to face the newcomer, she hissed from the corner of her mouth, 'I thought this was between you and I. You never said anything about a man.'

'If you want to learn the sexual side then you need someone of the opposite sex,' Kate stated. 'It stands to reason.'

The young fellow offered a hand. 'Hello, Alice I presume. I'm Bob.'

The girl accepted the appendage. 'N-nice to meet you,' she stammered, complexion colouring.

'And you.' He glanced at Kate. 'You didn't say your friend is so attractive, Kate.' His eyes audaciously roamed her body. 'Yes, gorgeous, one might say. Lovely figure, Alice.' He let the hand loose and ambled to her rear. 'Delicious bottom. Shapely legs.' He slapped Alice's rump, and utterly shocked, she glowered. She folded her arms, unsure how to react. Peeved, she glared at Kate.

'Oh, what's up now, Ali?' her friend snapped.

'I'm not a piece of horseflesh, Kate,' she grumbled through gritted teeth. 'Your friend seems to think I am.'

'No, he doesn't. They're compliments. Of course, you're not used to the ways of men, are you?'

'And you are, I suppose.'

'I'm used to the ways of Bob,' she divulged with an inference.

'You don't mean…?'

'Mmmm. Last Easter. And I'm not sorry about it either.'

'And what would dear daddy say if he found out?'

'He won't, will he? I mean, he's not a gynaecologist, is he?'

'Get one thing straight, Kate,' Alice said determinedly, 'I intend to remain intact.'

'There was never any suggestion that you should go the whole hog.' She leered. 'Not unless you want to, of course. And you won't object if I do, will you?'

'Not a lot of point, is there, Kate? You'll do whatever anyway.'

'Finished?' enquired Bob, hands resolutely stuffed in trouser pockets.

'I think so,' replied Kate, slipping an arm about Alice's slim waist. 'Come on, we haven't got that much time.' She ushered the nervous girl into the disused tack room, Bob following, representing the spare part.

'Right, Ali, Bob is going to give you a lesson in hand spanking,' Kate announced. 'He's very good at it. He won't hurt you. It will be done sensuously. Give you an insight into how erotic it can be.'

'Tell you what, Kate, you go first,' Alice suggested. 'You show me how it's done.'

'We haven't got time, Ali.'

'You first, or not at all.'

'Oh!' Kate ground her teeth. 'Okay, Bob, spank me like I was a novice.'

'No,' intervened Alice. 'Spank her like she wasn't.'

'That's not an initiation, Ali,' argued Kate.

'I want to see you take it. I want to see you *writhe with pleasure*.' Alice emphasised the last three words.

'You still don't believe me, do you?'

'I've felt the cane, Kate. I know how it smarts. If you're

telling me the truth then it will be a pleasurable experience, won't it?'

'All right then, I'll bloody well show you.'

Then, to Alice's disbelief, Kate began stripping. Off came her blouse, the girl obviously indignant. She slid the skirt to her ankles. Expression petulant she unfastened the bra and tossed it to the floor, her ample bosom wobbling. She slipped off her panties and turning, offered herself to Robert.

The young man sat on a stool, and happily took the naked girl over his knees. One arm placed over the small of her back, he raised the other. Alice observed with more interest than she would have admitted, Robert's gambit. His large hand descended with speed and slapped noisily on those wide buttocks, the flesh shuddering dramatically. Kate offered no protest.

He treated the opposite number similarly, Kate remaining limp, showing no reflex as far as Alice could see.

He persevered, that rump colouring swiftly, Kate's breathing rapid, expression intense. The slaps rained more briskly, the hand heavier, Kate gasping with each blast of heat. Alice watched intense, unable to take her eyes from the spectacle, the buzz in her groin undeniable.

Her backside hot, a brilliant scarlet, Kate finally tensed. Her whole body rigid she lifted herself until she lay horizontal. Face demonstrating the pleasure she gasped, 'Wicked! Oh, bloody wicked!'

Alice thought so as well.

'Now Bob, show Ali how you please a girl,' Kate panted. 'With your hands, that is.'

The arm that had held her down slipped beneath that buxom torso and fondled those pendulous breasts. The spanker pushed apart thick thighs to gently stroke the vaginal folds. Kate moaned in an exaggerated fashion, the pretence not lost on Alice.

The naïve and inexperienced girl considered the manipulation, her own mind in turmoil. Her strict moral upbringing screamed at her it was wrong, that carnal forays outside of marriage were a sin. The woman in her, however, twisted the knife, Alice longing to trade places, to be touched like Kate. To be felt and petted, private places invaded. She shivered as Bob's digit slid deep into Kate's vagina.

How could she place herself at the man's disposal? How could she expose those parts of the body she had always been told were intimate, which were for her future husband's pleasure only? Not to be offered before marriage.

'I'm sorry, Kate,' she blurted. 'I can't go through with it.' Offering no time for argument Alice fled the tack room and ran back to the school. There she dwelt on what she had seen; trying to deny to herself that she had been tempted.

She didn't see Kate that evening, her friend's absence seeming strange. Come bedtime the girl had still not shown. A worried Alice laid her head on the pillow, and concerned, she succumbed to a fitful sleep.

The next morning she rose to find Kate's bed still empty. Alice pondered over breakfast on whether to say anything or not. As far as she knew she was the last person to see her friend. What if something had happened to her? What if the staff hadn't realised the girl was missing? Alice spooned porridge, her stomach in knots.

Eventually she decided to opt for speaking up. She could broach the subject with diplomacy, not drop Kate in the mire.

'Miss Jenkins,' she began to the duty staff member, 'has anyone seen Kate Howell this morning?'

Jenkins looked down her nose at Alice. 'The least said about Miss Howell the better. Don't worry about her; she has an interview with the headmistress this morning. I think one could say her days at Carters are numbered.'

'Why, what's happened?'

'All will be revealed.'

Rumours abounded, and at morning break something near the truth emerged. Mr Howell had been seen arriving in his Bentley. Word had it that Kate had been caught red-handed in a compromising position. The grapevine whispered there was a boy involved. Oddly, no one seemed surprised or shocked.

They had to wait until midday break before the mystery started to unravel. All senior pupils were requested – that meant ordered – to attend a special assembly in the main hall at six that evening, and filed into the hall at five forty-five. They took their places, seated on the floor.

Five minutes later Teresa Lake took the stage, the other members of staff dotted about the assembly. Serious, pallid, Lake fumbled for words. She glanced up at the windows, a tear in her eye. 'I have asked you all to come here this evening to hear firstly a testimony by one of your fellow scholars.' She coughed, and then cleared her throat. 'Although *scholar* in this case is probably the wrong inference.'

To Alice the woman seemed distraught. She had never known Lake to be lost for words.

'This girl was caught with a boy from the village last night. Not only with the boy, but involved in what one might term, a sexual clinch. I tell you this as I am sure you are all old enough to understand the immorality of the situation this girl has involved herself in. Also because I don't want rumour to distort the truth.'

Again she took a moment to compose herself. 'I have been in conference with the staff, governors, and the girl's parents. A decision has been reached. One that was not easy to come to. But having said that, all parties are agreed, including the girl herself.

'We cannot condone the pupil's continued education at Carters. The matter is far too serious for that. Especially when you consider that the authorities might take action against the young man involved for assault. I won't have this school dragged through the courts, or its good name sullied.

'The girl will be expelled. She will leave these grounds tonight. But first she will be disciplined. This is not only a requirement by the governing body, and myself, but by her parents as well.

'Kate Howell will be summarily thrashed by cane before all. Any girl that feels she does not wish to witness such a punishment is free to leave. I feel it necessary for you all to understand what to expect if any other girl ever considers entering such a relationship, and that is the polite phrase.'

Lake faced the wings. 'Kate Howell, please take your place.'

No girl rose. No girl left. *Bloodthirsty lot*, thought Alice, who herself remained seated.

Kate breezed jauntily onto the podium, that wicked knobbly cane held before her. Alice breathed a sigh of relief, for there but for the grace of God went she. Had Alice been weak enough to accept Kate's dizzy proposal, then she would have surely been lined up alongside.

'You have something to say, Kate?' urged Lake.

'Yes, ma'am.' She smiled at her audience, seemingly unperturbed by the immediate future. 'I'm a bad bugger that deserves a whacking.'

'Kate Howell!' Lake bellowed. 'How dare you?'

'I dare, miss. I'm to be expelled. I'm to be whipped. What else can you do?'

Every face other than Lake's struggled to remain straight.

'You do yourself no favours whatsoever, girl! You are an incorrigible rogue. And this attitude only reinforces my decision to sack you. Now bend over, Howell, and take your medicine.'

Kate wore the punishment smock, a rare sight at Carters. The dress made from white muslin covered the body from neck to knee. A collar fastened at the back encircled the throat. A loose bodice draped the torso, and gathered tight to the waist. The pleated skirt when raised would reveal an honour saving g-string sown to the lower hem of the bodice. So, when the dress was stepped into the scant panties automatically assumed their place.

Kate passed the rod and about-faced, a definite spring in her step. She dutifully doubled and touched her toes. Alice wondered what would have occurred if Kate hadn't been a devout masochist. And what Lake would have

58

said if she'd known she was.

The headmistress stepped forward and raised the skirt high over Kate's back, those buttocks naked except for the slip of material deep in the cleft. A definite excited murmur buzzed about the crowded hall. Eager eyes watched and waited. Anticipation ran high.

'Feet apart, Howell, and grip those ankles.'

Kate complied, that bottom taut.

Face drawn, jaw muscles tight, Lake demonstrated the lack of flex in the rod. At twelve millimetres thick it terrified most to the extent they avoided it at all cost. Slowly she brought it to bear, the cool wand resting on proffered bottom.

Alice held her breath along with everyone else. Would Kate be able to take it? Or would it prove too much even for her?

Lake took an inordinate amount of time adjusting her stance; the rod pressed into flesh that would soon reel to its consequence. Alice guessed correctly that she mentally prepared herself, that the stroke when delivered would be close to her limit.

Lake drew the cane up, her torso twisting, arm held high, eyes not moving from the target. It hovered a second or two and then flashed to the objective. The slice of air phenomenal it slapped bare bottom with an awesome crack, five inches of rump surrendering to the force. The rattan quivered silently as all waited on a reaction.

Kate offered none. She posed there in complete defiance. If it did scald then she wasn't about to broadcast the fact.

Pupils at the front, in a better position to view the flogging, had seen the shudder of flesh and sat quietly as a vivid red stripe developed. Lake swung into action again, the rod slapping, the echo careering off the far walls. Still Kate refused pained comment.

Alice swallowed. Feared for her comrade, she thanked God that she had the sense not to get involved. There was no way she could take such a beating.

Lake powered a third in, meeting and marking stinging

59

nates. One stripe stood thick and proud. A second burgeoned. The third coloured. All blazed within a half inch of each other. The rod slowly climbed those cheeks.

Alice winced as the fourth hurtled in. She screwed her face at the almighty impact, and then opened an eye to see the cane rising. How could Kate take that without so much as a whimper?

A frown on her face, Lake aimed the fifth, adding to the cauldron that had to boil below those trounced flanks. The cut so violent, Kate teetered a second before settling back on plimsoll encased feet. Lake cast a furtive glance at her deputy, the expression telling. She couldn't fathom the girl's lack of protestation.

Six struck, indented and retreated, Kate's behind mauled, the first stroke discolouring, turning mauve.

The hall so quiet a pin would have deafened, Lake's intake of air proved audible as she powered the seventh to those ample cheeks. That copious flesh leaping, Kate finally grunted. Her hands moved, and then realigned themselves on her ankles.

As if Lake feared losing the minor advantage she swiftly revisited, the cut extricating another grunt. Her face relaxed, and pure determination replaced the consternation. Nine admonished, Kate seeming to struggle with the consequence.

No word had been spoken about how many strokes the girl would have to endure. As with many others, Alice assumed it would be the proverbial dozen. Kate knew different. Most would have been mortified at the announcement, but not the masochistic, irrepressible Kate. She had not battered an eyelid when Lake informed her in authoritarian tone, that she would be whipped no less than eighteen times.

So as ten approached, the shrill whistle preceding a violent detonation, Kate was fully aware she had only coped with half. Her bottom corrugated, she battled against the gut-churning torment, that dense rod reaping a harvest of absolute purgatory. Kate would never admit it. Having boasted of her ability to take anything, she would find it impossible to concede she had met her match.

Eleven struck, a thousand hornets in unison. The meagre padding amplified the torture well beyond her tolerance. Kate could do nothing about the squeal that informed her audience on how much it really hurt.

Sustaining that intolerable position proved evermore difficult as the cane slammed against welted posterior, cutting into pronounced stripes. Twelve extricated a wretched yelp, relieving the knot in Kate's chest. Breathing hurried, intake of air insufficient, Kate's head swum. Bright lights darted before eyes either opened in horror or squeezed in agony. Thirteen bit deep into the sensitive joint of cheek and thigh. A strangled cry pierced the quiet.

Not a girl envied her. Not a girl would have traded places, not even for a term's pocket money. Every one sat in awe. Kate rapidly approached heroine status, but sadly she wouldn't be permitted to bathe in it.

Fourteen stole the air from her lungs. Her backside burned continuous and furious. The flogging surpassed the unbearable. Katy sniffed. Tears wetted the lower lids, squeezed out by a distorted expression.

Determined not to waiver, Kate clung tenaciously to those ankles, her fingers delving to the bone. Fifteen slashed, the wake a nightmare. Her behind felt as if it had been coated in oil and set alight.

Wishing the ordeal over, resolve finally floundering, Kate reeled to the sixteenth; a dynamic slash that took her over the edge and tipped her into Hell's kitchen. She partially rose, her back almost horizontal, her mind set on seeking clemency. *Two left* flashed in her mind's eye. *Don't give them the satisfaction.*

Kate reached for those slender joints. The seventeenth ripped into her upper thighs. 'God!' she hissed.

Lake prepared herself for the ultimate, that she determined to be an absolute stinger. The rod flashed, the headmistress's feet nearly leaving the floor. An almighty *swack!* startled all, including the martyr Howell.

The girl slowly straightened, that in itself pure hell. The skirt fell to conceal that ravaged rump, eighteen mauve welts smothering the once fair haunches. She sucked air, shuddering as a sob escaped. She rubbed the tears from her eyes, stuck a smile on lips that wanted only to tighten, and turned. She curtsied and took a slight bow.

Lake shook her head. She had always liked Kate regardless of her undisciplined behaviour. Something about the girl brightened the day.

Jaw set, Katy Howell struggled to the three steps leading down from the stage, and descending made her way along the central aisle. She paused as she came alongside Alice. Looking straight ahead she grinned and imparted, 'It glows, Ali. By Christ, don't it too.' With that her legs folded and she collapsed.

Members of staff quickly lifted the wretched girl and carried her from the hall. Alice whispered goodbye, firmly believing she would never see her friend again.

Chapter Three

Pulled from Carters, and with six weeks' wait until her new school opened its gates, Alice had to spend the interim with the loathed Uncle Richard. She thought it would have been a nice gesture if he had collected her, but instead she caught the train and walked from the station.

She kept a low profile during her last weeks. Instead of striving for infamy as Kate had suggested, she sought obscurity. Alice regained her penchant for hard work and left Carters with a glowing reference, her one and only blot forgotten or ignored.

Richard opened the front door and bid Alice enter. He pointed up the stairs. 'You have the back room. Go and unpack. Leave your clothes laid out on the bed. I will check for unsuitable items in due course.

'When you are done, join me in the parlour and we will talk, lay down a few house rules so you will have no excuse for unacceptable behaviour.'

Heart heavy, still missing her quirky friend, Alice ascended the poorly lit staircase and sought her temporary lodgings. She readily found the back room, sparsely furnished with bed and single wardrobe. The floor bore no carpet, a piece of tatty linoleum the only comfort against bare boards. Dingy, threadbare net curtains hung from a drooping wire. The walls had been distempered somewhere in the distant past, a filthy discoloured brown.

The iron bed bore two ex-army blankets and a crocheted bedspread. She turned the covers back. A single sheet covered the mattress, with nothing between her and those abrasive blankets.

She had travelled in her school uniform, believing that tactful. Her Sunday best and casuals she folded and lay out on the bed, along with her underwear. Two pairs of fancy briefs and a matching brassiere she carefully hid beneath the mattress.

Checking her attire the best she could without a mirror, Alice took a deep breath and headed downstairs. Richard waited, back to the fireplace and hands clasped behind.

'The house rules,' he stated as she emerged. 'One. You will behave in a ladylike fashion at all times. Two. You will obey a curfew of eight o'clock. Should you return even one minute late you will be punished. Three. You will dress as someone of your age, not as a slattern of twenty. Four. You will attend Mass. Five. You will obey my command without hesitation or protest. Six. You will study every night between eight and nine. Seven. You will wash in the kitchen sink every night and morning and bath every Sunday night. Eight. You will not cuss or take the Lord's name in vain. Nine. You will earn your keep; you will cook and keep house. And finally, ten. You will not, under any circumstances, adopt any male friends. Do you wish me to write these down for you?'

'No uncle, I think I can remember them.'

'Not only remember them, Alice. You will obey them.'

'Yes, sir.'

'Very well. We will inspect your wardrobe.'

Alice followed the martinet upstairs. He cast an eye over the clothing. Picking up a pair of trousers he tossed them out of the door. 'Not suitable for a young lady, are they?'

Alice pulled a face. 'No, sir.'

The man found no further fault. 'I'm glad to see you have embraced suitable underclothing, Alice.' The girl smiled, but that said, he abruptly lifted the mattress and seized on the illicit underwear. 'And what's this?' he demanded.

Alice said nothing. She could offer little in defence.

'Ten minutes beneath my roof and you have sought deceit. Did you think you could pull the wool over my eyes?' His voice remained calm, all the more unsettling for the hapless Alice. He handed the garments to the girl. 'You will go into the garden and burn them while I contemplate on what I shall do with you.'

Clutching the forbidden fruits Alice headed for the rear of the house, Richard calling after her, 'The matches are by the oven.'

With tears rolling she set the panties and bra alight with the aid of some kindling. The future had never looked so bleak. Six weeks with the ruthless Richard would prove arduous, to say the least.

What was he conjuring up in there? She glanced at the back door. Hopefully not the strap again. Please, she thought, not that.

Her bum squirming, she returned. Richard reclined in an armchair reading the morning editorial. She waited, nerves fraught, and eventually he put the paper to one side. 'Well Alice, what shall I do with you?'

She shook her head. Fear had her tongue.

'You knew possession of that sort of underwear is against my wishes. You hadn't forgotten or else you wouldn't have hidden them. Or perhaps the fairies did?'

'No uncle, I hid them.'

'No point in asking why, is there?'

'Because I have reached an age where I like…'

'Sexy lingerie,' he finished for her.

'No, uncle, not sexy.'

'Then what, Alice? Come on, tell me. Conjure another adjective that will save your hide.'

'Fancy?' she tried.

'Tell me, Alice, are lacy brassieres and panties as comfortable as plain ones?'

She guessed where the debate headed and merely wished to get it over with. As an intelligent sensitive person she despised bad feeling. 'In my opinion they are no less or more comfortable, sir.'

'So why wear them? Where is the benefit?'

Alice felt an old familiar knot in her chest. Storm clouds gathered. Anger simmered.

'Well, Alice?' Richard persisted. 'What is the benefit?'

'So when I show the boys my tits they're well presented,' she retorted in a crude, gutter accent.

The man leapt from the armchair, Alice cringing,

immediately regretting the challenge. 'You little tramp!' he growled. 'Showing your true colours now, I suppose. Well, you little trollop, you'll regret that outburst. Tonight you can sleep in the garden shed alongside the creepy-crawlies. But before you go we had best check what you're wearing.'

'My uniform, uncle.'

'Beneath your uniform, Alice.'

She glared defiantly.

'Well? What have you on?'

The mouth engaged before Alice troubled to think. 'Why don't you have a look, uncle?' she challenged. 'I'm sure you'd get a kick out of that!'

The smarmy expression faded. Richard straightened, chest out, body trembling, face the colour of beetroot. 'You never learn, do you?' he hissed, Alice cowering. 'There's not one ounce of respect in that offensive body of yours.' He grabbed at her, the girl evasive, backing away. 'Come here, you tramp!'

She ran for the door, but only managed to open it an inch before his fist slammed it shut. He seized her by the hair and dragged her back, Alice screaming, terrified.

Richard hauled her to a table, pushed her over and wrenched the blazer from her shoulders. Alice wriggled. She pulled free, the jacket left in his grip. Again she tried to make her escape, his hand grabbing her by the back of the blouse.

'What are you trying to do?' she cried, face ashen.

Teeth grinding in the effort of holding her, he promised, 'I'm going to ensure you never wear ungodly lingerie again. I'll see the trash burned. You will remember this day. The memory I will etch into your mind and your backside.'

He caught her flailing arms and held her by the wrists, those pressed to the small of her back. He reached around and loosened the tie before tearing it from her neck. That he used to bind her wrists, the material biting deep into the slim joints.

Breathing laboured, veins standing proud from face and

neck, Richard ripped the blouse open, buttons popping and fingers clawing soft breasts as he executed the degrading act.

'You've ruined it!' sobbed Alice. 'You've torn my blouse.'

Richard's reply was abrupt and unexpected. He slapped her head with the flat of his hand. 'Shut up,' he snarled, yanking the starched white garment down her back, the shirt pinning her arms.

He spun Alice, forced his hand between her breasts, and grasping that troublesome brassiere hauled her to the sideboard. There in a fit of pique, a drawer refusing to open he wrenched too hard. Cutlery and oddments scattered as the drawer cleared its compartment.

The man stooped, picked a pair of scissors from the shambles and cut the elastic between the cups. Distraught, Alice looked away. Tears streaming down her flushed cheeks she felt him separate the cups, her breasts laid bare.

Shirt rent, undergarment divided and handhold lost, Richard shoved the defenceless girl to a chair. He forced her over the back, and lifting the skirt inspected the scant, fancy panties.

'Disgusting!' he spat. 'Filthy slattern! Your bottom is all but naked. Have you no shame? Temptation flaunted in such a filthy manner.'

No more said, he cut the elastic over each slender hip and snatched the panties from her. Breathing heavily he warned, 'You stay there. You remain like that. Do not move if you know what's good for you.' He knelt, and glaring at those naked buttocks, firm and full, he removed her knee length socks.

'Part your legs, girl.' Her ankles he bound to the chair legs, the white cotton the ligatures.

'Now, Alice,' the temper seemed to calm, 'you remember the strap?'

'No uncle, please. Not again. I don't understand why you despise me so much. What have I ever done to you?'

'Nil comprehension,' he said, tutting and shaking his

head. 'How am I ever going to ingrain any discipline? You don't listen to a word I say, do you?'

'If you beat me I'll scream,' she warned. 'And I won't stop screaming. Your neighbours will think you're murdering me. They'll call the police.'

'I'd best shut you up then, hadn't I?'

'What do you mean?' Her heart pounded.

'This.' Richard used her rent panties. He leant over her back, his groin pressed to those naked buttocks, Alice certain she felt something hard. He forced the gusset between her lips and knotted the remains behind her neck. 'The tramp silenced,' he announced, the smile bitter.

Then, that fearsome strop in hand, he began, the slap of leather on fragile rump harsh, Alice reared, the skirt falling. She twisted, bound hands attempting to tend and protect.

Richard wrenched the interfering cloth down, the buttons surrendering. He forced her back over, holding her there, the strop returning, taking its toll of vulnerable buttocks.

That time Alice counted the strokes. She noted every sickening clap of leather. Mind dizzy with the blood rush, bright lights darting before her eyes, she suffered twenty dreadful lashes. Struggling for breath, backside numbed, exertions ineffective, the relief proved undeniable when Richard finally desisted.

But that comfort proved short-lived as he reached to caress those trounced cheeks. A growl of protest surged from her throat to be muted by the gag. Richard ignored the indignation, believing her too sore to bear his touch.

Considering her butt sufficiently stoked, he removed the wet gag and released her. 'Now get upstairs and put your nightdress on.'

Alice fled, hands rubbing the trauma. The reserved, cold Richard proved fearsome. The irate Richard terrified her. In that stark room she quickly changed, carefully hanging blazer and skirt in the wardrobe and donning the cotton nightshirt.

Still sobbing, she examined the torn blouse and ruined

bra. 'Animal!' she whispered. 'Bloody, animal!'

Five minutes later, suitably humbled, she presented herself. 'To the shed, Alice,' he coldly informed her. 'You stay there until breakfast tomorrow.'

A hot, clammy July day and Richard led her to the bottom of the garden. There he had sited a wooden shed some eight by twelve feet in size. Obviously a hobby of the past, the structure had been allowed to fall into disrepair. The solitary window was filthy, cracked, with a jagged piece of glass missing. The hinges had rusted, the door resting at an acute angle. The roof lacked a weatherproof covering, the thin boards bleached and twisted.

Richard yanked open the door, and gripping Alice's arm, marched her inside. Everything with regard to the garden had been thrown to the far end. There a clutter of debris hid God knows what. Against the wall opposite the broken window sat a crude bench, the only tool upon it a rusty old vice, bolted down.

Richard pushed her to the centre of the available space. He reached out and took a switch from the bench. 'First though, foul-mouthed brat, there is still the matter of that initial deception and your whore's remark when challenged.'

Alice eyed the switch with trepidation. He bent it, showing off the flex. 'An Ash wand, Alice,' he explicated. 'As good as any rattan cane. Now turn around and bend over.'

'No.' She shook her head. 'No, I won't. I'm not spending my holidays being beaten at your whim.' Her heart pounded. Alice had spirit. Frightened as she was she knew she had to challenge him, or her life would be an absolute misery.

'No?' he questioned, his voice a whisper. '*No?*' he iterated, a touch louder. 'You dare to say no? After I have explained where you stand in the eyes of the law? You have the temerity to stand there and defy your legal guardian? You ungrateful guttersnipe. Bend over this instant or I won't be held responsible for my actions.'

She backed cautiously away, shaking her head. 'No,

uncle, you'll not beat me again.'

Richard took a deep breath. The anger abated. 'Very well, Alice, we'll see how you feel in the morning.' He left, slamming the shed door and locking it.

Alice peered through the filthy glass as he strode back up the garden. She had no watch, although she had noted the time on leaving the house – half-past three. She had no idea of what time Richard deemed breakfast to be. Assuming seven, she had fifteen and a half hours to while away. And what would he do the next morning if she again refused his demand?

Come to that, what would he do about her tea? She was already thirsty, and as far as she could see there was nothing to drink in the shed. The structure stood at that time in the shade of a large elm. Soon the protective foliage would cease to shield her prison from the sun. How hot would it get then?

Alice perched her petite bottom on the bench, squirming with the touch. In her mind that would be safer, sore as she was. She knew not what lurked in the tangle of disused lawn mower, plant pots and other assorted junk. There might be mice, or large spiders. She shuddered at the prospect.

And the night would be infinitely worse. Then the lack of light would deny her the privilege of sight. Anything could crawl over her. She decided upon sleeping on the bench; preferable to the floor, she concluded.

A tedious two hours passed. She counted the knots in the wood. The planks in the floor. She even summoned the courage to poke amongst the flowerpots, a large piece of wood in hand.

The sun fell directly on the shed roof, the temperature climbed. Mouth dry, her throat sore, she mopped at her brow with the hem of the nightdress. She had been sure that Richard would return, if only to give her another chance. Six o'clock came and went, and then seven. Alice realised the man meant what he said. She would have, by that time, given almost anything for a cool drink of tap water.

How could he do that? A person could die of thirst. She peered out into the garden for the umpteenth time; still no sign of the man. Alice approximated the temperature by then to be in the high nineties.

Perspiration wetted her body. The cotton nightie clung, the air claustrophobic. She ambled to the door and gave it a hefty kick, past caring about what Richard thought. That door held firm; she couldn't know her uncle had rammed a piece of six by two against it.

She examined the window to see if it could be opened, but the two by two had been glazed directly into its frame. Fear and anger gripped her. Alice struggling to breathe, and panic amplifying, picked up a small clay pot and hurled it at the glass. The window shattered, fragments scattering on the grass outside. She lunged for the opening and gulped air.

Climbing out teased, but the inherent dread of Richard restrained. Instead she remained, head protruding.

By eight, thirst worrying, empty stomach calling, she noted the sky darkening. Heavy rain clouds obscured the hot sun. The atmosphere became electric, the heat sultry and overbearing. She pulled the nightie from her sweat-soaked body, and naked, tossed it onto the bench. She cared not to find something unsavoury in it later.

The sky darkened overhead. A cooling breeze sprung up. Alice stood cruciform to appreciate the blow. Then the first heavy raindrops spilled, striking the roof like lead pellets. She poked her head out, open mouth seeking succour. The impetus increased rapidly, a deluge shaking the building with its force. She remained, water soaking her hair and cascading down her face.

Those potent droplets stinging, she withdrew to settle on the bench and witness that mighty force of nature. Arms folded, ankles crossed, she squatted – naked as the day she was born.

She noted the first drip, drip, striking the dusty floor, the uncovered roof surrendering to the tide washing over it. Alice sought her nightie and quickly hauled it over her head. Within minutes that deluge discovered every slit and

71

gap in the aged roof above. Soon water poured rather than dripped, the girl finding it impossible to evade.

Sweats gave way to shivers as the nightdress slowly soaked, clinging to her curvaceous form. The thirst slaked, she faced the prospect of spending the night cold and wet. The bench offered some protection, but clambering beneath only served to delay the dousing.

The immediate storm over within the hour, the rain assumed a steady rhythm for the rest of that dreadful night. Alice cowered, eyes owl-like, seeking any movement in the almost impenetrable gloom. She huddled, trying to keep warm.

First light at five brought no respite from the rain. Reduced to a drizzle, the drips were plenty and constant. The floor soaked, Alice chilled, she longed for the warmth of her bed, a steaming mug of tea, and even a plateful of the dreaded school porridge.

Richard proved an early riser. Raincoat donned he strode purposefully down the garden, removed the timber and unlocked the door. His small frame filled the portal. 'Spend a comfortable night?' he enquired.

Alice crawled from beneath the bench and rose, arms trying to cover the transparency of her nightwear.

'You appear a trifle damp, Alice,' he mused. 'It was rather a wet night and this old shed hasn't been weatherproofed for years. So, young lady, have you reached a decision?'

'I'm hungry, uncle.'

'A decision first.'

'What if I say no?'

'Then you stay here until you change your mind.'

'What, with no food or water? I'll die.'

'I wouldn't be that callous. No Alice, should you settle on six weeks imprisonment then I will supply bread and water for your diet. I have to admit I don't care one way or the other. Bread is cheap, water free. And I won't have to suffer your capricious whims.'

Alice could not face six weeks of that, and she had no doubt that he meant every word. Richard had already proved himself a callous and indifferent tyrant. 'If I let you cane me, then will that be it?' she asked.

'Let me?' he sneered. 'Not quite, Alice.'

She stared at him, aghast. 'What then?'

'You challenged my decision last night and I see you have broken the window.'

'The window was already broken,' she replied, indignant.

'It was cracked, not broken.'

Alice threw her hands apart, forgetting the see-through effect of her nightdress. 'The bloody place is falling down,' she protested. 'How can you accuse me of damage?'

Richard swallowed as his eyes fell upon her bosom, and Alice quickly covered herself again, arms folded.

'That's the offer, Alice,' he went on, tearing his eyes back up to her face. 'Punishment for your deceit. Punishment for your disgusting language. Punishment for your audacity and for breaking the window. What's it to be?'

She shivered, partly from cold and partly from apprehension. 'If I agree, what then?'

'Breakfast. A hot cup of tea and I might even let you catch up on your sleep.'

'I meant, what punishment?'

'Deceit warrants the switch. Foul language requires the mouth to be washed. Audacity necessitates humility, and wanton damage the strap.'

Alice shuddered.

'It will warm up one part of your anatomy,' Richard offered, smiling.

'Mouth washed?' Alice questioned.

'Soap and water.'

She pulled a face, but what choice did she have? Alice realised that if she were to have anywhere near a decent life she would have to adopt a halo. So she nodded.

But that was not good enough for her sadistic uncle. 'Say it, Alice.'

'I... I agree.'

'And you won't challenge my authority again?'

'No, sir.'

'Very good.' He stared at her for the best part of half a minute. 'Put your arms out in front of you, Alice. Hands together.'

Not daring to question, the girl obliged, and Richard bound them with a thin rope. He placed a hand beneath her arm and guided her to the bench. The free end of the rope he tightened in the vice. 'Now bend over, Alice.' The girl shuffled her feet backwards until in position. Richard then secured her ankles, tying them together.

'The rope is to ensure you don't change your mind.'

'I won't,' she assured.

'Oh, you might, Alice. I have in mind a rather prolonged flogging. You see, I intend to sort out our differences here and now. I will penetrate that thick skin one way or another. You, my girl, will jump when I snap my fingers. You, my girl, will learn obedience.

'In two years from now you will take up unpaid employment with Mr Hassan Al-Awadi. He will expect you to serve his every whim without question or favour. In the intervening years you will be prepared. You must learn to not only expect discipline but to advocate it as well.'

What was Alice in for? Serve? Discipline? An Arab? Her heart sank.

Richard picked up the switch, the end of an Ash branch. It began in his fist at a half-inch thick, tapering over forty inches to a whippy three-eighths. Her bottom he would leave covered, for he knew the wet material would accentuate the bite.

Katy's flogging flashed through Alice's mind, and she felt sick. Would he render her senseless, as Lake had Kate?

Richard, however, had other ideas. He had sold the girl for a princely sum, an insurance against old age. There was no fixed term as he had said, but the gentleman in question required an intelligent and subservient young woman – one that would pander to his 'needs'. Richard had only a few years to train Alice. He knew the consequences should he fail.

The funds for Alice's education would come directly from Richard's pocket, hence his choice of faculty; one that would provide the correct stimulus to succeed without bankrupting his account. Alice would learn to appreciate the finer points of corporal punishment, for that was his client's main fetish. She would yield to his demands. He would snap her spirit like a dry twig.

For the next six weeks Richard would find every excuse to admonish the girl. He would subject her to every humiliation he could devise. Alice would leave his house in September chastened and subjugated.

And then there was Chatswood. The learned Chatswood. A master of education and of corporal punishment. He had cost Richard a few pounds. But there again, Chatswood had begat Chatswood junior, inveterate bully and perfidious academic at Heptonstall.

A visit to inspect the facilities and enrol Alice provided more than Richard could have hoped for. He recognised Chatswood senior immediately. They served in the Royal Artillery together. Richard casually reminded the Don of his moneymaking schemes during the war. The deputy headmaster laughed, asking Richard not to make too much noise about the matter, as he had a position to think of.

Richard bargained a favour for a favour. The deal haggled over a dinner at the local hostelry cost him a few pounds, but assured of an ally in his schemes. He held reservations about the sexual side of the plot, but Chatswood junior, he was assured, did not.

Trying to ignore the unmistakable outline of Alice's bottom, the wet cloth adhering to the flesh, Richard commenced the girl's ordeal. Lacking severity he whipped her bottom, the cut stinging, wrapping to the hip, leaving the girl in no doubt she had been striped, but no more.

Alice grimaced, unsure whether he had misjudged or his arm had weakened. The stroke proved nowhere near as debilitating as Stagnant's. But what the whipping lacked in strength it more than compensated by quantity.

Her ears assailed by the constant swish and smack of rod on wet bottom, she flinched and grunted to the incessant lathering. Her bottom warmed, stung continuously. It reddened, took on a deeper hue, Alice wondering if the man would ever tire. To her own surprise she tolerated. To her consternation as her spheres began to glow, she even found the drubbing somewhat stimulating.

Could this be, she wondered, what Katy experienced?

Her backside smothered in fine welts, a general numbing induced, she sensed the glow that Katy and she had joked about. Each subsequent stroke accentuated the sensation, the feeling a mild but interesting tingle, akin to having a soft comb drawn over a sexually responsive part of the anatomy.

And that didn't waver or increase. Had Richard known he would have seen his prayers answered? Alice had no idea how to benefit or accelerate the wonder. Her fantasies and dreams were limited, sexual adventure almost non-existent.

For ten minutes she bore the flagellation until her uncle desisted, the interval short-lived. He withdrew that fearsome strop from an inside pocket of his discarded raincoat. Placing that on the bench he reached down and drew her nightdress up and over that scarlet bottom. The strop would be delivered on the bare as on previous occasions.

Alice sought a deep breath as she heard the dull rush of air, the leather cracking hard on flogged cheeks. She gasped as the fire intruded, a strip of flesh ignited.

What would Katy do now? How would she turn this awful smart, make it into something sensual?

The strop revisited, the burn nearing untenable. She tried to concentrate on her vulnerability, to imagine how he saw her. That rosy backside, stripped of all covering. Her very private nether region exposed to one of the opposite sex. However, the jolting explosions to her backside checked those imaginative notions. She found it near impossible to retain lucid thought.

Instead she tried to dodge the incendiaries, moving her behind left and right, anticipating the dire impact and thrusting forward as the leather struck. All to no avail. Wherever her rump dived so the broad hide followed, the consequence sickening, the aftermath unbearable.

Tears cascading, chest heaving, she sobbed and cried, squirmed and writhed, howled and yelped. All music to Richard's ears.

The punishment duly executed, he replaced the strop in the coat pocket and released the wretched Alice. She wriggled the nightie back over stricken hips, and demoralised, awaited instruction.

He led her out into the rain and back to the house, Alice finding some relief in that. At the sink he lathered a bar of soap, Alice quailing at the prospect. He faced her. 'Open your mouth. We'll clean the filth from it now.'

Reluctant, Alice obliged. Richard seized her jaw and inserted the soap. He scoured her mouth, ensuring he left a heavy residue of suds. Then he clamped the jaw shut, the taste foul.

She heaved. He let her go. Alice rushed to the sink and vomited.

'No more filth from that mouth, I hope,' he said.

She shook her head. In a way it was worse than the thrashing.

'Good. Now as an act of humility and contrition you can take off your nightdress and stand in the corner of the kitchen, hands on your head while I make us breakfast.'

Without argument Alice went from the scullery and into the kitchen. She removed the garment and faced the wall, hands on her head. She stood there for the fifteen minutes it took Richard to cook bacon and eggs.

She couldn't see his furtive glances, the admiration of his handiwork, as he studied from a distance that beleaguered posterior.

Nightdress back on, Alice sat gingerly to partake of the edibles, glad to fill her belly and gratify her thirst with a hot cup of sweet tea – that going some distance towards ridding her of the taste of soap.

Richard forked a piece of streaky bacon into his mouth.

'You see, Alice, behave and I will treat you well. Misbehave and I will punish you severely.'

'Yes, uncle,' she whispered.

The meal vanquished, Richard collected up the plates. 'When you have washed up, Alice, you can clean yourself up. Use the kitchen sink, and I don't mean a cat's lick, either. A proper wash. All over.'

'Can I wash my nightie as well, please? It will smell tonight if I don't.'

'Of course, and you can do my laundry at the same time.'

She forced a smile.

She washed the plates and cutlery, cleaned the frying pan and wiped down the cooker. Then she refilled the sink. She cast a glance at her uncle, sat at the table reading the paper. It seemed obvious to her he intended to stay. Modesty was a word she had to forget. She guessed she would have to get used to him being there, her privacy invaded.

She washed her face, utilising a cloth perched on a shelf. Again she checked her master. The man sat unabashed, reading. Resigned, embarrassed, Alice pulled a face and caught the hem of the nightie. She eased it up, the cloth still damp adhering to her skin. The garment rose, first buttocks still discoloured and sore came into view, then the slim waist and lean back. She sighed and tugged the cotton over firm, full breasts. The nightdress temporarily covering her head she missed Richard's admiring glance, her nakedness clearly pleasing.

Alice dropped the item to the cold tiled floor. She lathered the soap on the facecloth and began washing her torso. Richard spied furtively over wire-rimmed glasses. He held a side view and ogled the generous movement of breast. The suds-covered wet tit entranced.

Alice's back crawled; she knew he studied her. She turned her head in his direction hoping to embarrass, but Richard simply smiled.

Galled, she resumed, attending to abdomen and the best part of her back. She rinsed the cloth, and re-soaping delved between her legs, her uncle to all intents and purposes reading again.

Her bottom she approached with caution, the touch of rough material abrasive, aggravating the countless raised welts. Carefully she doused the cheeks, Richard's attention re-captivated.

She wanted to scream at him, to vent her exasperation, to call him a sick bastard, to tell him she despised and loathed the very sight of him. But she knew what the result would be and cared not to invoke it.

Finished, she bent to pick up the soiled nightie, realising too late that she offered an intimate view. She crouched and collected the garment in her arms, the rag carefully draped to protect her modesty.

She faced Richard and asked politely, 'May I go and get dressed now, please?'

'Not yet, Alice; I couldn't help noticing how sore your bottom looks.'

'It has been thrashed, uncle,' she pointed out, unnecessarily. 'It's hardly surprising, is it?'

'Don't be facetious. In that cupboard you will find a tub of antiseptic. Bring it to me, please.'

He admired the wiggle of hips, the tremor of cheeks and the rosy tint inspired. The tub in hand she returned, Richard savouring the jostle of breasts.

She handed it to him. 'Over my lap then, Alice.'

'I'm sorry?'

'Over my lap, girl. I'll spread the lotion for you. You can hardly do it yourself, now can you?'

Not believing her ears, his outrageous behaviour beyond her, she lowered herself and lay over those thighs, feet and hands trailing the floor.

With a self-satisfied smirk Richard opened the tub. Humiliation he maintained, denying to himself he enjoyed it. Finger supporting a healthy dollop he spread the greasy salve. Methodically he massaged the fleshy rump, lingering on the warm, compact buttocks, deliberating on their youthful constitution.

Alice found the attention repugnant. The cream soothed,

that she could not deny, but his touch on such an intimate place teased, Alice attempting to ignore the inner desire.

Richard loitered, persisted with the unwarranted favour, refusing to cease until all trace of the cream had been absorbed.

Then he slapped her rump playfully and allowed Alice to rise. 'All done. You can get dressed now. Nothing decent, mind you; you have work to do.'

Seven days passed without further aggression. The man nagged, kept a vigilance on Alice, the girl subsequently always on edge. But he refrained from punishment.

Involved in a round of endless chores, Alice was interrupted by a postman delivering a long cylindrical tube wrapped in heavy brown paper, the item addressed to Richard. As the man was at work she left it on the sideboard, only slightly curious about its contents.

She had been left a pound to shop with, her uncle telling her he expected dinner cooked and ready for the table by the time he got home. Her problem? She couldn't cook, had never been taught how.

She opted for bangers and mash, believing that to be the easiest to prepare. Cheap, as well, she thought. That would please the tight-fisted scrooge. A pound of pork sausages purchased along with a pound of potatoes, she added a tin of baked beans for the vegetable.

Upon her return she sought a cookery book, expecting one to lie somewhere within the kitchen cupboards. There was none, but not one to be easily defeated she applied commonsense.

Richard always came home at five-thirty, and Alice configured the cooking time for the ingredients to be about a half-hour. At five-ten she was disturbed by a knock on the door, and opening it revealed a door-to-door salesman.

The man entered upon his spiel; Alice too inexperienced to slam the door in his face. Some ten minutes later she finally convinced him he was wasting his time.

Heading back for the scullery she caught the definite reek of burning, and dashing into the room she found the sausages blackened on one side. Worse still, the potatoes had disintegrated and the beans were a dried lump adhered to the bottom of the pan. She panicked. She pulled at her hair convinced the world had come to an end.

What would Uncle Vicious say? More to the point, what would he do? Desperately she tried to scrape the black from the sausages. She sieved the potatoes, hoping and praying they would still prove edible. The beans were lost.

She checked the wall clock a moment before a key in the front door alerted her to Richard's arrival home. Shaking, Alice wiped at her tears and laid out the plates.

In Richard walked. 'Something doesn't smell delicious, Alice. Something smells burnt. I do hope for your sake that is not my dinner.'

She backed to a cupboard as if that would protect her bottom. Holding trembling hands out she begged more than excused. 'I… I'm so sorry, uncle. I had a caller just at the crucial moment. When I came back the dinner was burnt.' She hung her head and added in a whisper, 'I'm not very good at cooking, I'm afraid.'

'That's obvious.' Richard sat and held Alice with a fixed gaze. 'Women cook and clean, Alice. Men work for the bread. That is the way of the world. Has been for centuries. What good is a woman that can't cook?'

She shook her head; defence, she knew, to be pointless.

'Too much airy-fairy in that head of yours. Instead of learning the basics to be a good wife and mother you chase a dream. Do you really think the world is ready for you to displace the accepted head of the household?'

'How do you mean?'

'All these qualifications you study. What's the point? Are you after a man's job? Don't you want to be a mother and wife? Is there something wrong with you?'

Mien cold she retorted, the inference clear, 'There's nothing the matter with me.'

'Mind your tongue, young lady; you hover on insubordination. Now answer my question.'

'I want to prove I can. Simple as that.'

'At what expenditure? A costly point to make, don't you think?'

'Why worry, you're not paying?'

'Insolence again. Will you never learn?'

'I'm not being insolent!' she near shrieked, as Richard stood.

'You will speak to me with the utmost respect, Alice. And until you do, you will suffer the consequences.'

Her hands went to her bottom without prior thought. She held the cheeks, the previous marks only recently faded.

'You burn the dinner through neglect or stupidity. You fail to inform me you can't cook in the first place. And you react with insolence when challenged. After the last time I thought you might comprehend. But it is obvious your skull is thicker than I believed. Tell me, Alice, is your hide as thick?'

She stared at the floor, eyes wide, mouth open.

'Did I receive a parcel today, Alice?' he suddenly asked, and she nodded. 'Then where is it, girl?'

'In the parlour, on the sideboard.'

'How opportune. How appropriate.'

Slowly her head lifted, and she gazed at the devious tyrant, puzzled.

'Come, Alice, you can open it. It is primarily for you. Or should I say, for use on you.'

She followed, heart in mouth.

In the parlour she unravelled the tube, ripping the brown paper away. She removed the cap and then a ball of tissue paper stuffed in the end.

'Tip the contents onto the table.' Richard smiled, self-satisfied.

Dreading what lay within, she complied. Three rattan canes, straight, without crook, emerged. She gasped. Her heart rate sped even faster.

'What, not pleased?' asked Richard, his tone cruel.

Alice stepped back. Memories of Lake's rod slashing her backside flooded her mind. The three rods differed in thickness – one of five millimetres, one of eight, and one of ten.

'I thought I might require a decent deterrent, something that would make an impression on you. It seems I will have to buy dinner tonight. That displeases me considerably. Especially when I've already paid out once. Still, you will reap the fruit of that mistake.

'I shall take a stroll to the fish and chip shop. Whilst I am gone think about what I have said. Feel the rods. Dwell on their embrace.'

She listened to the front door closing. Slumped on a chair, her head fell to comforting hands. How could a brother and sister be so different? Mother was so kind and understanding; Richard was a vindictive bastard. How could they leave her in his care? Surely they knew what he was like?

She let the tears roll, distressed mind returning to happier days. She envisioned how life had been; a loving mother, a doting father.

Perhaps she was spoilt. She'd had everything a girl could wish for. They said Uncle Richard was a pain, a sponger, but they never intimated he was downright cruel. So perhaps it was her. She did run off without a word from Carters, and she had been insolent to Richard. Perhaps she deserved that caning. Maybe he saw something in her that she could not. Perhaps he wanted to change her for her own good. If she tried really hard to please him, he might even grow to like her – or even love her.

Alice wiped away the tears and made for the scullery, and there she cleared away the wreckage of dinner and washed up. She took a seat and waited on her uncle.

Twenty minutes later he returned, a wrapped bundle in hand. Selecting a plate, knife and fork he opened the package. Alice's heart sank. Exceedingly hungry, the threat of a thrashing not having diminished her appetite, she noted only one portion of fish and one of chips.

Richard grinned. 'Not hungry are you, Alice?' he mocked.

'Well actually, I am,' she replied.

'Oh, I'm sorry. I thought your imminent caning would

have put you off eating.'

'Um, no, it hasn't.'

'What happened to the food you burnt?'

'I cleaned up. Washed up. It's in the bin.'

'Terrible waste, that.' He sprinkled salt and vinegar over his dinner. 'I would have thought you could salvage enough to feed yourself.'

'It seems I made a mistake, uncle.'

'You're making a habit of that.'

'I thought perhaps you might have just the slightest streak of humanity in you. It would seem I was wrong.'

The piece of fish heading for his mouth stopped short. Richard blinked. He glared at her. 'What did you say?'

She reached out and took a chip. Placing it in her mouth, she iterated, 'I thought perhaps that you might have just the slightest streak of humanity in you. It would seem I was wrong.'

Richard shook visibly. He threw down his cutlery; face a deep red, implosion seemingly imminent.

'Oh, not hungry, uncle?' she said sweetly. 'Never mind, I am.' Alice reached over and pulled the plate towards her.

His mouth opened but no words came forth. Alice began to eat.

'I,' he stammered. 'I wi… will thrash you for that, you wretch,' he finally growled.

'Oh, I thought you were going to anyway,' she goaded.

Stricken, Richard could do no more than watch her eat. Then seeming to gather his wits he struck out, the plate and dinner sent flying.

Alice examined the mess. 'Uncle, what a waste!' she exclaimed. 'Good food thrown on the floor. You should be striped for that.'

'You disrespectful slut!' he seethed. 'Get in the parlour!'

'Oh, I don't think so, uncle. Not unless you physically drag me there.'

'What the hell has come over you?'

'You, uncle. I was set to try. I was going to give it my heart and soul. And then you waltz in here and start eating without a thought for me. I'm a girl. I have recently lost both my parents. I need love, understanding and guidance, not tyranny.

'You seem to think that beating me is the only answer. I have not up until now been wilfully disobedient. I accept I have had outbursts, and I also accept I should be punished for those.

'However, flogging me for doing my best I cannot accept. I didn't burn the dinner on purpose. I really tried to do something constructive. I accept I must pull my weight. But you must see some good in me in return.'

'Have you finished?'

'Yes.'

Richard leapt up, seized Alice by the arm and dragged her squealing to the parlour. There he sat on a wooden chair still holding the girl. He forced her over his lap, pulled her skirt up and wrenched her panties down, her bottom bared. He then lay into those cheeks passionately, slapping her bottom as hard as he could.

His jaw set firm he said nothing as Alice wriggled and writhed, that hand pounding, striking each buttock alternately, finger marks rapidly appearing. Within minutes the pain grew beyond her, such was the rapidity of his rough handout. Alice began to punctuate each detonation with a yelp. Struggling to free herself, Richard determined she wouldn't.

Alice had said her piece. She had allowed the urge to retaliate to better commonsense. She paid. The sting in her rear continuous and sickening, she accepted that come whatever she had to curb her tongue. Richard would retaliate; saw physical discipline as the answer to all problems, large or small.

Between slaps she kept her eye on the mantelpiece clock, watching the seconds tick by, the minutes, her backside crimped and exceedingly sore. Richard seemed to have lost that cold control. He vent his anger on her; the strength of delivery not diminishing, the pain and fire excruciating.

Her legs kicked with every discharge, fingers clawed thin air. Her expression twisted in constant turmoil, the riot in her rump beyond comprehension.

Five minutes of hell she endured before Richard desisted – and then only due to fatigue. He pushed her from his lap, Alice landing heavily on the thin carpet. Modesty beyond her she remained there, her scarlet behind thrust up, the heat there prolific.

Richard rose, and face warped with anger, ordered, 'Remain in that position, Alice. You *will* treat me with deference. We *will* sort this out here and now.'

He selected the medium cane, and after flexing it cut the air, the slice unfavourable. Alice shifted her head from comforting hands and stared up at him, eyes pleading. 'But you've spanked me!' she protested. 'Isn't that enough?'

'I don't believe it is, no. It should be, but Alice, you are not normal. I have noted that after I have chastised you we enjoy a period of calm. An interval where you seem to accept your place. However, after a few days you regress. It appears that you possess a short memory, and I have to constantly remind you.'

She buried her head again as he raised the rod. The swish awesome, her butt reeled to the import. The cane slashed and wrapped, the fire in its wake dreadful. The position she had innocently adopted proved to be the most untenable.

Richard lashed that upturned seat a half-dozen times, Alice near screaming with each trial. He then stood astride her back and beat her from above, the cane cutting vertically, a cross hatch of welts the result.

Twelve strokes in all administered, the man placed the cane back on the table and left. Alice lay awhile, waiting for the smart to ebb. Cautiously she rose, still sobbing. She felt her whipped backside, recoiling at the touch. Her panties kicked off during the fracas she stooped to pick them up, the brief flirtation of skirt and tender buttock enough to dissuade her from putting them on.

With no idea of where Richard had gone, she climbed the stairs to inspect the damage in her uncle's bedroom, each step a nightmare. With her back to the wardrobe door she lifted her skirt. Her buttocks shocked; deep carmine they exhibited the horizontal and vertical bites of the cane, those marks raised and discoloured. Those laid to her from above terminated a few inches below her cheeks, her thighs etched.

The front door closing snapped her to her senses. With a glance to check she left no evidence she hurried to her own room. There she picked a book to read.

Five minutes later Richard entered without knocking. 'Have you been in my room?' he asked, the usual chill to his voice.

Alice shook her head.

'Then what are these doing there?' He held up the panties, and Alice dropped the book such was her fear. The evidence incriminated. She must have dropped them in her haste to leave his room. She could offer no lie, only the truth. 'I-I'm sorry,' came her admission. 'I used your mirror. It's the only one in the house.'

'You just can't help yourself, can you?' he sneered. 'Always the lie first, then when faced with undeniable proof you come clean. But only when you have no other alternative. So Alice, why were you in my bedroom?'

'As I said, to use your mirror.'

'Admiration?'

'No, not at all; I wanted to see what you'd done to me.'

'As I said, admiration.'

'Curiosity.'

'I see. I'm not going to punish you this time, Alice. I was remiss in not mentioning my room is out of bounds. I didn't think for one minute I would have to tell you. I thought that a lady of breeding would automatically know. But of course, you are no lady of breeding, are you?

'In future, Alice, you stay out of my bedroom. It's bad enough you invading the privacy of my home, without you snooping in my private domain.

'Now as for lying to me, that is a different matter. In the shed you will find a garden fork. You will take that and turn over the weeded area you will see lying adjacent. It is now six forty-five. You have until nine. In that time I

87

expect to find it completed.'

'And if I don't?'

'Don't even think that way, Alice. You will do it. That is the way you must conduct yourself from now on.'

Chapter Four

Alice delved amongst the debris that had intimidated her so. There she located an old rusted fork, the shaft bleached with age. Out into the evening she carried the tool, dressed in shorts and a T-shirt, plimsolls on her feet.

The plot Richard referred to lay behind the dilapidated structure. She estimated it to be some fifteen by ten feet, the patch overgrown with nettles, thistle and couch grass. Dejected, Alice slammed the fork into an unforgiving ground. There was no way she could turn the plot in the time allotted. So what would Richard do when she failed? Alice cared not to contemplate that.

She toiled, and as she worked so the first spots of rain fell. She gazed up at the heavens, the clouds thick and foreboding.

Not a storm this time, more a persistent drizzle. Rain that soaked the weeds she waded in. Drenched the clothes she wore and soaked the plimsolls on her feet. Working as if the devil possessed and keen to avoid whatever Richard held in store, the water mixed with her perspiration.

A half-hour elapsed. Alice had turned over three of that fifteen-foot strip. Her own mathematics informed her she couldn't make the deadline. Her stamina flagged, arms, shoulders and back ached. Her legs bitched continuously, Alice close on exhaustion.

In the scullery Richard squatted, a pair of binoculars to his eyes. He ogled her every movement. Telling himself he monitored her progress, her diligence. Never for one second did he admit he drank of her body, the translucence of her attire, the mobility of feminine flesh.

Dirt adhered to hands, nettles stung uncovered legs, thistle heads probed where no man had laid a hand. Alice stretched, her back to the house, oblivious that another watched.

And equally intent on her every movement, Malcolm the boy next door gazed in sexual appreciation. Malcolm, the teenage son of Janet, a widow.

Cosseted, pandered Malcolm, a boy whose only acclaim to carnal fulfilment was a copy of an illicit magazine and five sisters at night. And those five fiddled continuously through the material of corduroy trousers as he scrutinised every movement of the girl next door.

Malcolm, certain she wore no underwear, brooded on what sort of young woman she might be. He could clearly see the pink of her bottom through the wet shorts. And when she turned, oh he hoped she would again soon; he could determine the outline of pert breasts and nipples.

He watched her bend again, those pants so tight to that lascivious backside, the material stretched almost to bursting point. Malcolm grunted, and unable to resist, pushed a hand inside his trousers, seizing the meat within. Eyes unblinking he rubbed the crown of that inflexible torpedo, the erection sensitive to his feverish manipulations.

Lust at first sight. Alice drove Malcolm insane. Breathing ragged, he mentally placed himself with her, naked bodies entwined, her softly giving breasts hard to his chest, full buttocks in his grasping hands.

With a wheezing sigh he shot his lot, too late to extricate the tool from his pants. The slimy warm seed wet, Malcolm bothered not. He had to get to know Alice better. Somehow he would have to overcome his natural shyness and make a gesture.

Hair saturated, clothing dripping, Alice neared the halfway mark. She had no idea of the time but estimated she hadn't long.

Richard appeared shortly after, umbrella shielding him from the rain. 'Not a very good showing, is it Alice?'

'I've done my best, uncle,' she assured.

'Perhaps if you had put your back into it the outcome would be different.'

She showed her hands. Large broken blisters marked the palms and thumbs. 'I'm not a navvy, uncle. Honestly, I did my best.'

'You'd better go in and put the copper on. Take a hot bath. I don't want you going down with pneumonia.'

'And what then?'

He shrugged. 'You can finish it tomorrow.'

The copper boiled, Alice dragged in a zinc bath, the only means for some in those days. The boiling water in the tub, she added the cold to suit. As expected, Richard took up his usual seat in the kitchen, the evening paper in hand.

'Can I ask you something, uncle?' Alice dared.

'Fire away.'

'Would it be possible to take my bath in private?'

'You've nothing I haven't seen all ready.'

'I know. It's just that I would like to be left alone.'

'Why? What do you intend getting up to?'

'Uncle, I'm a female and you're a male. Even my father didn't watch me washing.'

'I'm not watching, Alice. I'm reading, as you can see. And, young lady, I don't care for your insinuation.'

'There's no insinuation.'

'Good. I might get annoyed if I thought you inferred I got some pleasure out of you being naked.'

'Uncle.'

'Yes.'

'I don't sit reading the paper when you're taking a bath.'

'It wouldn't bother me if you did.'

Alice pulled a face; she knew it pointless to argue.

'Don't you believe me?' he asked.

'Of course I do. You wouldn't lie, would you?' Her intonation was clear.

He folded the newspaper, took off his glasses, and carefully placed them in a case. Then he unfastened his shirt. 'No, Alice, I wouldn't lie. So I'll prove it to you.'

Her mouth opened in disbelief. She had never seen a man naked before, and she wasn't sure she wanted to. Undaunted Richard stripped shirt, shoes and socks. He unfastened the trouser fly and they fell to the floor. Unhesitant he lowered the white Y-fronts, his privates revealed.

Alice should have looked away, if only for decency's sake. Something, however, a lurid fascination, kept her riveted. He approached the tub, ensured the temperature met his preference, and then climbed in.

'You see, Alice, there is nothing to be ashamed of. There is absolutely nothing wrong with the naked body. I don't suggest you show yourself off to all and sundry. No, that would be wrong. It would be misconstrued. However, within the family it is quite acceptable. And we are family, Alice.'

'Can I read your paper, uncle?' She felt the need to disassociate herself.

'Of course, but you'd best take off those wet clothes first.'

She started for the kitchen.

'No, no, girl, you'll drip all over the floor. Take them off there and hang them over the sink.'

Alice kicked off the plimsolls and then eased the shorts over her hips. Still not convinced, she turned her back and removed the shirt.

'Where's your underwear, Alice?'

'I didn't put any on.'

'So I can see. And most likely half the neighbourhood has as well. Are you some sort of exhibitionist?'

'No, uncle, I didn't want to get them dirty. Since I had to burn half I don't have much left.'

'In that case I had better buy you some, hadn't I? I see the cane made an impression.'

'In more ways than one.'

'Do as you're told and you won't have to suffer it again. That is entirely down to you.'

She waited for him to finish and then used the water he left. Alice was in two minds; the more trusting side of her nature assured he took no interest in her nudity, but a voice from the darker side warned that his actions were just a prelude to more sinister goings on.

The next morning, Richard having departed, Alice resumed her toils in the garden. She wore the same clothes as the previous evening, again without the underwear. With no interfering uncle she could very much please herself.

She had all day and adopted a leisurely pace, unawares the boy next door kept a vigil. Malcolm watched eagerly from his vantage point, tucked behind the net curtains, begging for a glimpse of something erotic. He prayed the seam of her shorts would split. He hoped she might feel secure enough to strip to the waist. Oh, God, he did yearn for that!

Alice, unfortunately for him, was well aware that houses overlooked, and did not intend to draw unwarranted attention. However, the thought of being naked beneath her skimpy outfit aroused. She was sensitive to the movement of her bosom as she dug and weeded, knowing how it rippled within the tight T-shirt. Had Alice realised Malcolm writhed in rapture to her labours, she might well have accentuated the act.

During the last few weeks her attitude had changed radically. Hormones assaulted her chemistry. She deliberated more on the opposite sex, at times finding it hard to keep her mind off them. Confusion reigned, a virtuous upbringing at odds with desires.

Malcolm took a deep breath and advanced on the dividing fence. He leaned on the top, and finding a voice, hailed Alice. 'Hi there.'

The girl looked up, and seeing no one, turned. 'Yes?' she said, startled.

'I'm your neighbour,' was all he could think of.

'Oh,' answered the equally shy Alice.

'Malcolm.'

'What?'

'I'm Malcolm.'

Alice managed a smile. 'My name is Alice.'

'Nice name.'

'Is it?'

'I think so.'

Unimpressed, the boy not her ideal, she replied, 'I'm

sorry, I can't talk, I've got work to do.'

'Are you a relative of old grumpy?' he persisted.

'Niece.'

'Are you staying here? Only I haven't seen you before.'

'Just for the holidays. And then I'm back to college.'

Malcolm couldn't take his eyes off the prominence of her bosom, and Alice noticed, an idea forming. 'You look a strapping young man,' she said. 'Are you as sturdy as you look?'

Malcolm straightened, his shoulders back. 'I use chest expanders,' he said, proud. 'Look,' he flexed his biceps.

'Looks impressive, but how strong are you?'

'I could dig that patch over in no time at all.'

'No, I don't think so, Malcolm. The ground is rock hard. These roots go down for miles. You'd have to be really strong to dig this.'

Keen to impress, and looking for any excuse to get closer, Malcolm leapt the fence. 'I'll show you,' he said without malice, and Alice gladly passed him the fork. Richard wouldn't loom large for at least another seven hours.

Malcolm dug, turned the sod like a man possessed, his only purpose to please. And please he did. Alice smiling egged him on.

'Are you finished school now?' she enquired.

'For good. I'm looking for a job now.'

'Any idea what you want to do?' She practiced idle chitchat.

'Not really.' He turned several more clods. 'You're very attractive,' he mumbled.

'Sorry?' Alice didn't hear.

'I said, you're very attractive.'

'Am I?'

His face burned. He returned to digging. 'I think so.'

'I thought I was quite plain.'

'Oh no. Anything but plain.'

'You're quite good-looking yourself,' she lied.

He shook his head. 'No, you need glasses.'

Alice didn't pursue the matter. 'You've got a good body,'

she offered instead.

'And so have you.'

'Are you flirting with me?'

Malcolm tossed another clump of couch onto a pile. 'Yes, as a matter of fact. I think you're gorgeous.' He couldn't keep the eye contact. The boy was no Don Juan. 'I watched you digging yesterday evening,' he admitted.

'You didn't offer to help then. Was it because it was raining?'

'No. I didn't like to. I had to summon the courage, and besides, old grumpy was at home.'

'You don't like my uncle then?'

'It's not that. He doesn't like anybody. Miserable sod, if you ask me.'

'Why do you think I'm gorgeous?' Alice was intrigued. The only other compliment she had received from a boy was the reference to her body by Kate's friend.

'You don't mind if I'm honest?'

'Of course not.'

'First, you're pretty. That red hair, those green eyes. The rest of you is very nice as well.'

Stirred, seeking flattery, she said, 'Tell me, Malcolm, why is the rest of me nice?'

He continued to labour. 'You're slim, in the right places. You've shapely legs. You've a pleasing, er…' He pointed at her midriff.

'Belly?' She teased, straight faced.

'No.' He shook his head.

'Waist?'

'Lower.'

'Bottom? You mean bottom?'

He nodded.

'And is that what you were looking at last night? When I was wet through?'

Malcolm swallowed uncomfortably, and nodded.

'Oooh, naughty Malcolm.' His interest pleased her. 'My shorts were so wet you could almost see right through them.'

'I know.'

'Not the gentleman, is it? Looking at a girl when she is disadvantaged.'

'I'm sorry. I shouldn't have…'

'Admitted it?' Tongue wrapped in knots, his brain inadequate, Malcolm floundered, and amused by his inability to riposte or flirt, Alice took pity. 'Don't worry, Malcolm. You're a young man, and men are generally beyond chivalry, or so my friend Kate says. You liked what you saw, though?'

Realising she held the intellectual upper hand he tried caution. 'I couldn't see that much, really.'

'You didn't answer the question, Malcolm,' she pressed. 'You're prevaricating.'

'I'm what?'

'Oh, it doesn't matter.'

Thinking he had upset her, he altered his plea. 'I did.'

'You did see, or you did like?' She eyed him coolly.

Malcolm didn't look up. 'Both.'

'Would you like a cold drink?'

'I don't need cooling down, if that's what you mean.'

'You're not hot and bothered by my presence then?'

'You're playing with me, aren't you?'

Alice crossed the cleared soil and stood directly before his lumbering form. He glanced up, her middle meeting his eyes, the shorts tight, outlining the crotch. 'I wouldn't do that, Malcolm.'

The youth slowly licked his lips. 'All right, I'm hot and I am bothered.'

'Perhaps you should take your shirt off.' She reached out and felt his shoulder. 'For now.'

Proud of his physique, content to let Alice lead, he removed the garment, torso glistening with sweat.

Shortly after, he finished. 'There you are, Alice, all done,' he proudly announced.

She smiled. 'I think you deserve a reward, don't you?' Something other than commonsense drove her – a mixture of her natural rebellious nature and the effect of an overbearing guardian.

'What have you in mind?'

'Come inside the shed and you'll see.'

Malcolm followed, the lapdog, his eyes riveted to Alice's swaying bottom. 'Shut the door,' she said. 'I don't want anyone to see.'

'I don't think there is anyone. You're uncle is at work, so is my mum. The neighbour on the other side is away on holiday. But...' Malcolm closed the door.

Alice wasn't quite sure what to do. Unsophisticated, she had no clue as to what to offer. 'Come here,' she beckoned.

Malcolm closed the distance, expectant. Alice leaned forward and kissed him on the cheek.

'We had to hide for that?' he groaned.

'Oh,' Alice frowned, 'I'm sorry, I'm not very good at this.'

'You haven't been with a man before?'

'No, I've been too busy studying.'

'You could kiss me properly.'

Her heart thumped. 'Okay.' She leant again, hands behind her back and placed her lips to his. They hung in expectation. Time stood still. Neither took the advantage.

Alice settled back on her heels. 'Well?'

Malcolm shrugged. 'It was like I kiss my mum. You're supposed to do it with a bit of passion.'

'You show me then.'

The youth grinned. He took Alice in his brawny arms, held her to his muscular body, her breasts firm to his chest. 'Like this, Alice.' Lips touched tentative, then pressed together. They roamed in passionate embrace. Malcolm withdrew. Alice breathless.

'That's a kiss.'

'That didn't quite touch the spot. Want to try again?' She closed the gap.

The lad readily obliged, the clinch lasting, his hands chancing to roam. They descended to her bottom, cautiously traversing the contours, Alice pretending not to notice.

The girl pulled away. 'You mustn't tell anyone. Not ever.

If you do I'll be in terrible trouble. I'm not even supposed to be alone with you. If Uncle Richard found out he'd go mad.'

'I promise.'

Alice opened the shed door. 'Er, is that it then?' Malcolm asked, disappointed.

'What else did you want?' she returned, knowing exactly what he hoped for.

He shrugged, too shy to elucidate. 'Can I see you again?' He held his breath.

'I'm here for six weeks. You can't really not see me, can you?'

Unsure where that left him, Malcolm climbed back over the fence.

That night Alice lay awake, unable to rid her mind of Malcolm, and more to the point, what might have transpired. She permitted the possibility of going the whole hog to enter her thoughts. She imagined what that must feel like. That rigid length thrust into her. Her vagina stretched.

Alice pulled back the covers and in the gloom peered at her naked lower half. She felt herself, pushing a finger between the folds. Sexual psyche awoken she gasped at the provocation. She longed to know what it felt like to receive an erect penis. To be pierced, stretched, filled. The urge nagged, would not desist.

Sleep refused her. The clock beside the bed ticked louder than she could remember. She recalled Kate's caning and then her own. What if a desirable man had done that, would she have felt different? Should she have let Kate's boyfriend spank her? Over his lap, her hips devoid of all covering, her bared bottom proffered for his hand. She shivered, the frustration worsened.

Alice rolled to one side, hand traversing buttocks in search of the welts Richard had laid the day before. They had subsided. Only tramlines remained. She pictured Malcolm whipping her with a supple rod, the image soon dismissed.

Confused, Alice sought clarification. What was her sexuality? Why did the scent of a beating excite, but not the threat and reality? Where were her morals? She knew that sex before marriage was a sin, so why long for it? Oh that her mother still lived and she could approach her.

Were her tendencies regards Malcolm against the Almighty's creed? Was the finger playing with her vagina wrong? Perhaps Satan visited, tempted. Perhaps she should cleanse her soul, seek the priest and confess her sins. Would the urges that plagued then retreat?

But there again, it was only her mind – her very private and intimate aspirations. Why should she feel guilty? If only Katy were available, she could confide in her.

The nub responded, grew, the pre-orgasmic sensations pleasing. She let her mind drift back to Malcolm, imagining his penis. She focused on that stiffening, then mentally placed it between her legs, the folds spread, his shaft within. She didn't really want Malcolm, but in her dreams he would do.

That image faded, Alice appearing before him fully clothed. The thickset lad advanced, with piggy eyes, mousy hair and prominent nose. He grabbed at her, pulled her to him and without consent kissed her, his mouth to hers, his lips on hers.

Hands, yes his grimy paws, lifted her skirt and gripped the buttocks beneath. She couldn't fight; he was too strong. Releasing her he pushed her against a wall, the rough brick hard to her back. He seized her blouse and rent it, buttons popping. Eyes glazed he sneered and felt a breast, groping through the thin cotton of her brassiere.

That support was then torn from her, those fleshy orbs jostled, the quiver egging him on. Bowed, he pushed his head between, separating the warm breasts with his face. Then he licked and nibbled, gratifying his lust.

She felt his hand between her thighs, the callous palm stroking upward. Legs forced apart, he felt her through the gusset of her panties.

Alice's breathing sped up, each exhalation accompanied by a whisper of a sigh. Her finger aroused more energetically, the burrow wet. Eyes closed tight, the vivid images sped through her mind. Malcolm wrestled her to floor, her panties down around her knees. His hand played rough and uncaring with her exposed sex. His mouth suckled a nipple.

He rose and knelt before her, a massive erection levelled. She watched in horror as he lowered his hips and then felt the penetration, a hot shaft filling her.

The climax overwhelmed. Her back arched from the mattress. Wave after wave of passion swept through her groin, Alice moaning, succumbing. She couldn't give herself, but if taken would be blameless.

The following day gave way to a hot sun. Mid-morning saw the temperature edge into the eighties. Alice sifted through a limited wardrobe and finally selected a thin sleeveless summer dress, the hem just below the knee.

Richard had organised some of her day with regard to cleaning the house. She could leave that for a couple of hours and still have time to complete it, so drawn by curiosity, she sought Malcolm.

She barely set foot in the garden when the lad appeared at the fence. 'Morning Alice. Sleep well?'

'Did you?' she returned.

'I tossed and turned. I was thinking about you.'

'That's sweet.'

'I was thinking.'

'And?'

'Would you like to go for a walk?'

'Anywhere in mind?'

His face lit up; Alice didn't turn him down flat. 'The common?' he proposed, hesitant.

'We'll have to be back by one.'

'No problem.'

They strolled a well-trod path, the boy strangely quiet, Alice's attempts at conversation met with a nod or a grunt. He pointed to a track leading into dense undergrowth. 'Let's walk that way,' he suggested.

The lad let Alice lead, eyes riveted to the roll of her

hips, the shape of her bottom and the gentle jostle of buttock flesh beneath the flimsy dress.

She entered a clearing, noting an apparent cul-de-sac. 'It's a dead end, Malcolm,' she pointed out.

'I know,' he admitted.

Before she could face him, he wrapped his arms about her waist. 'Thought we could snog without worrying about who might see.'

'That's called taking liberties, Malcolm.' She pulled the grasping hands apart and turned to face him. 'I don't care for assumption. What next, eh? Thought you might put your hands inside my dress?'

He coloured, guilt etched in his ugly face. 'No,' he whispered, suitably chastened. 'I'm sorry. I just thought...'

'A girl likes to be asked, Malcolm. She likes to be wooed. Made to feel she's important.'

The clod shrugged, unable to look Alice in the face.

'Well, Malcolm?'

'What?'

'Ask me?'

'Can I kiss you, Alice?'

'Yes, Malcolm. Wasn't hard, was it?'

Face lit he threw his arms about her, and lifting her clear of the ground nigh on crushed her lips in his enthusiasm. Alice struggled, the hulk not seeming to notice, then gradually she succumbed and ceased wriggling to return his ardour.

One arm still supporting, the other moved down, his large hand grasping a buttock. Malcolm desisted to permit protest, but Alice immediately closed the gap, offering none.

Aware of her breasts, soft and yielding, Malcolm risked all. Taken by the madness of pent-up lust, he inched the dress up then dived beneath the cotton covering of panties, his hand groping naked buttock. Surprised the beauty didn't remonstrate he assuaged his carnal thirst. The hand roamed, fondled that luxuriant rump, intoxicated he lowered her, feet touching barren grass. That free paw rose, pushing between he and she to fall upon covered breast. There he fumbled, testing the water.

Incited by his random touch, Alice responded by unfastening his fly. Mouth flapping in astonishment, the boy froze as Alice delved inside. Those cool fingers found stiff flesh, the pants no protection.

Open day declared, Malcolm loosened the buttons on her dress, fingers almost incapable. Pulling back the dress, finesse beyond him, he gasped at the revelation. Her fancy bras all burnt by Richard, Alice had decided to do without. Although of ample proportion her breasts were lithe, and in no need of support. Alice merely conformed with propriety.

Shaking his head in disbelief, Malcolm first stroked and then grasped the yielding tissue. He filled his hands with tender mammary, drifted into sublime ecstasy, his cock in spasm and firmly in Alice's grasp.

Words beyond him, his mouth moved but delivered no utterance. Instead he lifted the straps from the girl's shoulders, the dress falling to her ankles. Drinking of her divine body he reacted without realisation. Alice's fondling below produced a damning reaction; he oozed semen, the viscous seed spewing over playing fingers and grass alike.

His orgasm receding, Malcolm gazed stupidly at the result. Alice inspected her fingers. 'Sorry,' he tendered, voice box back in action.

'Spunk,' the girl determined, neither asking nor stating.

'I didn't mean to. It sort of happened.'

Alice stooped and wiped the secretion on the grass. 'It was you, Alice. You turned me on so much. I couldn't help it.'

She rose again. 'What about my turn?'

Malcolm stammered. 'Wha… what d-do you want me… me to do?'

She took his hand and inspected the forefinger. Without verbal explanation she lowered her panties, Malcolm bug-eyed. His hand recouped, she placed it between her thighs. Alice smiled, green pools sparkling.

'I… I'm sorry, Alice. What now?'

102

The girl demonstrated. She aimed his finger, that parting the vaginal lips. She located her clitoris and manoeuvred the prod. Malcolm, penis still exposed and limp, imitated the example. Alice closed her eyes and let the mind wander.

A spark of interest still persuasive, he leant and kissed a breast, detecting the shiver that induced. Alice gasped, and pulling his hand free, sank to her knees.

'Good?' he enquired, little else on his limited mind.

'Yes, Malcolm, very good.' She reached for her dress.

'No, please, can't you stay like that for just a few minutes longer?' he pleaded. 'You are so beautiful.'

'I shouldn't be here at all,' she pointed out. 'I don't know what came over me. Don't you ever tell a soul what we did, Malcolm.'

'I won't, honest. I can't believe what we did do. It was fantastic!'

Thankful he didn't see the marks, for explanation was beyond her, Alice dressed. The pair walked home in silence, the girl brooding on her actions.

That night Richard attended bowling practice, a regular event by all accounts. Alice had the house to herself. She deliberated on that flirtation, angry with herself for having exceeded self-imposed moral boundaries. She tried to read, there being little else to do, but the excursion nagged, guilt and spice.

Spice won. Her thoughts were private. Only the Almighty could read those, and he made her the way she was, didn't he? Or did Satan tempt? Those kisses, his hand in her knickers, feeling her bottom.

Alice tossed the book aside. She closed her eyes. Malcolm's face when she let him undo her dress! His eyes bulged, and that wasn't the only thing. She could not believe she actually undid him and felt that horny shaft. The thrill when he groped her breasts! She recalled the ejaculation, the slimy seed, the way his cock lurched.

'Oh, God!' she whispered, recollecting what she had him do. He actually had his finger in her. What would his cock have felt like?

The demons took her. She checked the time – eight-thirty. Richard would be hours yet. Alice climbed the stairs, and ignoring the out of bounds edict, she utilised Richard's bedroom. Before that full-length mirror she studied her body – the prominence of her bust, the taper of waist and swell of hips. She conjured Mr Perfect, tall dark and handsome. Eyelids blanking the light she laid her hands to that waist, imagining he stood behind. Slowly, sensuously they ascended, to settle on the covered bosom. She squeezed those supple breasts, the fingers not her, but his.

The tide of passion rising, Alice unbuttoned the dress, then pulled it apart. She drank of her reflection, breasts bared, hands kneading those flawless tits. 'Ah, shit!' she uttered, a flood of eroticism invading.

She eased the dress from her shoulders, the garment falling to the floor. Posing naked but for the panties, she let her hands wander. They roamed, stroking, caressing, petting. Pushing aside the elastic they probed the soft curls. Enraptured, oblivious to all else, Alice discarded the panties and offered her bottom for inspection.

Fingers inciting sexual response, she visualised her ideal suitor. He threatened a whipping, a supple tail about to punish. She conceived the whistle of parted air, the crack of punitive leather on fragile bottom. She perceived the biting cut and stinging aftermath. 'Uh!' she gasped, as the effect added to the furore.

She lay back on Richard's bed, deaf to a key unlocking the front door. Game rained off, her uncle sought trouble. Silent he searched the lower floor, before stealthily ascending the stairs.

Stark naked Alice writhed on his bed. Legs parted, fingers titillating the vaginal lips, she had strayed from reality.

Richard checked the bathroom. He glanced about Alice's bedroom. Puzzled, he approached his own.

The teenager lost to her own manipulations, mind in blissful repose, persevered on the road to Nirvana.

Hearing Alice sigh, Richard stopped short of throwing

the door wide. Frowning, he edged it open an inch, and there on his bed he witnessed his niece in the full throws of masturbation.

The initial anger thwarted, he monitored, avoided confrontation. Notes he would take. Punitive measures he would consider. He brooded on the girl's act of self-gratification as she teased voluptuous breasts. Mouth ajar, he sighed unheard as she delved those fleshy tits, fingers probing deep.

Affected, he witnessed the leisurely rise of curvaceous legs, bending at the knee, and their spread to reveal the intimacy of her sex. His heart thumped as she first fondled and then slipped a finger deep into that succulent fissure. Mouth dry he savoured the gentle movement of hips, the motion of finger, the female form in rapture.

He stayed until the conclusion. The rapid breathing. The throes of passion. The final shudder and the girl's subdued squeal.

He left, carefully closing the door, admittance of his proximity beyond him.

Unaware of the spectator and full of self-reproach, Alice sat on the edge of the bed, composing herself. She felt dirty – wretched about that salacious act and ashamed of her escapade with Malcolm. If Kate had been there, she could have told Alice that her feelings were normal. That once the roar of climax had thwarted the indiscriminate assault of hormones then rationality returned. Without that awareness Alice would continue to blame the demons.

Once dressed, a cup of tea beckoned, but entering the kitchen horror pounced. Richard, ensconced at the table, read the holy bible, always an ominous sign. Expression churlish he remained tacit. Alice lit the gas, and having filled the kettle placed it on the ring.

'Would you like another one, uncle?' she asked, amiable. Sullen, he shook his head. 'I didn't know you were here,' she continued.

'That's obvious,' he replied, tone laboured.

Alice spooned sugar from a bowl, hand shaking so violently she scattered granules over the surface.

'Have you been home long, uncle?' She had to know.

'A while.' The man refused to look up from the book.

'I was upstairs having a lie down.'

'I know.'

Alice grimaced. Her backside crawled. God! What would he give her for masturbation? Why didn't he interrupt her in his usual violent manner?

She made the tea, and shaking like the proverbial leaf in a strong breeze sat, the beverage spilling.

Richard glanced up from his studies. 'What's the matter, Alice? You seem to be trembling. Not cold, are you?'

She sensed he knew, that the bastard played with her. Better he had made his assault, rather than drag it out. 'Because I've been asleep, I suppose.'

'Possibly. Will you be attending confession tomorrow?' he asked, Alice wondering when he would punish her. She nodded. 'Nothing too serious, I trust.'

'Minor matters, uncle. I would like to talk with the priest anyway.'

He frowned, feared that she might divulge the discipline he administered. 'Why's that?'

'I need guidance, counselling. I hope the father may be able to help.'

'Can't I? I am your guardian, after all.'

A light smile flickered. 'It is a matter I would have taken up with mother. A girl becoming a woman, if you understand my meaning.'

'Oh, I see. Do you think the priest will be able to help with that?' Richard assumed she spoke of the menstrual cycle, having no idea when a woman began, and not knowing Alice had some years before.

'Only one way to find out.'

Richard didn't pursue the other matter. He would keep his eye on her.

In the years before mass television hobbies preoccupied. Richard read, and Alice sank in a mire of tense boredom. So she took to her bed early, feigning a headache.

The night hot, the air sultry, she slipped beneath the blankets naked. Unable to sleep she turned, kicking the covers clear. She lay there, back to the door, peering out at a star-studded sky. She did not hear that portal open, and lay unsuspecting of her uncle's presence.

Richard checked to see if she slept. Curiosity battled religious indoctrination. He rued the lack of action. He should have seized the opportunity and punished Alice for her excess and trespass. Shame sat heavy. The girl evoked something in him that he despised.

He said nothing as he drank of her body, the gentle divergence of calves to knees, of knees to thighs. The lustrous sheen of those limbs in the half-light. The culmination of posterior, the division of buttocks, generous with resilient lower cheeks. And then the rapid dive to slim waist. The gradual rise to shoulders, the arm tucked beneath the pillow. Just beyond that ridge of ribs he knew lay the bosom. A bust that still defied gravity, that trembled rather than lurched.

Richard licked dry lips. Appetite not wetted for some time he could not tear his eyes from the naked girl. The pious conscience rebelled but the beast controlled. The cane's image hovered before him, smooth, sleek, thin and whippy. He drew a sharp breath as he visualised that cutting into those plump buttocks, the flesh jostled, a red stripe given a short existence.

Richard quietly closed the door and aimed for his own privacy. There he switched on the light and scrutinised his reflection. He didn't care for what he saw – a frustrated middle-aged man. A pathetic shadow that no woman wanted to know. Slowly he released his belt and let the trousers fall. Eyes closed briefly, they fell reluctantly to digest the bulge within the pants. Disgust etched on his countenance, he lowered those white Y-fronts and glared at the erection facing him.

Jaw set, Richard removed the belt from the trouser loops and carefully folded it. He raised it high, and determined, brought it down with strength. The doubled leather struck his penis, slapping the shaft with force. He sucked air through clenched teeth, a whimper escaping.

Again he lifted the leather and brought it down hard.

His face twisted in pain. He checked the image. Not content he struck again. 'Get from me Satan,' he growled. 'Get from me!' The strap hit for a fourth time. The erection surrendering he staggered back and slumped on the bed. Richard would not accept the fact he could be attracted. He found it repugnant, beyond his control. He wanted to rule Alice's life – not her, his.

As suggested by Richard she attended Mass in her new school uniform. It was the first time in nearly six months, her parents not being anywhere near as religious as her uncle. The service over she waited for the congregation to clear, telling Richard she would walk home.

The priest having seen his flock off approached the lone girl. 'I haven't seen you at Saint Michaels before, have I?'

'No, father. I am staying with my uncle.'

'And that would be?'

'Richard Barker.'

'Ah yes, a good and devout Catholic.'

'He is, yes.'

'And your name?'

'Alice Hussey.'

'Well Alice, what can I do for you?'

'Two things. The first, I haven't been to confession for ages. The second, I'm confused.'

'Confession you can come for anytime I'm here. As for confusion, is this a religious matter?'

'I'd like to confess now, father. And no, it isn't a religious matter.'

'If you confess now, child, you will lose all anonymity. And as for your problem, I'm not sure I would be worthy.'

'Father, you know all your parishioners well. Can you honestly say that when they are in the confessional they are anonymous?'

Father Doolan smiled.

'And as for my problem, I think that may become evident with my confession.'

'Do you wish to take the box, or would you sooner sit before the Almighty?'

'I'll sit before the altar, father.'

They both crossed themselves and bowed before taking a pew. Alice composed herself. What she intended would not come easy, but she accepted she had to do something.

'Father, I have sinned,' she started tentatively.

'And do you seek forgiveness?'

'I do.'

'There is always a price for forgiveness, child. That will take the shape of atonement.'

'I accept the Almighty's penance.'

'Then speak your sins.'

'I have told untruths. I have harboured deceit. I have acted vainly. I have been ungrateful. I have used my...' she paused for breath. There the strength failed her.

'Yes, my child?'

'I have used my body in a manner which goes against my understanding of the Holy doctrine.'

'Are you telling me you have entered upon a sexual liaison?'

'Not fully, father. I am still as the Virgin Mary.'

Doolan leant forward, his hands clasped together. 'Do not confuse normal urges with the work of the devil, Alice.'

'But father, they are not normal urges.'

'Who says what normal is?'

'My parents are dead. My uncle has no comprehension of the young. I cannot know what normal is. But I do suspect the devil himself visits at night.'

'Perhaps you best be explicit, if it troubles you that much.'

'I don't know that I can.'

'It is of a sexual nature though?'

'Very much so.'

'I have a colleague. A brother that specialises in cleansing the spirit, so to speak. I understand he is a good listener. That he has a way of winning one's confidence. His achievements in the field of purging the soul are legendary. Would you like me to refer you?'

'Yes please. And my other sins?'

'You recognise them. They are the traits of humanity, I'm afraid. Fear not, for a teenager you seem very level-headed.'

Alice walked home, feeling slightly better. Perhaps this Father Cavenny would help her further. Richard eagerly enquired how she fared, and she told him about Cavenny.

'And you can't confide in me?' he asked, disappointed.

'I'm sorry, uncle.'

Alice received a phone call on the Monday from the priest in question, and an appointment was fixed for the half-term holidays in October – apparently Cavenny was a busy man. With little to occupy her, Alice's fancies returned. Disturbed, she sought Malcolm, but not until she had tried desperately to assuage the demons, specific fiends that haunted her nightly.

A harmless game she convinced herself. Maybe with sexual connotations, but no actual participation.

The boy quickly appeared at the fence. 'Want to play?' she asked with a sly smile.

'What have you in mind?' Malcolm's pulse rate increased.

'Do you have any rope?'

'I think so. There's an unused washing line in the shed.'

'Cowgirls and Indians is the game.'

'I take it I'm the Indian?'

'You're quick aren't you?'

'In the shed?'

'No. Let's live dangerously. In the parlour.'

'What if your uncle comes home?'

'He won't. He never does.'

'He might get sick.'

'Not Richard.'

'If you're sure.'

Malcolm fetched the rope and followed Alice to the parlour. 'Right, what do you want me to do?'

'Use your imagination?'

'Am I really beastly Indian?'

'Oh yes.'

'Take off your clothes.'

'No.'

'Oh, all right.'

'That's not the correct answer, Malcolm.'

'But…'

'I won't because I am a proud cowgirl. Although I'm frightened of you, I will not surrender. But you want me naked. So, what do you do?'

He smiled, the penny dropping. 'I make you.'

'That's it, Malcolm.'

'How do I make you, exactly?' he asked, frowning.

'I'm wearing a really old shirt. It's no good for anything now. My skirt has an elastic waist. I'm not wearing a bra. Any bright ideas?'

'Oh.' Embarrassed as usual he saw the solution. He reached out, Alice slapping his hand away.

'Don't you dare touch me,' she squealed. 'Don't you dare.'

'That's part of the game, isn't it?'

'Yes, Malcolm, it is part of the game.'

He lunged, not knowing quite what he intended, and Alice stopped him in his tracks with a smack to the face. 'That bloody hurt.'

'So what are you going to do about it?'

'I'll show you.' The lad used his strength and seized her wrist. He twisted it, Alice having no option but to turn. Arm up her back he reached around the front with the other hand and ripped open her shirt. Alice felt the tide of excitement rise. Still holding her he pulled the cloth from a shoulder and then the arm. Letting her go he clung on to the garment, and as Alice pulled away so the shirt came off. She covered the exposure, forearms crossed, those charms compressed.

Malcolm stared stupefied, the shirt trailing from a fist.

'What is it, Malcolm? You've seen me before.'

'It's you covering them like that. You look defenceless, vulnerable. Really sexy.'

'Is vulnerable sexy?'

'I think so.'

'So what now, Malcolm?

He rubbed his crotch, the discomfort there undeniable.

'I'm going to have you.'

'Have me?'

'Tie you up.'

'That's a relief. But I'm not giving up that easy.'

Malcolm let the shirt fall. He circled Alice, the girl keeping her face to him and her teasing forearms in place. His gambit took her by surprise with regard to the speed and agility of it. Alice had him down as cumbersome, not one who could move rapidly. Bowing, he caught her midriff, his arms encircling her waist. Straightening he lifted the girl onto a shoulder, then spun her. By the time he returned her to her feet her head reeled. Seizing the advantage he tugged the skirt down.

Malcolm took advantage of the opportunity, Alice still floundering, completely naked. Grabbing her from behind, his arms about her ribs, those soft breasts against his flesh stimulated.

He hauled her back and seated her on a dining chair. The rope to hand, he caught a wrist and tied it, Alice not relinquishing the fight. Those hands he tied behind her, the rope then looped about the rear leg brace.

Both revelled in the heady scent of sexual horseplay, the thrill potent, urges undeniable, frustration lurking. Malcolm tied her ankles to the front legs, her limbs forced slightly apart. He then secured her torso, ropes about her waist and tied to the chair back.

'How does it feel?' he asked.

'It's very arousing,' she admitted. 'I can't move and I like it. I can feel the roughness of the rope digging in. I'm helpless. Are you going to take advantage of me, you savage?'

'Not half.'

Malcolm went behind and reaching over mauled her breasts, Alice enjoying every second.

'Gag me. Stop me from screaming for help.'

He used one of her socks, separating her lips and delving the corners of her mouth. He stood before her, struggling

112

against an impulse. Slowly he unfastened his fly, Alice entranced. He eased the stiff cock out and holding it, rubbed the tip.

Astonished, she watched. He worked on himself, his impetus increasing, clenched fingers speeding back and forth encouraging a climax, Alice enthralled. Then he froze. The front door opened and closed. Alice stared in terror at the parlour entrance. Then she heard the voice, a faint nearly taking her.

'Alice. Alice. Are you there? I forgot my sandwiches.'

Malcolm tucked the rapidly deflating piece away and fled for the cover of the settee, hiding behind it.

All colour draining from the girl's face she waited for the inevitable. Richard's frame appeared in the doorway. Initially puzzled he merely stared at her, unable to comprehend.

'What's happened?' he finally managed, regardless of the fact she could not answer.

His eyes ran around the cheap furnishings to check nothing was amiss. He strode forward frowning, the scenario beyond him. Alice nearly wet herself with fear as he removed the gag.

'What has happened, Alice?' he asked. 'Who tied you up?'

What could she say? Malcolm cowered behind the settee and it would only be a matter of time before Richard discovered him. Her mouth opened but no words issued forth.

For some reason Richard did not untie her. He hovered, scratched his head, continuously glancing about the parlour, eventually demanding, 'Are you going to tell me what happened?'

'I can't,' she confessed.

'Why?'

'Because it is too embarrassing.'

'Ah,' he snapped, 'no good. You've been up to no good.'

He took a seat opposite. 'Well, girl, I am not releasing you, or leaving this house until you offer me an explanation.'

'What is there to explain?' she returned. 'I'm naked; tied to this chair. What can I say?'

'Why, for a start. And who, for seconds.'

'Because I wanted to, uncle. Because I'm perverted. Is that what you want to hear?'

He shook his head, expression grave. 'What on earth have I taken on? What sort of harlot are you? I have never in my life come across such depravation. You are sick, Alice. Did your parents know what you are?'

Malcolm's knees ached. He tried to turn to ease the discomfort, nudging the couch as he did so. Richard noticed the movement. 'Whoever is behind that settee had better show themselves now. And I mean now!'

Malcolm rose, his ugly face pushed over the parapet.

'Good grief! You! This gets worse. And how long have you been carrying on together, might I ask?'

Malcolm, hero to the last, pointed a finger at Alice. 'It was her, Mr Barker,' he squealed. 'She made me do it.'

'Oh, you coward!' spat Alice.

'I should ring the police,' threatened Richard.

'No, please Mr Barker, don't. My mother will have a fit.'

'I suspect she'll have one anyway, when I tell her what a reprobate she has for a son.'

The boy hung his head in shame. 'Does she have to know, sir?'

'The good lady has raised a deviant. I think she should know that.'

Ravaged with fear he sought clemency. 'Is there no other way? Can't I make it up to you somehow?'

'And what would you suggest? You should be crucified, boy!'

'I've never done anything like this before, sir.'

'Tell me, Malcolm, have you had sex with my niece?'

His eyes widened in horror. 'No sir, never.'

'But you have played around, haven't you?'

'No sir, I just tied her up. She took her clothes off. She asked me to do it.'

Richard rose and took the few steps to Malcolm, stared

hard into his eyes and then slapped him about the face. 'Liar!'

Tears welled. 'I'm not, it was her. She's a Jezebel. I didn't stand a chance!'

Richard hit him again. 'I said liar! You have touched her, haven't you? You have laid your filthy paws to my niece's body, haven't you?'

'Only because she wanted me to.'

'Where, boy? Where have you touched?'

'I felt her bosom, sir.' Malcolm folded completely. Not the smartest of boys, he surrendered unequivocally.

'And where else?'

'Nowhere sir.'

That backhand struck his smarting cheek again. 'Where else, you bastard?'

Unable to look the dominant Richard in the eye, he pointed to his own crotch.

'You disgusting wretch! You filthy sewer rat. I'll have the law on you for this!'

That was it, in a flood of tears Malcolm fell to his knees, hands clasped together he begged. 'Please Mr Barker. Please let me go.'

'You'll not go unpunished.'

'I'll do anything, I promise. Just please let me go.'

'Anything?'

'Yes sir, anything.'

'You must be punished.'

'Yes sir, you punish me.'

'Go into the kitchen, Malcolm. Wait for me there. We'll sort this out here and now.'

An escaped rat, the boy darted from the room. Richard stared at Alice. 'You, I will see to later.'

She listened to the goings on next door. 'Right, Malcolm, drop your trousers and pants and bend over the back of that chair.' At least the cowardly shit would get his comeuppance.

'What are you going to do, Mr Barker?' came the boys strangled reply.

'Flog you, Malcolm. Thrash you with this cane.'

'But sir, I've never been caned before.'

'You will be now, boy. Unless of course you want me to telephone the police.'

'It'll hurt!'

'That is my intention. Now are you going to do as I ask, or shall I…?'

Silence fell. Alice pictured the craven Malcolm baring his behind.

'How many, Mr Barker?'

Richard did not answer. She heard instead the unmistakable crack of rattan on naked buttocks and Malcolm's scream.

Alice smiled. Oh, she knew she would eventually replace him and receive her lot, but for the moment she savoured the wretch's agonised cries. Each hefty stroke was punctuated by a mortal squeal, Malcolm having temporarily discovered hell.

She counted the lashes. One to twelve. Would that be it? No, the purgatory continued. Fifteen, then eighteen. Alice understood what Malcolm suffered. She gloated, her only regret being she had allowed him to touch her sexually.

Twenty-four gruelling cuts Richard administered, the dolt sobbing his heart out, begging and pleading her uncle to stop. He left there in a rush; Alice only wishing she could witness his marks and the tearstained face.

Richard appeared shortly after, hands deep in trouser pockets. 'That is that piece of gutter trash attended to. I don't think we'll see him on this side of the fence again.

'And now you, Alice; what am I going to do with you?'

Her bound state stirred something, the unseemly image he suppressed. 'I shall contemplate your punishment this afternoon. Be warned, I cannot deal with this lightly. Furthermore, I shall have to look into this disgusting affair more deeply. A young woman that wants to be tied up and assaulted? I have never in my life come across the like. Still, as you obviously appreciate your predicament you can stay like that until tonight.'

Richard fetched a blanket and wrapped it about the

hapless girl. He then lifted her, chair and all, and carried her to the garden shed. Inside he set the chair down and removed the blanket. Expression disgusted, he replaced the sock gag.

'See if you still feel the same in…' he checked his watch, 'in four hours time.' He left, closing the door behind.

Alice felt empty. She should have been scared, but she wasn't. Numb was more the word. Humiliated didn't suffice. The worst thing in her life next to losing her parents had just occurred. Even the caning from Stagnant didn't come close. The pain from being discovered in such a compromising position tore her apart. How could she ever look Richard in the eye again?

She needed a psychiatrist, not a priest. What on earth was wrong with her? Was it hereditary? Did her parents tie one another up in the privacy of their bedroom? She couldn't see that, somehow. So why was she inflicted with such a horrendous craving?

Alice needed a wee. She could not go for another four hours, so what could she do? She hung on another forty-five minutes before deciding that she could not possibly humiliate herself further, so she peed where she sat.

Startled, she looked up as the shed door opened. Malcolm stood there. She could say nothing; the gag prevented discourse.

'I saw him bring you in here,' he explained. 'I gave it enough time to make sure he'd gone.'

Malcolm moved towards her. 'He hurt me, Alice. In fact, he fucking crucified me.' He turned his back and dropped his trousers. 'Look. Look what he's done to me.'

His meaty rump was smothered in thick welts, the marks turning blue, bruising imminent. What a lovely job, thought Alice. He deserved every stripe and more, the cowardly shit.

'It'll be days before they go. I can't even sit down. I've never felt anything so painful in all my life.'

He replaced his trousers. 'And it's all your fault. Live dangerously, you said. Go in the parlour, my uncle never comes home early. I believed you. You stupid bitch.'

Had she been able, Alice still would have said nothing. For what was there to say? Malcolm was irresponsible. He would never accept part of the blame.

'I hope he whips you tonight. I hope he whips you good and proper. Let's see how you like it. I'll tell you, Alice, it's like being covered in boiling tar. The agony rips through your backside like molten lava. Oh, I wish I could watch. I'd love to see your arse striped.'

Alice shook her head and looked away.

'I'm talking to you, you cow!' he shouted. 'You fucking listen to me.' His voice levelled. 'I reckon you owe me. I reckon you ought to do something as recompense.'

Slowly she faced him again. Malcolm released his penis. 'I know what will really get to you.' He leaned forward and released her gag.

She spat the fluff from her mouth. 'Fuck off, Malcolm.'

'Oh, I intend to *fuck* off.' He straddled her thighs, and then pulled his foreskin back. Placing a hand behind her head he pulled her forward. 'You're going to suck this, Alice. You're going to bring me off.'

She clamped her mouth tight as he pressed the smooth tip to her lips. Keeping it there he held her nose, the pressure still applied to the back of her head. Eventually she had to gasp for air and Malcolm took advantage, thrusting his cock into her open mouth. 'Now suck,' he demanded.

Alice didn't. She bit instead. Worse still, she kept her teeth there, refusing his release.

'Bitch!' he roared in agony. 'Let me go, you bitch!' She did eventually, having taught him a lesson first, and he backed away clutching at his vitals.

'The great shame is, Malcolm,' she told him, 'that if you had supported me against my uncle I would have treated you. I would have sucked your penis. I would have repaid the debt. As it is I never want to see your ugly face again. And if you ever come into my garden again I will tell Uncle Richard.'

'I bloody hate you!' he growled immaturely as he left.

Richard returned at six that evening, the puddle long since dried. He picked up the sock and held it in front of her face. 'Well?'

No point in lying, it would only make matters worse. 'Malcolm saw you bring me down here. He came to tell me how much he hated me.'

'He needed to take this off for that?'

'He wanted me to apologise. I didn't.'

'I see. So how do you find the bindings now, Alice?'

'Uncomfortable, uncle. My hands and legs have gone numb. I ache and my bottom is complaining.'

'Not as much as it is going to complain. I have decided on your punishment. Such a disgusting act warrants a sound and prolonged thrashing. Hodges Wood. There you will harvest birch twigs. You will manufacture a rod. And there I will drive the perversion from you.

'Not tonight, though – tonight you can stay here, tied to that chair. We'll see if you're as keen in the morning. Perhaps an overindulgence will curb your appetite.'

'I'm hungry and thirsty, uncle.'

He thought for a moment before his face gave to a vicious smirk. 'Very well, Alice, I will release you to eat. That you can do in here. Now I seem to recall an utterance that could not be construed as ladylike. So after dinner I shall warm your behind with a slipper. And as you seem to enjoy exhibitionism, I do believe I might let that oaf next door witness it.'

'I didn't watch him get his, did I?' The prospect of the abhorrent Malcolm gloating as she suffered exasperated her. He had all ready expressed his vengeful wish for her to be thrashed. It seemed as though he would not only be granted that, but would receive a ringside seat as well.

Richard's eyes narrowed. 'Is that another twist, Alice; a desire to see his bare backside caned? You feel left out? Perhaps I should make it up to you. I shall double the slipper.'

Alice diverted her eyes. 'I didn't mean it that way. He's obnoxious, and the thought of him watching galls.'

'All the more reason, then. Humiliation may counter

your natural arrogance.'

'And you have no objection to him seeing me naked?'

'How can I, Alice, when you have already shown him everything you have?'

Untied she rubbed her arms, wrists and legs, attempting to revitalise the numbness. Why did she do it? She might have known Richard would choose that day to come home unexpectedly. Why did she do it, anyway? It wasn't the night demons, not in broad daylight. At times she was like the alcoholic with the bottle, denying the health risk. She deserved the slipper. She deserved worse. She even merited a beating before Malcolm.

Richard returned with a bowl of steaming broth and two slices of bread. 'You eat that. I shall return in fifteen minutes.'

Her appetite had bolted, but Alice knew the night would be long and she would be hungry, so she forced it down.

Richard knocked on his neighbour's door, Malcolm's mother answering. 'Sorry to disturb you,' he bid. 'May I have a word with your son?'

'Malcolm?' she asked, as if she had another.

'If I may.'

'He hasn't done anything wrong, has he?'

Richard shook his head. 'No, of course not. I need a favour, that's all.'

She shouted up the stairway. 'Malcolm! Mr Barker wants a word.'

Complexion ashen, he descended.

'Ah, Malcolm,' greeted Richard. 'I wonder if you could spare me a few minutes of your time? Nothing to worry about, I can assure you. It's just that I have a problem I need to deal with, you know, similar to the one you had earlier today, and I would appreciate your being there.'

Richard's expression implied the invite could not be refused, so the boy nodded acceptance and followed.

Within his own house Richard expounded on the 'favour'. 'You blame Alice for your misfortune?'

'Yes sir,' concurred Malcolm.

'So would you like to see her punished?'

The youth could not believe his luck. 'You mean whacked like I was?' he asked, not even attempting to hide the glee.

'Not exactly so, but whacked will suffice.'

'Yes sir, I would sir.'

'Then follow me.'

Richard armed himself with a slipper, Malcolm envisaging the punishment. Alice bent over, her pert little bum cocooned by skirt. She would feel that thick rubber sole. Her arse would sting terribly. Perhaps her uncle might even give it to her on the knickers. That would be a sight, but not in his wildest dreams did he think she would get it on the bare.

Trailing Richard, his organ reacted on spotting the girl, naked at the bench, empty bowl before her.

Determined to appear unabashed she stood her ground. 'Well, ugly,' she sneered, 'an unexpected treat, eh?'

'You're only getting what you deserve,' the boy retorted, revenge in sight.

'How's your behind, then? Can you sit down yet, Malcolm?'

Jaw set, he glared.

'That's quite enough, Alice,' scolded Richard. 'Now let's get this done. About turn and bend over. Touch your toes.'

So aware of her bottom, she complied. The nerves in those cheeks tingled, making her aware of every inch of tight flesh. She bent, proffering that rump for punishment, seeing in her mind's eye the sacrifice.

Malcolm's observance intensified the developing tendency. An acute buzz coursed through her groin. An engaging electric storm nagged at her stomach. She concentrated on that exposed *derrière*, the sensation intensified. The possibility that Malcolm could see her vagina occurred, and she gasped at the carnal assault.

Then those fancies were devastated as the slipper forcibly met with her rump. A loud crack assailed her ears. A fierce smart filled the left haunch. She tensed as the fire flooded her arse.

Malcolm's piece stiffened as that rubber sole hit, buttock flesh fleeing from the impact. He rose to the rapid coloration that followed, and watched enthralled as the slipper sped toward the opposite cheek.

Richard held nothing back. He struck with speed, the implement slapping and quitting, the consequence painful in the extreme. Alice swayed with each explosion, the collisions upsetting her balance.

Her rump burned furiously, the torment almost as intolerable as that stirred by the strap. The third abused both haunches, slapping low, ripping into the division of flanks. The whisper of approach barely audible, she winced to the fourth delivery, stinging the haunch, toe close to the hipbone. She sucked air as the tidal wave of searing fire tore through her flesh, and she thanked God the birch had been postponed.

Out of the tormentor's line of sight Malcolm rubbed his stiff. Never had he been treated to such a display and most likely never would again. His gaze riveted to that suffering rear he savoured each hearty slap, every tremor of flesh, and Alice's subsequent grunts and whimpers. He took pleasure in the reddening, the rapid heating, the mottled appearance that soon emanated.

Malcolm wished the thrashing could go on indefinitely. He dwelled on the separation of vaginal lips that poked enticing from straining thighs. He wondered what it would feel like to thrust his hard meat within. Delight and frustration played together.

Richard covered every square inch of available posterior, her hide induced to the deepest scarlet. Eight frightful connections she had suffered. Her bum fair blazed. That punishing slipper turned her stomach, the sting excruciating. Richard kept up the fusillade, rigorously pounding her buttocks, the slaps strident, debilitating. Fourteen flesh-pulverising strokes battered her resolve. Alice sobbed. Tears fell like autumn leaves. She howled, if only to appease her taskmaster, but the bully persisted. Malcolm demonstrated his delight with the broadest of grins.

Eighteen belaboured, Alice sure she could not tolerate any more. Nineteen seemed to strip the very skin off her rump. She felt flayed; butt so sore sitting would be out of the question.

Finally the twentieth crucified and Richard made his withdrawal. Slowly Alice rose, buttocks complaining. She stared at the shed end panel, resisting the temptation to comfort those trounced cheeks. She cared not to offer Malcolm the satisfaction.

'As you are so adept at bondage young man, you can tie her again.' Richard handed the boy the rope. 'I shall come back in thirty minutes to inspect your work. Do not disappoint me.'

Malcolm held the rope in his hands, mouth open, comprehension beyond him. Richard had given him the chance to do virtually what he wanted. He could carry out any amount of delving mischief, and the trouble Alice had roused would most likely keep her quiet.

A malicious smirk on his countenance, he whispered, 'I bet your arse ain't half sore, bitch.'

'At least it wasn't the cane,' Alice retorted bravely. 'And I didn't scream and beg for mercy.'

Malcolm's eyes fell to the neat curls of pubic hair, and licking his lips, he said, 'Fancy leaving me to tie you up. I mean, anything could happen, couldn't it?'

'It better hadn't,' Alice warned defiantly. 'Not unless you fancy having your fat backside whipped again.'

His body stiffened, the rope snapped taut between tensed fists. 'Sit on the chair, Alice,' he sneered. 'And I hope it hurts.'

Gingerly she lowered her bottom, the cool contact comforting at first, but as her body weight compressed those beaten haunches so the discomfort settled. Alice refused to reveal her distress. Instead she smiled enigmatically.

'Your uncle doesn't want to be disappointed. What do you reckon he meant by that?' His tone held an inference.

'Keep your grubby mitts to yourself.'

'I think he wants the ropes tight and you extremely

uncomfortable.'

Alice guessed he was right.

'Put your arms behind you.'

Seemingly unruffled she did so, and Malcolm tied them. Three loops about one and then three about the other, savagely he wrenched them together, the fibres burning her skin. He knotted the cord.

Justice, thought Alice. You reap what you sow.

The rope secured to the rear cross-brace, he severed the ligature. He studied her, Alice knowing what he looked at. Reaching forward he placed a length about her chest, above her breasts, which he pulled and knotted before letting it fall between them, nestled in her cleavage.

'Part your legs.' He rubbed the sweat from his palms, as the smooth pale thighs drew apart. 'Now lift your bum off the seat.'

With difficulty she managed to raise that savaged rump an inch. Malcolm led the rope beneath and behind her. 'Now sit.' He yanked on the line, then wound the tether about the brace and secured it. The means pulled Alice slightly forward and down. The rope dived between her legs, parting the labia and sitting abrasively within. Alice bit her lower lip.

He bound her ankles to the rear chair legs, keeping her legs parted, preventing bodily support. To ensure her bottom remained in firm contact with the hard seat he forced the bond beneath one thigh, a few inches below the groin, looped it and tied it off. He fed that beneath the seat and in a similar fashion secured it to the other limb.

'Comfy?' he asked.

'Very,' replied Alice.

'One final touch.' With that he placed a rope about her elbows and drew them closer, forcing the girl's chest out. Alice gasped as Malcolm knotted that ligature.

'Oh,' he said, 'I nearly forgot.' He gagged her, using the sock.

'Oh, very nice, Alice. If it were up to me and me only, then I'd make you a damn sight more uncomfortable.' He checked his watch. 'Look, still fifteen minutes to go.

124

How shall we pass the time?'

Alice had already presumed, and closed her eyes in repulsion as Malcolm pawed her, his hands squeezing her breasts. He moved in close, tongue darting out, licking a nipple. The girl could say nothing; remonstration was beyond her. She sensed his lips, felt him suckle, but cared not to view the obscenity.

A hand crept below. Fingers played, then dipped between her thighs, feeling the rope biting her vagina.

'How's your bum, Alice?' he asked, seeking to upset. 'Sore? It'll get a hell of a lot worse. Not being able to move and all. Think about that bite. If you hadn't done that I might have bound you a little less tightly.'

Malcolm moved away and perched on the edge of the bench. He would not be caught interfering with Alice. No way could he endure another caning.

Richard arrived in due course and inspected the bound figure. 'Very good, Malcolm. Kept your hands to yourself, I trust?'

'Yes sir, of course, sir.'

'And if I was to remove the gag and ask Alice, would she say the same?'

Malcolm felt his backside crawl. 'Yes sir, she would.'

A cold glint to his eye, Richard removed the sock. 'Alice, did this lad touch you improperly in any fashion?'

Malcolm held his breath.

The girl took her time answering, knowing what the effect on the hapless idiot would be, but not seeing any point in providing further fuel to the fire she replied, 'No uncle, he didn't.'

'Good,' whispered the man. 'Then it is time to run along, Malcolm.'

The lad legged it.

'So why say that, Alice?'

'What uncle?'

'That he didn't touch you.'

'What would you have done to him if I had said he did?'

'Why save his hide when he was so quick to see yours

125

flogged?'

'You seem certain about your suspicions.'

'Oh, I know my delinquents. You have a forgiving nature, Alice, and I'm not so sure that is a good thing.'

'Are you going to leave me trussed like this all night, uncle?'

'I should do, if only to teach you a lesson. Uncomfortable, is it?'

'Yes.'

'As it happens, you have a visitor,' he informed her. 'So it would seem you are let off for now. I will birch you tomorrow as promised. However, tonight you may sleep in your own bed.'

'A visitor?' she asked. 'Who?'

He tossed a shopping bag on the bench. 'There are some clothes in there. Get dressed and you can go and see.'

Chapter Five

Curious, relieved, Alice ran to the house. She headed directly to the parlour knowing that her uncle would use that as the reception. Then shocked, Alice stared in disbelief at the girl lounging in an armchair. 'What the...?' she gasped.

'Hello, Ali.'

'K-Katy!' Alice stammered. 'How? Why?'

'I wanted to see you, Ali. I missed you. I needed a cuddle.'

As Kate rose so Alice leapt upon her, throwing arms about the girl's neck and hugging her.

'You're not pleased to see me then?'

'Katy,' she said, 'I'm so happy I think my heart is going to burst.'

'Definitely not pleased to see me then?'

'How did you find me?'

'You said.'

Alice frowned. 'No I didn't.'

'You said your uncle lived in Southport. That's all I needed. When father has got money, and father loves his little cherub, then anything is possible.'

'But Uncle Richard hasn't even got the same name as me.'

'What, Richard you mean?'

'No, Hussey silly.'

Kate grinned. 'It only took the private detective three days. Cheap really. It would have been far more exciting if you'd emigrated to Timbuktu.'

'Why go to all that trouble, Kate?'

'Oh Ali, you're the best friend I have. I couldn't go for six weeks without seeing you.'

'Six weeks?'

'I'm enrolled at Heptonstall next term.'

Alice near screamed at her. 'You haven't!'

'Don't you want me there then?'

'Oh, Katy, course I do. But with your father's money why there?'

'Two reasons: one, because I wanna be with you, gel. Two, because I've heard it's a whacking school. And not only a whacking school, but whacking by men.' Kate shivered and pulled a face. 'Whacked by a man! What a thought.' She trembled again, then leant forward and whispered conspiratorially. 'Maybe even with the skirt up! Maybe even with the knicks down. Ooh, Ali.'

'Didn't that last caning teach you a lesson?'

'That were a humdinger, that were,' Kate acknowledged ruefully. 'Eighteen with the thickest rod, wearing the punishment dress. Almost on the bare bum and in front of all those people. That has to be close to the ultimate.'

'You fainted!'

'The blood went to my head. I came over all dizzy.'

'So it glowed, did it?'

'For hours, Ali. For hours. I used that to orgasm for weeks after. You know, going through it mentally over and over. But like all fantasies it became boring. Now I'm looking for something else.'

Alice smiled. 'Want me to whip you, Kate?'

The girl's eyes widened and she licked her lips. 'Now that could be interesting.'

'I was joking, Kate.'

'I wasn't.'

'What would you suggest? In front of Uncle Richard?'

'Come and stay with us.'

'Eh?'

'Come and stay at Howell Manor.'

'What would your father say?'

'Please, I expect. I'm driving him mental. He'd be glad of the distraction.'

'I don't think uncle would condone it.'

'Why not?'

'Look, Katy, let's go for a walk.'

Alice sought Richard and asked for permission. 'Don't be late back,' he warned.

Parked outside, Alice noted the gleaming chauffeur driven Jaguar, the driver reading a book. 'That'll get the neighbours gossiping,' she remarked.

'And seeing you leaving in it will make them talk all the more.'

'Katy,' Alice said as they turned out of the road.

'Yes, Ali?'

Alice stopped. She faced Kate. 'He's a cruel swine.' Tears filled her eyes.

'Who is?'

'Richard.'

Kate adopted a look of little surprise. 'Go on.'

'What he's done to me you wouldn't believe.'

'Try me.'

'My bum is so sore at the moment I can hardly sit. He gave me the slipper.'

'You lucky devil!'

'Naked and in front of the creep next door?'

'Oooh Ali, perhaps I should come live with you.'

'It's not funny Kate!'

'Sorry. That's me, I'm afraid. When I get upset I make a joke of it.'

'You're upset?'

'I am if you are. And you obviously are. What did you do to earn it?'

'Oh, God.'

'What?'

'This is so embarrassing.'

'All the better. Juicy scandal, eh? Tell me, Ali, what have you been up to?'

'I'll start at the beginning.'

'A good place.'

'When I arrived here I knew uncle didn't like fancy underwear, so I hid mine. He found it. Not only did he find what I hid, but he guessed I was wearing the rest. He bound me with my own clothing and strapped me. Afterwards...' Alice pulled a face, close to tears, 'afterwards he rubbed ointment in my bare bum.'

'What a sicko!'

'Well, one thing led to another and he took me to the shed in my nightie. He wanted to flog me with a switch, but I refused. Katy, he made me stay in that shed all night. It poured down. The bloody roof leaked. I was in a terrible state next morning.

'Anyway I had to give in to his demands or I'd still be in the bloody shed. He whipped me with that switch for nearly ten minutes. Oh, it wasn't as bad as Stagnant's thrashing, but it wasn't a pleasure either. If that wasn't enough he strapped me again on my bare bottom after. Then he washed my mouth out with soap. I was sick.'

'And all because he didn't like your knickers, eh?'

'Not quite. I got really angry. He kept on and on, so I said something about showing my tits off to all the boys.'

Kate shook her head and tutted.

'That, with my refusal, earned me the thrashing.'

'Unjust, Ali,' Kate decreed. 'Unjust!'

'He makes me wash in front of him as well.'

'What's wrong with that?'

'In the nuddy?'

'Oh.'

'Then I burnt the dinner. That swine went out and bought himself a fish and chip supper, nothing for me. So I gave him a piece of my mind.'

'Ouch!'

'Exactly. A thorough hand spanking followed by twelve strokes of the cane.'

'Oh, a spanking,' Kate beamed mischievously. 'I love a spanking.'

'Then he made me dig the garden because he found out I'd been in his room.'

'No whacking then?'

'No, and I cheated. I got Malcolm next door to do most of it.'

'Malcolm?' Katy grinned, reading more into the name than she should.

'He turned out to be a slimy barrel of tricks. We did

130

things.'

'Things?'

'Just petting – you know, kissing.' She checked her fingernails. 'Touching… my tits, his cock…'

'Cock? I haven't heard you use that word before. You've been sullied.'

'Sullied! Do you know after I dug the garden he said I should take a bath…'

'Who? Malcolm?'

'No, Richard. No bathroom like you've got, Kate. A bloody old copper and zinc tub. Anyway, he wanted me to take it in front of him. I argued. Nothing wrong with the human body says he, and proves it. He took off *all* his clothes.'

'Two in one week! Who's a lucky girl? Was it all stiff and hard?'

'Malcolm's was.'

'The slipper; how did you earn that?'

'Oh, back there again. Katy, I'm kinky, if that's the word.'

'Ali, kinky?'

'I got Malcolm to strip me and tie me up in the parlour. Of all the rotten luck Richard came home unexpectedly. He caught us. Malcolm got two dozen of the cane on the bare bum and I got the slipper later.'

'Did you see him get it?' Kate fair gushed.

'No. He got it in the kitchen. But I heard it all.'

'You probably deserved that one, Ali.'

'Yes, but he whacked me in front of Malcolm. Even went around to get him special. And he left that specimen to tie me back up again. Of course he had a good old prod and feel, didn't he?'

'Lucky you.'

'No, I wasn't.'

'If you didn't like Malcolm why play in the first place?'

'He seemed all right at first, then turned out to be a cowardly piece of slime. Blamed me completely for what we were doing.'

'All men are cowardly slime, Ali. And it was your fault,

wasn't it? I mean, you did ask him to. And you got off lightly in comparison. The slipper as opposed to the cane.'

'Not really, I get the birch tomorrow.'

'Never had that. Still, worry not, I've seen drawings. They're only little twigs all tied together. It couldn't possibly hurt that much.'

'Do you think I'm perverted?'

'No, Ali, I think you're waking up sexually. It's all very confusing for a while. Me, I was very precocious, I went through that years ago. I'm better off than you. I have no inhibitions whatsoever. If I like, I do it. I quite like the idea of being tied up. Where did Malcolm touch you?'

'He felt my tits, then he put his hand between my legs.'

'And you didn't like that.'

'I'm not saying I didn't like it. I'm saying I didn't like him.'

'Perhaps we could get even with this Malcolm.'

'How?'

Kate winked. 'Leave that to me.'

The Howell standing impressed Richard. Money impressed him. He was the type of man to doff his cap to the local lord of the manor. So Katy possessed an advantage. The exact opposite to Alice, loud, outgoing, vivacious and streetwise, she also dazzled the quiet man.

'Mr Barker,' she said immediately on their return. 'I need a favour.'

Richard peered through his glasses, puzzled. 'What can I do for you?'

'Mother is in America and father has to go to London for a very important meeting. I do so hate to be left at home on my own. I know there are the servants, but it's not the same as being with your family. I was wondering if you would let me stay here with you for a day or two.' She sat, crossed her legs, ensuring a goodly proportion of thigh showed.

'Oh.' Richard frowned. 'I don't have a spare room. Well I do, but there is no bed.'

'I can squeeze in with Alice. She won't mind. Will you, Ali?' Kate leant forward, elbow on knee, chin resting on hand, the cleavage he couldn't avoid.

'No, of course not,' replied the girl, sceptical. She didn't believe Kate could pull it off.

'But it is only a single bed,' pointed out Richard.

'I would be eternally grateful, Mr Barker. And so would my father. You know, me being in good hands while he's away.' She winked suggestive.

'Eternally grateful?'

'Oh yes, father does like to show his appreciation, and so do I.' Kate smiled, tempting.

'I can't let you sleep two to a single bed. No, it would be far too cramped.'

'Have you any shopping to do, Mr Barker?' She checked a stocking, pulling the skirt further up a shapely leg.

'As it happens, I have.'

'Harry could take you in the Jaguar tomorrow. He could take you into Manchester if you liked. Or even up to Blackpool. With father away he hardly has anything to do.'

'And where would Harry sleep tonight?'

'He'll go back to the house.'

'I would like to help you out, Miss Kate. But as I said, I don't have the room.'

'Do you know, Mr Barker, to find Alice I had to engage a private detective.'

'Expensive.'

'And revealing. He had to check out all the records to find you. You know, your mother's birth and marriage certificate. Your birth certificate. It's amazing what they can turn up, *isn't it?*' Kate emphasised the last two words.

Richard's jaw tightened. His eyes glazed. 'You have a persuasive tongue in your head, young lady. Alice, change the bedding in both rooms. I shall use yours tonight and you and your friend can sleep in mine.'

'And tomorrow, uncle?'

'What about tomorrow?'

'That trip to the woods you promised.'

'Ah. That is a private matter, Alice. One between you and I. But as you have raised the subject I must assume you have been talking to Kate. I dare say, Miss Howell, that Alice has made me out to be the villain. That I can assure you is not the case. I do not wish to embarrass Alice so I will not go into detail. However, I have promised to punish her tomorrow, and tomorrow I will.'

Katy shrugged. 'I'm sorry, Mr Barker, Alice hasn't said anything to me.'

Richard's eyes narrowed. 'Really? Whatever, tomorrow evening at six you will have to excuse us both. That is if you are still here then.'

'I'll go and speak with Harry.'

On seeing Kate's approach, the chauffeur leapt from the car and opened a rear door. 'No, Harry, I'm not going. In fact, I'm staying the night.'

Harry, inveterate snob, gave the house façade the once over. Unimpressed, he asked, 'Really, miss?'

'Yes really, Harry. I want you to go back to the house and return tomorrow afternoon. You are to take my friend's uncle shopping. Maybe Manchester. Maybe Blackpool. I want you to get lost, Harry. I don't want to see you back here before dark. No matter what, Harry, you don't come back before dark.'

'Of course, miss. Will there be any remuneration for the extra hours?' He winked. Harry, at twenty-five, presented a well-groomed figure.

Katy offered an alluring smile. 'The same as usual, Harry. Unless you fancy something a bit different.'

'Variety is the spice of life, young miss.'

'When we get home then.'

'I'll look forward to it.'

'Oh, so will I, Harry. So will I.'

Bedtime arrived, Alice having laboured to make sure the rooms passed muster. Katy gave theirs the once over, and Alice apologised. 'I'm sorry it's not what you're used to.'

'Not your fault, Ali. Anyway, I'm used to school dormitories remember. Oh, I wish you could come and live with me.'

'So do I, Kate… You've no luggage. What are you going to wear in bed?'

'Nothing of course.'

'What if you need the toilet in the night.'

'Where is it?'

'Downstairs.'

'I'll slip something on.'

'You can use my dressing gown.'

'Will it fit?'

'Try it.'

Katy stripped to her underwear then slipped the gown over her shoulders. The gap in front proved impossible to bridge. 'Big tits, I'm afraid,' she remarked, gazing at the gap.

'Well endowed is the word.'

'Same thing; big tits.'

'You daren't meet with uncle on the stairs looking like that, Kate.'

'Why not? Is he shy?'

'He'd go mad. He can't stand that sort of thing.'

'That's the same man you wash in front of, is it? The same man that takes his clothes off and bathes before you? The same man that whips you on the bare bottom? And he can't stand that sort of thing. Sounds a bit off his rocker to me.'

'He is.'

'Be interesting to see his reaction, wouldn't it?' Kate said naughtily.

'No.'

'Oh, he's a snob, Ali. If he found me naked on his breakfast plate he'd say nothing. The fact he knows my family has wealth and standing makes him a servant to his own principles. I bet he would just go red in the face and apologise.'

'Maybe, but I don't want to find out. It's my bum you're playing Russian roulette with.'

'He can't punish you for my misdoing.'

'I wouldn't bank on that.'

'Okay Ali, I promise to behave.' She tossed the robe onto the bottom of the bed, and without compunction took off her bra and panties. 'Left or right?' she asked.

'Eh? Oh, whatever. I don't mind.'

Alice stripped off her bra and picked up the baggy nightie.

'You're wearing that?' exclaimed Kate.

'I always do.'

'But it's hot tonight, Ali. Live dangerously for Christ's sake!'

So Alice dropped the gown and her panties and, feeling self-conscious, clambered onto the bed.

'You've a lovely body, Ali,' Kate purred, stroking an arm.

'Thank you,' accepted an embarrassed Alice.

'Come on, snuggle up.'

'But it's hot, remember?'

Kate grinned and turned off the bedside lamp. 'Ali.'

'Yes?'

'Do hot nights make you horny?'

'It's when the demons come.'

'Demons?'

'They make you do things you wouldn't normally do.'

Kate rested her head on a hand. Silhouette outlined against the window, she asked. 'What things, Ali? What do the demons make you do?'

'You won't laugh? Or think less of me?'

'Promise, silly.'

'They make me touch myself. You know, down there.'

'And you think that wrong?'

'It's against the church's creed.'

'Oh, Ali, so naïve. Do you enjoy touching yourself?'

'At the time. I can't sleep until I do.'

'Ali, that is what becoming a woman is all about. If you don't feel horny then you won't want a man to fuck you. If the man doesn't fuck you then bang goes the human race. It's normal. I do it every night. Sometimes I don't even bother waiting for night. Mind you, I've been fucked a fair few times now anyway.'

'Kate! You're not even engaged, let alone married.'

'So hang me. Why wait for the chain about your neck before enjoying yourself? Sex is wonderful. And to feel a cock hard in your cunt is something else.'

'You're talking like a common whore.'

'I'm not common, Ali. In fact, I'm getting very good at it. I know what a man likes now, and I do it for them.'

'Them?'

'That buffoon I got caned and expelled for. I took his seed before they caught us. Then there's the gardener's son at home. And of course, Harry. Harry's a big boy, if you know what I mean. Massive glands.' She lay back giggling.

'Aren't you frightened you'll get pregnant?'

'There are times of the month when you can do it quite safely.'

'I'd sooner not risk it.'

'You don't know what you're missing.'

The two lay quietly for some minutes. Alice broke that peace. 'What do men like, Kate?'

'They like a whore, that's what they like. They won't marry one, but they like to fuck with one. They like bras that lift and push your tits together, and thighs above stocking tops. They like skimpy panties encasing buttocks.' Kate sighed. 'They like you to play with their knob, and feel their balls. They like their sex coarse. Harry just loves it when I climb on top and shag him that way. He can lay there and watch my tits bounce up and down.'

'Ever sucked a penis?'

'No, not yet. I haven't been licked, either.'

'I had Malcolm's in my mouth.'

'You never. You sly devil. What was it like?'

'Horrible. I bit it.'

'Ouch!'

Again silence descended. Kate pierced it next. 'Ever thought about being with another woman, Ali?'

'What, a lesbian you mean? That's illegal.'

'A girl knows what a girl likes, though.'

'What are you suggesting, Kate?'

'Nothing.' Her hand fell to Alice's tummy and slowly stroked the flat stomach.

'What are you doing, Kate?'

'Don't you like it, Ali?'

'It's soothing, but I'm not so sure it's right.'

'I love you, Ali. Don't you love me? I mean as best friends, of course.'

'I feel very affectionate toward you, yes.' Alice did nothing about the caresses.

'Same thing. So if we love each other in mind, why not in body? What's wrong with that?'

'I don't understand what you're saying. I can't even come to terms with playing with myself, let alone what I think you're suggesting.'

Kate slid her hand lower and toyed with Alice's pubic curls. She noted the shudder of the girl's body and breath. 'What does that do to you, Ali?'

'Oh Kate, please don't.'

'You're getting excited, aren't you?'

'Yes, my tummy is full of electricity.'

The hand inched down to the vaginal lips, and Alice gasped.

'I'm your friend, Ali. I would never hurt you. Not physically, and not in love.'

Alice wanted the attention, so her mind found a million excuses to let Kate continue. That wandering hand enraptured. Provided a thrill that Alice couldn't deny. Her lips parted. She sucked air. 'Oh Katy, don't,' she whispered.

A finger parted her vaginal lips and probed inside. Alice tensed. Kate moved closer. For a second she gazed at the face before her. A beautiful countenance, she thought. Then she sought the full lips of Alice. They kissed tentatively, Alice not protesting. All the while her finger toyed below.

'It's wrong,' muttered Alice, as Kate moved down her body, nipping at her nipples, kissing her breasts.

Kate straddled the girl. 'Why Ali?'

'Because…'

'Because you've been told it's wrong. All I'm doing is touching you. If I put my arm about your waist would that be wrong? If I kiss you on the cheek would that also be wrong? Prejudices Ali. Made up by people that are not inclined as us. You tell me where it says in your bible that a woman cannot love another woman.'

'I'm not so sure it is love that drives us.'

'Lust, you mean?'

'I'm not sure.'

'What would you like to do to me? This very minute?'

'I don't know, Kate.'

She took hold of Alice's hands and placed them on her breasts. 'Feel me, Ali. Feel my tits.'

Alice snatched her hands away. 'It's because it's wrong. That's why it's exciting.'

'Or because deep down you want to. It's possible, you know – to like both men and women. There's nothing wrong with it. Only the objections you raise in your own mind, because others have drilled it into you. Free yourself. Do what your heart tells you.'

Her hands slowly returned, and Alice gently felt the girl's breasts. 'You're firmer than I thought you'd be.'

'I'm wet as well. I'm really wet. I've fantasised about this for ages, Ali. I've wanted to bed you for months.'

'Why didn't you say something before?'

'Because I knew exactly what your reaction would be.'

'You're probably right.' Alice giggled. 'Can you imagine what uncle fart would say if he knew what we're doing at this minute, in his bed?'

'Probably, can I join you?'

'Oh, I don't think so, Kate. More like a double bum thrashing.'

'I wouldn't mind.'

'You are incorrigible.'

'I know. Kiss my tit.' She lifted the breast before Alice's mouth. The girl reciprocated, tongue licking the nipple and surrounding areola. Kate sighed and placed a palm behind Alice's head, pressing her face to that ample bosom.

Passions rose, Kate unhindered by concern, Alice fast

subduing hers. Both wanted to discharge the sexual tensions. Both desired to make love. But they ran aground on the rock of inexperience, a fundamental lack of knowledge, and the pair finally found sleep. Both lay naked, the sheets and blankets kicked to the floor.

At seven the next morning Richard thought to impress. He laid a breakfast tray with cereal and tea and climbed the stairs. Opening the door he expected two nightwear attired girls cosseted beneath coverings, but jaw dropping he stared in disbelief at the vision before him. Alice sprawled face down, breasts compressed to the mattress, bottom in full view, legs spread wide. Kate reposed on her side, arms hugging the pillow beneath her head, bosom lolling.

He retired, closing the door behind him. Placing the tray on the floor he fled downstairs to seek solace in the holy bible. His aspirations were to him, less than honourable.

Richard worked the morning and booked the afternoon off. He sought every means to impress his colleagues, mentioning the Howell family and the Jaguar that would be taking him shopping. He decided on Blackpool, the lure seductive.

Malcolm ranked high on Kate's agenda. She swore revenge on Alice's behalf, but also sought some sexual kindling. Wearing what she had arrived in – a thin, curve-clinging summer dress – she pounced as soon as the creep reared his head.

Leaning on the fence she waited until he inevitably looked her way. She smiled, that Katy Howell you can't resist me cock-twister. To her consternation Malcolm stayed put. As far as he was concerned she stood on Barker terrain, and most likely represented trouble.

'You're Malcolm, aren't you?' she asked in friendly tone.

Sullen he nodded.

'I'm Katy. I've been hearing stories about you.'

'Lies I expect.'

'Oh maybe.' She pouted. Pools of brown engaged the

boy. 'Muscular, she said. Fit and strong. Knows how to use what he's got. I suppose they were lies.'

'Alice said that?'

'Hmmm. She thought about what happened, and realised it was all her fault. Even said she deserved to be slippered in front of you.'

'Some whacking that was.' Malcolm's face lit up.

'Why don't you come over here and talk to me? Who knows who might be listening.'

Cautiously he approached. 'What are you to Alice?' he asked. 'Sister?'

'Do I look like her sister? I'm her friend. I'm staying a day or two.'

'Friends stick together. How do I know you're not scheming?'

'I'm just talking. Offering Alice's apology.'

'Why don't she do that herself?'

'She didn't think you would talk to her.'

'She said some horrible things.'

'People do under stress. She told me some other things as well.'

'Like what?'

Kate straightened, thrust out her considerable chest. 'That you're not shy when it comes to playing.'

'You're a big girl,' he observed.

'You saying I'm fat?'

'No. Big in the right places.'

Kate reached out and with a finger traced a line down his chest. 'I've plenty for the right boy to get hold of,' she cooed.

'Are you suggesting what I think you are?'

'Maybe. Depends on what you're thinking.'

'Why don't you come over here, off that Barker territory? Mum's at work, so we won't be disturbed.'

'Can I trust you, Malcolm?'

'I wouldn't do anything you didn't want me to.'

'Should be an interesting morning then.'

He stood back and watched as Kate clambered over the fence. 'Are you inviting me into the house?'

141

'As I said, we won't be interrupted.'

Kate followed Malcolm to the back door. Intrigued by the roll of his backside she remarked, 'Ali said her uncle caned you after he found you together.'

'Yeah. That bloody hurt.'

'Haven't you ever been whapped before then?'

'No.' He opened the back door and held it for Kate to pass through.

'Oh, I have, many times,' she confided.

'Really?'

'Oh yes. Not that it deters me any.'

'It doesn't worry you?' The boy appeared astonished, and in the kitchen she faced him. Kate knew how to turn a man's legs to jelly; she had that natural ability. 'No Malc, to be honest I quite like the thrill. I mean, it's never with knickers on, always off.' By Alice's account she presumed he had a sadistic streak a mile wide; a tendency she could utilise. Kate had been without discipline since she'd left Carters. Her needs were urgent, and the mention of certain words along with a manipulation of body language incited the moron.

Malcolm began to believe himself irresistible. 'Caned on your naked bottom, you mean?' His mouth went dry.

Kate hoisted herself onto the table and crossed her legs, ensuring she exposed four inches of thigh. She nodded. 'Sometimes without a stitch on.'

Malcolm rubbed his jaw. How could he offer?

'What do you think about caning a girl without a stitch on?'

'Well, if she deserves it...'

'Oh she deserves it all right. The trouble is, Malc, no cane.'

'There is one,' he blurted without thinking. 'Mum used it on me when I was young.'

'Show me, Malc.'

He brought it to her from the parlour – a whippy rattan. Kate examined it. She flexed it. 'What shall we do now, Malc?'

'Cane you,' he offered, the prospect nearly stopping

his heart.

'Why? What have I done to deserve it?' She smiled enigmatically. 'Oh, I know; it's punishment for leaving my handprint on your face.' Kate moved too fast for the unsuspecting Malcolm, and he reeled from the hefty slap, his cheek stinging. 'See, you're ever so mad, aren't you?'

Tears in his eyes, his face stinging, he stammered, 'Th-that wasn't necessary.'

'Oh, it was, Malc. When you thrash my bare botty I want you to mean it.'

'So I cane you for slapping my face?'

'Not quite. A slap on the face would only merit a minor act of discipline. I want a major one.'

'So what else?'

'This.' She seized his hair and hauled him down, the lumbering ox not sure how to defend himself; upset Kate and his chance of sexual adventure would evaporate. Ensuring she hurt, she yanked his head this way and that, tugging the hair relentlessly. Malcolm yelped and then squealed as Kate punched that thick skull. She hauled him upright, a vicious snarl on her lips, and as Malcolm thought the assault over she brought her knee up to crush his testicles. Malcolm collapsed on his knees, tears streaming, his hands hugging the injured organ.

Calmly she sat again. 'See, an assault that warrants a thorough good caning.'

'You could have pretended,' protested Malcolm.

'Are you going to pretend to cane my naked butt?' she asked.

'No, I guess not.'

'Now, when you stripe my naked bottom you can recall just why the strokes should be hard.' Kate sneered, unseen by the stricken lad.

'It might be some time before I can,' he replied.

'I hope it's working all right, Malc. I've got the hots. I'm going to need a fully functioning hard cock before this morning is over. You won't disappoint me, will you?'

The boy looked up, an agonised smile on his countenance. 'You mean, you want sex?'

'I don't mean I'm going to sit and watch you wank yourself off, Malc.'

'Oh, right.' He struggled to his feet, hand still clutching the offended.

'Want me to rub it better?'

'You're kidding!'

'All right.'

'No, I mean would you?'

Kate reached out and slowly unfastened the fly. His heart went into overdrive as she flicked each button loose. Fingers probed the gap, the stiff within, straining for escape. 'Hard, aren't you Malc?'

'It feels like it's going to burst.'

The hand disappeared within. She held his tool then gently rubbed up and down. 'Been in Alice's mouth, hasn't it?'

Malcolm swallowed. 'Yeah, yeah, she bit it.'

'So she said. I won't though.' Kate slid from the table and knelt before him.

'Oh, God!' the lad growled as she freed his piece.

Kate held it there before her, sensually licking her lips. She had read about it. Harry had requested she do it. Alice had tested the water. She needed to know what it was like. She peeled back the foreskin. The dome gleamed a sensitive pink. The temptation to bite came and went. Kate filled her mouth.

'Jesus fucking Christ!' Malcolm cried out.

Kate pulled it out as if it were a lollipop. 'What, don't you like it?'

'I nearly came! What a sensation!'

'If I suck this, Malc, then you'll have to do the same for me. I've got a moist slit that wants your tongue in it.'

He pulled a face. 'I don't know…'

She eased his erection back into his pants. 'Okay Malcolm,' she stood and adjusted her dress, 'I've got things to do. See you.' She headed for the door.

'Kate, wait.'

'Yes, Malcolm?' she answered, her back to him, a smile of victory on her lips.

'I'll do it.'

She faced him. 'You don't have to.'

'I'll do it, Kate.'

'Cane me first?'

'Course.'

Katy unbuttoned the front of her dress, Malcolm delirious; a big-eyed, thirsty beagle. She eased the straps over naked shoulders and let it fall to her waist. Hands on hips she waggled her breasts, the cleavage deep, a lacy bra pressing them together. 'You like?'

'Oh yes, Kate, I like.'

The dress pushed over wriggling hips, it fell to the floor revealing a skimpy pair of matching briefs. She turned and wiggled her bottom, the panties concealing little.

'God, Kate, you've got a lovely bum.'

'I'm all yours, sir,' she said playfully.

'Bend over the table, Kate, er… what's your surname?'

'Jones will do.'

'Bend over the table Kate Jones.'

'Oh sir, how many strokes am I to endure?' she asked, batting her eyelids, acting the distressed damsel.

'A dozen.' Kate shook her head. 'No?'

'No.'

'More?'

'A lot more.'

'Ah, two dozen.'

'I think, sir, I deserve three dozen at least.'

'Three dozen?'

'At least, sir.'

'Hard ones?'

'Oh, very hard ones.' Kate eyed his crotch, ensuring Malcolm noticed.

The lad shivered. 'Okay,' he said, 'bend over the table.'

'Shouldn't I be tied down before you whip my bottom, sir?'

'Yes, of course you should.'

Within minutes he returned, a coil of thick rope in hand. Kate sashayed to the table, the roll of hips pronounced. She bent, thrusting her ample buttocks out. Sweat trickling, wetting face and shirt, Malcolm contemplated bondage.

'I should remove the panties, sir,' Kate offered helpfully. 'Tie my legs apart and my hands to the far table legs.'

The majority of her behind exposed, the act of revealing her completely induced the nerves. Hands tremulous he wrenched the briefs down, cheeks quivering. He wiped his brow and leant to remove the panties completely, her sleek buttocks inches from his face.

Her legs parted, Malcolm knelt and secured her ankles to the table legs, the division at full stretch. He gazed at the sexual difference before dealing with her arms.

Why anybody would want to be caned proved beyond Malcolm's comprehension. Why anybody would want to cane a girl's naked backside he understood. That is, he reacted. The testosterone in his body went berserk. His stiff cock ached as he raised the rod and dealt Kate an arduous stroke to her meaty rump. The smack of rattan on naked flesh filled the room. Her buttocks shuddered, waves of undulating backside sweeping from the cut. Kate grunted.

Wishing to make the most of that divine opportunity, Malcolm bided his time. He waited, the seconds ticking by, before repeating the exercise. Kate gripped the table edge, the pain excruciating. She knew though that it would soon transform, become erotically stimulating.

Three slashed her backside, the fire intensifying, Kate's brows knitting in concentration. Malcolm wiped the sweat from his palms, the threat of the cane slipping real. He studied the stripes laid ad hoc, scarlet and puffing. Thirty-six, he pondered. How could anyone take thirty-six?

Four induced a throaty rasp, the hurt close to the intolerable. Kate buried her face between forearms imploring the change. She pictured herself in times gone by. Malcolm a swarthy brute, a crowd of onlookers baying at every stroke. She focused on her nudity, between her legs, vulnerable and provocative. She thought of Harry's meat stretching her, thrusting into her, as if it were an unknown assailant. The cane slapped and wrapped, an inferno aroused.

She had suffered eight before the pain turned – before the fire sank to her crotch. Then sweet Nirvana visited. Each violent connection accentuated the fervour gnawing at her groin.

She twisted and writhed with each delivery, the sound of punished flesh pure music; the swish of hurtling rattan singing the tune of promise, the meeting of buttock and rod rewarding.

Three minutes passed, twenty cuts executed and Kate wanted the flogging to last indefinitely. Two hundred did not seem preposterous in her wildly aroused mind. Kate did not mark easily. Those rigorous detonations that Malcolm levied would be mere blushes by the morning. Kate could take a fearsome beating and not have to worry about the consequence.

Malcolm hovered in his own paradise, influenced by the whistle of rattan, the slap of rod on unprotected female rump, the jostle of flesh and the pain he thought he ignited. He also could have whipped her indefinitely.

That scalded backside turned a deep, hot scarlet. Thirty-six exacting strokes administered, Malcolm grudgingly backed off. Kate laid her head on outstretched arms and sighed.

'What now?' Malcolm asked, hopeful.

'Give me another eighteen,' whispered Kate.

'You sure? Your bum ain't half marked.'

'I'm sure. First though, have a good feel. Undo my bra and feel my tits. Put your hand between my legs and paw my fanny. Be rough. Be crude.'

Feeling as if a dozen birthdays had come early he battled with the bra catch. Having wrestled it free, he placed his hands about her ribs. 'You're lying on them.'

Kate pushed on her elbows and lifted slightly, enough for him to grasp. Breathing heavy he mauled the ample breasts. 'They're gorgeous, Kate. Much bigger than Alice's.'

'Ali has a lovely body.'

'Are you going to teach her a few tricks?'

'Maybe.'

Malcolm rearmed himself with the cane. 'Eighteen, you say?'

'You're the boss.'

'It looks sore.'

'Trust me, Malc, and cane me.'

The marked *derrière* he revisited, Kate groaning in bliss, the slashing rattan an aphrodisiac. Each detonation fuelled a tornado of energy that churned fervently from hide to core, constantly titillating, reinforcing the aroused, edging Kate to the brink of climax.

A weird and wonderful biochemical change; pain altered to unadulterated ecstasy. A shower of hot ice particles seemed to rake her flesh, delve beneath and besiege the very epicentre of her sexual being. A sensation that could prove, and had in Kate's case, addictive. She sighed and moaned her way through the eighteen extras, regretting the conclusion. One day she would find herself that special man that would whip her the way her hunger demanded.

'Enough?' asked Malcolm.

'I suppose so,' she replied, that climax having eluded.

The lad untied her. She lifted herself from the table, unconcerned as the bra remained on the polished surface.

'Bloody hell!' exclaimed Malcolm. 'What a bloody pair! They're fantastic.'

Horny, aroused, the urge pressing, Kate picking up the cane and coil of rope, seized his hand and dragged him to the parlour. There she lay on a hearthrug, legs spread. Malcolm hesitated. He hovered unwilling, sinking his cock in her his only desire.

'Well, I'm waiting,' she provoked.

He knelt.

'Aren't you going to take your clothes off first?' Kate asked. 'Let me see that virile body. Those honed muscles. Your big stiff cock.'

He eyed that succulent gorge with trepidation, the lips moist with her exudation. His stomach lurched at Kate's expectation. In no hurry, he unbuttoned his shirt.

Kate reached out to explore the exposed pectorals. 'Oooh, lovely muscles, Malc.' Her fingers stroked the smooth skin, before descending and tugging at the waistband of his trousers. 'Come on, don't be shy.'

Unfastened, he eased the grey flannels down, and then grinning nervously, he dropped the underpants. Kate immediately seized the profound erection, rubbing the underside of the head with her thumb. 'Think,' she said, 'that could be my tongue doing that.'

Malcolm gasped. 'For fuck's sake,' he groaned.

'Then down, boy.'

'Oh yeah.' Pulling a face he descended, his backside thrust up.

Kate surveyed the visible cane marks on his rump. 'Nicely decorated bum, Malc. Looks like Richard didn't hold anything back.'

He wrinkled his nose, his face an inch from Kate's slit. 'He didn't. The bastard really laid into me.' He stuck out his tongue, closed his eyes and licked experimentally.

Kate grinned maliciously, seized his hair, then brought her legs together, clamping his head between her thighs, ankles crossed, feet resting on his back. She listened to his garbled protests, laughing. 'I'm not letting you go, Malc, until you satisfy me. I don't care if you suffocate down there. You bring me off with your tongue or stay put.'

Desperate to escape he placed large hands on her thighs and tried to prise them apart, but Kate replied with a sharp cut to the boy's raised backside, the cane dissuading. She thought she heard him curse, 'You fucking bitch!' But with his mouth pressed to her fanny it was hard to tell.

'Lick, Malcolm,' she demanded, tone uncompromising, and listened to his objection.

'I 'an't 'eath.'

'There are men that would give anything to be where you are now, you ungrateful sod.' Kate added another livid stripe to his stinging nates. Desperately he dared to pinch her lower cheek, awarding himself another three rapid cuts. 'Are you going to please me or not, you thick ox?' she sneered.

''Lease let 'e out,' he begged.

'Okay,' she conceded. 'Another game then, Malc. Put your hands behind your back.'

'Why?' he managed to mumble.

'Because I said so, dimwit! Now do it or I'll bloody well suffocate you.'

His hands went to the small of his back. Kate pulled herself up by his hair, keeping pressure on his head. She leant forward with the rope and quickly tied his wrists together, then released her grip on him.

'What are you going to do now?' he pleaded.

'Stand up.'

He struggled to his knees, and then to his feet.

Kate noted the stiff cock had shrunk. 'Didn't you like having your face squashed between my hot thighs?' she laughed.

'You're like Jekyll and Hyde, you are,' he grumbled. 'Nice one minute, a bitch the next.'

'No, Malcolm, to you I'm a bitch all the time.'

'Why?'

'Hasn't it sunk in, stupid? Alice.'

'So it's revenge.'

'Oh, you'd better believe it.' She took the length of rope that hung from his back and pushed it between his legs, tugged on it, and then looped it about his privates. There she knotted it, ensuring the rough fibres bit deep into the penis, the rope pinching the foreskin. Malcolm winced. She led the tether up and circled it about his waist, securing it at the front with a double granny.

Kate dressed, and then watched him doing acrobatics trying desperately to free himself. She retreated to sit in an armchair and watched him a while longer, twist and turn, wriggle and writhe, but finally bored, she rose and walked to the door.

'Where're you going?' demanded the worried youth.

'Home, Malc.'

'You can't leave me here like this!'

'Oh, but I can Malc. I can.'

'But my mother will be home for lunch in an hour. She can't see me like this!'

Kate folded her arms and studied the lad. 'Gonna have a bit of explaining to do, aren't you? All tied up. Cane marks all over your bum. What you gonna say, Malc? How you going to excuse yourself?'

'I'll tell her it was you!'

'And will she understand? Her boy all naked, trussed like a Christmas chicken. That bad girl next door made me take all my clothes off, mother. She overpowered me and tied me up.

'You tell her, Malc. And when she comes round I'll let her know exactly what you've been up to.'

He slumped to his knees, head bowed, utterly defeated.

'Bye Malc.' Kate left him, and would have been a fly on the wall had she been able. How the hell would he placate his mother?

'How did you get on?' asked an eager but worried Alice.

'You won't have any more trouble from that one,' replied Kate, with a smug grin.

'What did you do?'

'Lots.' Kate lifted her skirt. 'Wanna see my bum?'

'Oh no, Katy, what have you been up to?'

'Four and a half dozen delicious stripes. Fifty-four scrumptious strokes. Heaven, Alice. I've been in heaven.'

'He caned you?'

'And how.'

'Is that what you call getting even – letting him whack your bum?'

'Bare bum, Ali.'

Alice shook her head. 'Hopeless! You're hopeless.'

'The jerk's now wandering about the house with his hands tied to his dick, wondering how the hell he's going to explain it to mumsy.'

'You what?'

'Hopeless, aren't I? Oh, and he's stark bollock naked as well.'

'She'll go mental. She'll come straight round here. Richard will be home soon.'

'No, I don't think she will, Ali. I told that cretin in no uncertain terms, that if she does then I will tell her all

151

about his goings on.'

Alice's expression gradually changed, she freed a nervous giggle. Hand covering her mouth she failed to stifle a laugh. She gave to hysterics until the tears ran down her cheeks, Kate unable to resist joining her. 'Oh Kate, what the hell is he going to tell her? Are you sure he can't free himself?'

'His hands are tied behind his back. The rope goes between his legs and around his bits. God help him if he gets an erection. I made double sure by tying it about his waist as well. He'll never get out of that.'

They witnessed the mother's arrival and armed with tumblers, listened at the partition wall.

'Malcolm, I'm home darling. Malcolm! Where are you, love?'

The voice faded and the pair guessed the woman headed for the kitchen. They ran to resume their positions in their own.

'Malcolm! What the bloody hell?!'

Absolute silence reigned for nearly thirty seconds. Malcolm seemed not to offer any defence.

'You disgusting pervert!' they heard her scream.

'Just like your father. A deviate. I had hoped you wouldn't turn out like him. I thought the good Lord would at least let me have a normal son. But no, I have to suffer a twisted offspring as well. Well pervert, have you nothing to say? Are you going to offer no excuses? What were you hoping for? To surprise me?'

'I didn't do it, mum,' the boy blurted. 'I was tricked.'

'What are you saying?'

Alice eyed her friend coldly. 'See Kate. Blabber mouth. No brain to come up with something, and no backbone to stand his ground.'

'See who he blames, Ali.'

'A girl I know. I thought she was a nice girl. But she tricked me.'

'Who is this girl and how did she trick you?' The woman's tone sounded sceptical.

'I couldn't possibly tie myself up like this, could I? And why would I wait and let you see me, if I had done it myself?'

'Perhaps it gives you a cheap thrill, like flashing your privates in the park.'

'Honest mum, I didn't do it.'

'So who did and why?'

'Her name is Kate. She pretended to like me. She tricked me into taking my clothes off. Then she tied me up and left me.'

'Your name has come into the frame, Katy,' Alice warned unnecessarily.

'Tricked you into taking your clothes off. What were you after, Malcolm? And what did you get?'

'Nothing, mum.'

'Nothing. You expect me to believe that? What was it, spot the difference?'

'I'm not a youngster any more. I'm interested in the opposite sex. It's only natural.'

Kate grinned at Alice, and tugged at an imaginary rope about her neck.

'So, this Kate came home with you for a bit of peek a boo, did she?'

'Sort of.'

'What is she, the town prostitute?'

'She knows you, Kate,' whispered Alice.

'I don't charge,' retorted the girl.

'No, just some girl I met.'

'When did you meet her?'

'Today.'

'And this strange girl you can't even know came home with you. Not only came home but launched into sexual horseplay?'

'Yes.'

'A tart. Did you do anything with her? She's probably diseased. You'll have to go to the VD clinic for tests.'

'No, we didn't do anything.'

'But you took your clothes off. Did she take hers off?'

'Yes. That's why I took mine off.'

'And you didn't do anything?'

'No.'

'You just stood there and looked at each other.'

'Yes.'

'How did she trick you, Malcolm?'

'She held my head between, er... we, er...'

'She held your head between what?!'

'Oh, God.'

'Between what, Malcolm?'

'Hung,' announced Kate.

'Her legs.' The girls could barely hear him.

'I'm going to untie you, my lad. And then I am going to flog you. Flog you for that cock and bull story you expect me to believe. Flog you for bringing a hussy home.'

'She knows about you too, Ali.'

'Cock and bull is apt, I'd say.'

'Flog you for using your body in an ungodly manner, and flog you for your stupidity.'

'Please mum, don't. What you going to use?'

'The slipper, Malcolm, and then the cane. And I will also give you a sound thrashing with the rope's end.'

A few seconds passed. 'What on earth are these marks on your backside?'

'She caned me as well.'

'Most of these are a day old. Explain.'

'I can't.'

'As I said, just like your father. A pervert. Did you pay for this to be done?'

'No, I hated it.'

'So why?'

'Can't say.'

'Won't say. I will tell you one thing, young man; you won't enjoy what I hand out.'

'Please, don't. Please, you can't spank me like I was a five year old.'

The girls listened to the fall of hand on naked bottom, and indulged in the prolonged spanking Malcolm suffered. They laughed at his cries of pain and pleas for mercy. They drank of the slipper pounding his sore behind. Then they concentrated on the several dozen cuts of the cane. Finally they saw revenge complete as Malcolm screamed to the tune of the rope's end.

'Well, Ali,' sighed Kate, 'I do believe that that is the jerk sorted. Summarily flogged and humiliated. Now all we have to do is let him know sometime that we listened to every painful detail.'

'Talking about painful details, I've got that birching coming tonight.'

'Don't worry about it; a lot can happen between now and then.'

'Divine intervention, you mean.'

'I was thinking more on Howell intervention.'

'What can you do? Use the family name or fortune?'

'I dare say if I offered him a hundred pounds he'd think twice.'

'And that would make me beholden to you.'

'You don't think I'd use something like that to have my wicked way, do you?'

'All I know is that you're devious.'

'Me? Whatever makes you think that?'

A key in the front door disturbed them, and Richard walked in seconds later. 'You're very quiet,' he said. 'What have you two been up to?'

'Taking in the rich atmosphere of this stimulating suburbia,' replied Kate.

'Does that mean you're bored? I know my home is not up to the standards of Howell Manor, miss, but it is all I can offer.'

'I wasn't being boorish, Mr Barker. I do find it interesting.'

'Good. Now, this afternoon, I think it only fair I take you both with me.'

The girls' expressions froze. 'Ah,' said Kate, 'can't I'm afraid.'

'Oh, why not?'

'Father is going to ring me this afternoon. He'll be worried if I don't answer.'

'Then ring him. Tell him you're going out.'

'I don't exactly know where he is.'

'I see. What about you, Alice?'

'I can't leave Katy on her own.'

'Very well. What time is your chauffeur picking me up?'

'Very soon.'

'I'll get washed and changed, then.'

Once the man was out of earshot Kate whispered, 'Not going to do it in front of us, is he?'

'You never know with him.'

'I don't fancy that.'

'I thought you fancied anything. And I mean, *anything*.'

Harry duly arrived and carried Richard off into the blue. Alice checked her watch. 'He said he'd be back by six. That gives us five hours, Kate. Are you going back with Harry tonight?'

Kate shook her head.

Alice smiled. 'You're staying over then?'

'No Ali, you are.'

'How?'

'Because Harry's going to break down or something. Well, at least the car is. I suspect in the middle of nowhere. By the time the recovery service has been out it will be well past nine. We will be worried out of our minds and both being so young will opt for a taxi to my house as soon as it gets dark. Of course, we'll leave a note saying what we have done and why.

'Our actions will be seen to be responsible, so there will be no repercussions. It will then be up to me to keep you with us. Once I've spoken to father I'm sure he'll aid and abet us. So what illnesses haven't you had, Ali?'

'Devious or what? Are you sure Harry will do what you ask?'

'I didn't ask, Ali. And yes, there's a little something in it for him if he does.'

'What, money?'

'More like a favour.'

'I can guess what, but I'm not going to ask.'

'I promised him you'd jump naked through hoops.'

'To get away from uncle until next term, it might even be worth it.'

'That would be really kinky, wouldn't it? Three in a bed.'

'Don't get your hopes up, Kate. I will say though, that I owe you one or two.'

'I can think of a way you can pay me back.'

'I thought you might. No sex, though.'

'The house grounds are immense. Gardens, pasture and woodland. We even have a small lake. We can do very much what we like in those grounds, nobody would be any the wiser.'

'Let's escape first. I wouldn't put uncle past getting a taxi home.'

A gloomy day, dark fell at nine. They had heard nothing from Richard, so Kate telephoned for a taxi. 'We're in luck, Ali. It'll be here in fifteen minutes. Pack a bag and make it quick.'

Kate wrote a note, explaining that she and Alice thought it best as Richard hadn't returned, and they hadn't heard from him, that they should go to her house.

Ten minutes after the taxi had left, Harry arrived.

'Some chauffeur you are, running out of petrol,' bitched Richard. 'I shall be having a word with Miss Howell about it. And I don't expect Mr Howell will be best pleased when he gets to hear of it, either.' Richard slammed the passenger door and stomped off. Harry provided a two-finger salute and drove away.

The house in darkness baffled the man as he searched for his key. Perhaps the girls had gone to bed. Inside he spotted the note Kate had written, and reading it quietly seethed.

'Don't think you're getting away with it, Alice Hussey,' he whispered. 'I'll have you back here tomorrow. And then I'll *really* thrash you.'

Alice had no idea what to expect. Kate had often talked of her mansion. Mr Howell appeared well heeled, but to be honest she had taken the stories with a pinch of salt.

The taxi swept through wrought iron gates. Traversed a driveway a half-mile long and pulled onto a forecourt that would have done service to a Park Lane hotel. Numerous expensive cars lined up before an immense house, that built of a yellow stone.

'Good grief,' Alice gasped.

'Looks like mother and father are entertaining,' Kate remarked, attaching little importance to the fact.

'I thought your mother was in America.'

'No, she never goes abroad.'

'What are they going to say when I walk in?'

'Hello, pleased to meet you?'

'Me in my glad rags and the house full of hoity-toity guests, great!'

'Influential guests, Ali. Who knows, therein might lurk a future husband. Don't knock the opportunity.'

'You don't give a damn, do you Kate?'

'Should I? Two minutes, mate,' she said to the driver, disappeared inside and re-emerged minutes later with a tall, good-looking man in his forties. The fellow paid the cabdriver and beckoned for Alice to alight.

'Good evening,' he said, offering a hand. 'Kate has often talked about you. And her praise, I have to say, is well founded. You, young lady, are very attractive.'

Alice accepted the hand and curtsied. The man oozed charm. Suave and sophisticated he captured her heart in seconds.

Mr Howell chuckled. 'I'm a businessman, not a lord. There's no need for the reverence, my dear.'

'You're Kate's father, I assume.'

'For my sins. You are staying, of course.'

'I would like to.'

'What prevents you?'

'My uncle.'

'Leave your uncle to me.'

Chapter Six

Jonathan Howell ushered Alice into the house. He led her to a large hall where the party throbbed in full swing. 'A drink?' he offered.

'Who are all these people?' Alice asked, wide-eyed.

'Associates. Customers. The odd earl and duchess. Anybody that may be able to aid the future success of my company.'

'What business are you in, exactly? Kate has never said.'

'Publishing. Magazines and books.'

'Perhaps I might know one or two titles.'

Jonathan grinned mischievously. 'I very much doubt it, Alice. Or should I say, I rather hope not.'

'Oh, that sounds ominous.'

'I produce for a specific market. An expanding market. Sales are better than expected and will be for the foreseeable future.'

'But you're not going to tell me, right?'

'I don't see why not. It's nothing I'm ashamed of. I produce and distribute pictorials of a sensual nature.'

'Dirty books, you mean?' Alice regretted the phrase immediately.

Howell gazed at her for a moment, Alice looking for a hole to fall into. He smiled, exposing gleaming white teeth. 'I do like your friend, Kate. Doesn't mince words, does she? Straight to the point.'

'I'm sorry, Mr Howell,' Alice apologised, angry with herself. 'I shouldn't have said that. I must sound rude and prudish.'

'And are you, Alice? Prudish?'

'I suppose I am in a way. I have led a very sheltered life.' Her expression jocose, she added, 'Boring, I suppose. I'm afraid you might find me naïve and dull, Mr Howell.'

'Never dull!' he said emphatically. 'And please, call me Jonathan.' He laughed. 'Dirty books, eh? I suppose they could be construed that way. Not the sort of thing you would expect a bishop to read, eh?'

'Oh, that wouldn't surprise me.'

Eyes sparkling, Jonathan agreed. 'Nor me.'

'So, is it just nude magazines you do?'

'I cater for various demands, the woman in all her natural glory being the mainstay. There are of course other requirements I meet. Fictitious novels and explicitly illustrated journals that you won't find in your neighbourhood newsagents.'

'Hardcore?'

'Not really, merely different.'

'Kinky?'

'That would define them, yes.'

'Perhaps I could broaden my horizons sometime.'

'As long as you don't see me as leading you astray.'

'No, of course not.'

'Well, it has been lovely talking with you,' he said. 'And we will again soon. But now I must circulate.'

'You never said,' Alice fired at Kate.

'What's there to say? Daddy sells pornography. What's the big deal?'

'I now know where you get your ideas from. Tell me Katy, what's the kinky stuff like?'

The girl shrugged.

'Come on,' Alice urged, 'you must know.'

'Like father like daughter.'

'I might have guessed.'

'Except father prefers to give.'

Alice frowned. 'Has he ever, to you, you know?'

Kate coloured; the very first occasion that Alice had witnessed embarrassment in her friend. 'We're kinky, Ali, not sick!' The retort came a touch too sharply for Alice's comfort. Had she settled upon a raw nerve?

'There are some beautiful women here,' Alice remarked, changing the subject. Are they by any chance models?'

'Most are, yes.'

'The others?'

'Chaperones.'

'Who are they chaperoning?'

'Important business clients.'

'Ah, to sleep with, you mean.'

'And you said you were naïve.'

'I'm curious, Kate. I'm not criticising. No, in fact I find it all quite exciting.'

'Father has taken quite a shine to you.'

'You think so? He's adorable, isn't he? Charming, handsome and intelligent.'

'Ali.'

'Yes?'

'When I said you might meet your future husband here, I didn't mean father. He's spoken for.'

Alice laughed. 'I don't know what you mean, Kate.'

'Don't get your fingers burned, Alice. Mother is a jealous woman.'

'I wouldn't dream of coming on to your father, Kate. I'm surprised you could say such a thing. Besides being married and my best friend's father, he's more than twice my age!' All the same, Alice did find herself attracted to him, her mind lingering on Jonathan for much of the evening.

In the early hours of the next morning, well-attired men began to leave accompanied by flirtatious women. The body language implied that they were not their nearest and dearest.

That night Alice slept well, a heavy burden lifted. For the first time since her parents' death she caught her first glimpse of happiness.

Late morning, having laid in until ten-thirty, she and Kate were summoned to Jonathan's study. Serious, he explained.

'I have just received a phone call,' he started. 'Your uncle, Alice; A rather gruff man, if I might say so. He seemed surprised to find me here. And he was even more shocked to discover Jenny is not in America. If you're

161

going to tell fibs, Kate, at least have the decency to forewarn me.'

'Sorry father, I didn't have a chance, what with last nights orgy and all.'

'It was not an orgy, Kate, as you well know. I managed to placate him, I think. I said I had been away, as had Jenny, but we had to be back for this evening. Something you didn't know about. I have also managed to talk him into letting Alice stay with us for the rest of the school holidays.'

'Oh father, you're superb!' Kate nigh screamed.

'There is a downside, though.'

'Oh,' moaned Alice.

'Apparently you have misbehaved, Alice.'

She nodded.

'Mr Barker sees your coming here as an attempted escape, and is determined you will not avoid the due punishment. I'm afraid I had to either let him come, or send you home post-haste. I'm sure you prefer the former.'

Alice nodded, grimfaced.

'I have offered the privacy of my study for the necessary. I hope, Alice, that it doesn't prove too painful.'

'Thank you, Mr Howell. What time can I expect him?'

'I have sent Harry to pick Mr Barker up. I would expect him to return at about two. Oh, and Kate, I do hope you had no connivance in our chauffeur running out of petrol. Mr Barker was none too pleased.'

'What do you suspect, father? That I siphoned the tank?'

'No Kate, of course not. However you do have Harry eating out of the palm of your hand. Should I discover that you put him up to it, then you can expect to visit the study yourself.'

'Yes father.'

Strolling the lawns, her mind on Richard and his promise, eyes alert for the Jaguar, Alice said, 'Well at least you tried, Kate.'

'Look on the bright side. We won half the war. You get to stay here until term.'

'And no more Richard Barker for eight weeks after

that.'

'Ever, Ali. I'm going to ask father if you can stay here holidays until you qualify.'

'That would be terrific.'

Richard duly turned up with what looked like a cricket holdall. Jonathan welcomed the man into the house and showed him to the study.

'As Alice will be staying here until September, I feel it my duty to point out that she is headstrong,' Richard stated curtly.

'Then I shall have two like it under my roof.'

'I'm sorry?'

'Katy. Always a handful.' Jonathan searched for a glimmer of humour in the man's face, but found none.

'Should you feel the need to discipline Alice, Mr Howell, then you have my permission.'

'I shouldn't think there will be any need for that.'

'No? Then why do you think I am here?'

'You intimated corporal punishment.'

'The birch, to be precise. I found Alice naked and—'

Jonathan held up a hand. 'Should you be telling me this, Mr Barker? I think that discipline should be a private matter and the reasons confidential, don't you?'

'You should know what you are dealing with. The girl is out of control. She has been under my care for barely three weeks. In that time I have had to reprimand her on a number of occasions. As I was saying, she was naked and bound. Tied up by the youth next door. At her request, I might add.'

'A stage, I suspect. She has recently suffered a traumatic loss. That is bound to affect her. Give her time, Mr Barker. She'll adjust. Alice seems a very nice, well balanced young lady to me.'

'Remember what I said. You have my permission to punish her if you see fit. By any means at your disposal.'

'I'll get Alice. Then Harry can take you home.'

That final remark did nothing to improve Richard's mood. He had hoped to impress Howell. The request to stay for tea not forthcoming, he determined to take it out on Alice's behind.

The girl thought to knock first, hoping it might placate Richard to some degree, but the second she saw his face she knew she would be in for a gruelling time.

'So Alice, you thought you could run away, did you?'

'We left a note explaining our reasons.'

'That was complete codswallop as you well know. The only reason I am letting you stay here is because I am well rid of you. You are nothing but trouble. I have instructed Mr Howell not to put up with your malarkey. So don't think you're going to have an easy time of it.'

He unzipped the holdall and laid three birch bundles on the desk. Alice scrutinised them, stomach rolling. Why three?

The unasked question he promptly answered. 'The birch breaks up very rapidly, so one wand will only last for about ten strokes,' Richard explained.

'Thirty?' Alice gasped.

'Think yourself lucky it isn't more. The perversion must be thwarted. The devil driven from you. What you did was completely unnatural. And then, of course, I have to take into account running away under false pretences.'

Richard picked up a chair and placed it against the desk, the surface clear. 'Remove your skirt and pants and kneel on the chair, Alice.'

As she knelt she assessed the birch bundles. Each three-foot long and consisting of roughly a dozen twigs, she considered them ineffectual. How could those fine sticks possibly hurt?

'Lay over the desk, Alice,' she heard Richard order.

The man surveyed that bared bottom and took hold of the first wand. The bound handle sat snugly in his clenched fist. The upper reaches spread to seven inches and would cover the majority of her bottom at each cut.

She listened to him slice air a few times, the sound intimidating. And nothing could prepare her for the pain that ineffectual rod would inflict. Alice was in for a shock.

'Right girl, you will acknowledge each stroke by its

number. Also, you will thank me for showing you the error of your ways.'

'Yes, uncle,' she whispered meekly.

She felt the twigs rest against her naked flesh, rough and abrasive. She took a deep breath as the birch withdrew, readying herself. The approach shrill, the twigs slashed, a dozen ends delivering misery. They bowed to the contours, driving a scalding fire deep into that fleshy rump. Taken aback, horrified, Alice inhaled deeply. 'One,' she exhaled, adding, 'thank you.'

The second added to the furore, the tips stinging mercilessly. Alice gasped then quickly counted in a single breath. 'Two, thank you.'

The third seemed to rip the skin from her. The girl yelped, the smart torturous. 'Th-three,' she stammered. 'Th-thank you.'

How she would endure thirty proved beyond her at that moment. Hands clasped together, fingers interlocked, she struggled with the hurt. But Richard rekindled that with a fourth, the pain completely beyond her. 'Uh, uh, uh four, th-thank you,' she gasped.

Five whipped flesh already in murderous turmoil, the stroke excruciating. Alice squealed, unable to contain her suffering. She counted and tendered the demanded gratitude, not seeing the smirk that lit Richard's face.

In dread she reeled to the sixth, still disbelieving of the brutal capability of that wand. Pieces of broken twig lay scattered about the room, the tips already decimated. A scarlet glow radiated, fine whip marks smothering her butt. 'Nooo!' she squealed, before uttering the expected.

She reached out for the table's edge and gripped with tenacity, her knuckles white. Eyes squeezed tight and teeth clenched, she faltered as the seventh slashed, her bottom so sore she wanted to die.

So much for ineffectual twigs. So much for Katy's opinion. Alice let the tears roll, knowing that nothing in the world would melt the callous brute's heart. Eight lashed. Alice sobbed.

She envied Kate with all her being. How did she convert

the awful pain to pleasure? How could anyone indulge in such a beating?

Ten strokes administered, her backside feeling torn to shreds, she watched Richard discard the decimated birch and select the second. That he practiced with, ensuring it met with his approval. He took up position on the opposite side. Alice's left haunch would bear the brunt of the renewed assault.

'Eleven, thank you,' she yelped as that fresh bundle savagely whipped, those unforgiving ends raking unmarked buttock. For a stroke or two the scorch returned to tolerable. A much needed respite. Soon though the fire strengthened, her left haunch screaming its anguish as had the right. By the time that rod had reached its end so had her end. Alice could not face the last ten.

'Pl-please uncle,' she begged. 'Please, no m-more. I'm so sorry for what I did. I promise I won't ever do anything like that again. Just please, don't beat me any more.'

She heard the reply. Richard swished the bundle. 'No Alice, I don't think you will. You will recall this punishment and deny Satan. But it will be this flogging that places you on the path to righteousness, not your pathetic self-centred pleas.' He whipped that tortured rear, Alice screaming in reply. 'Tw-tw-twenty-one... th-thank you.'

Richard cut low with the next, Alice's thighs receiving, the coarse sticks scathing. The girl shrieked. Richard smirked and repeated the episode.

'Aah... twenty-three,' she groaned. 'Thank you.'

'No Alice, you failed to count the last. So twenty-two, I'm afraid.' He wasn't really. Alice groaned. 'Say it girl, before I give you another.'

'Twenty-two, thank you.'

Her legs refusing to calm, Alice winced to a savage stroke across the loins, the flesh there relatively clear of welts. She writhed. Perspiration joined the tears. 'Twenty-three, thank you.'

Richard adjusted his position and stance, dealing a devastating angled cut that whipped from upper left haunch to right thigh, the twigs locating and delving the protruding vulva.

'Nooo!' she screamed, as the full implication sank in. Gasping, struggling for breath she sought the words, but before she could utter them he struck again. 'Aah… twenty-f-four, thank you.'

Alice felt sick. Throwing up seemed a very real possibility. She clung to that desk, the end in sight. Richard leant into the following stroke, the reach extended, those vicious twigs scouring to the hip and beyond. 'Bloody hell!' Alice yelled. 'T-t-twenty…'

'I beg your pardon?' growled Richard. 'What did you say?'

'Sorry uncle, it hurt so much.'

'It is supposed to. That gives you no reason to cuss.'

'I forgot myself.'

'Obviously. That demonstrates just how incorrigible you are, doesn't it? It would seem this flogging is inadequate. You have learned nothing. I foresaw this possibility and equipped myself with two more bundles. You shall feel them both.'

Alice leapt from the seat, and fell to her knees before Richard. Hands clasped in supplication she begged. 'Please don't. I can't take any more. Please uncle, I beg you, don't add any more. I didn't mean to swear. It was only because the birch caught me in a sensitive place. The pain was so fierce. My bottom is so unbearably sore. Please have some mercy.'

'Get up, girl.' He pushed the chair clear of the desk, Alice daring to think for a second that he relented. 'Now Alice, bend over the desk and place your legs apart. You have another twenty-five strokes to receive.'

'I can't! I can't take that. Please uncle, don't.'

'Perhaps I should take you home with me and continue this in the potting shed.'

Reluctant, dismayed, Alice climbed from her knees. Staring incredulous she sought those ravaged cheeks. Wincing at the touch she gauged the damage. Her backside felt stippled, the once sleek flesh whipped to the texture of bark.

167

Stomach hollow she lay over the desk, and parted those curvaceous legs.

'Not so close to the desk, Alice.' Richard cruelly sought the most indelicate posture.

She shuffled back, parting her legs again.

'Further,' he demanded. 'Now stick your bottom out. No, further. That's it.'

Richard lifted the tail of her blouse and placed it up over her back, baring her to the bra strap. Then, still using the third birch he resumed the murderous castigation.

Alice, fully aware of her exposure, mentally placed herself in his position. She pictured herself as he surely saw her – almost naked, bottom scarlet and welted, legs straight and parted, and her vagina exposed. That consideration set a tingle roaming.

Richard laid into her, that birch cutting air like a demon, the twigs slapping with a dull smack. Those tenderised buttocks quivered, the flesh ignited. Alice reared, pushed up on both arms. Tearstained face screwed, she stammered, 'Tw-twenty-six. Th-thank y-you.'

'Down,' snapped Richard.

Alice lowered herself.

Again the sharp whoosh, the dull slap and the slicing fire. 'Ah, ah,' she huffed, rolling her head between outstretched arms. 'Uh, twenty…' she ground her teeth, 'seven, thank you.'

Twenty-eight landed with equal force. A layer of hot ice seemed to coat her mauled rump. Alice frowned. Where had the sickening pain gone? Why didn't it hurt? 'Twenty-eight,' she recited. 'Thank you.'

Richard noticed her lack of reaction and inspected the birch. Most of the ends had gone, leaving frayed stems. Enough left to leave an impression, he concluded, and proceeded with the next.

That whipped high over the coccyx, the twigs wrapping to her side. The fury revisited. 'Tw-twenty… nine… thank you.'

That smart lingered, persisted as Richard whipped her there again. 'Aaaah…' she whimpered. 'Thirty,' she spat.

'Thank you.'

Richard tossed the demolished bundle aside and delved in his bag. He inspected a new birch, one that presented a mixture of thick and thin. Six uncompromising stems bound within a ring of nine willowy shoots.

Tempted to harass the girl he decided to shock instead. Selecting the middle portion of that carmine posterior he dealt a hefty blow. Those half dozen rods slashed the beaten, whilst the remaining nine whipped about the flank.

Eyes thrown wide Alice sucked air, the icy fire a most peculiar sensation... and agreeable one. Had she discovered Kate's bliss? 'Thirty-one,' she stated. 'Thank you.'

Richard lashed her again, those numerous twigs spreading, pounding the roasted sphere. The phenomenon rekindled she relaxed, indulging in its influence, enjoying the tantalising effect.

'Thirty-two,' she almost whispered. 'Thank you.'

Richard detected the change in tone; that 'thank you' almost meant in earnest. Perplexed, he moved closer to the desk. From there he expertly laid the birch in a diagonal path, those fine twigs flexing to impress her vagina, that cruel and deliberate act serving only to accentuate the fervour boiling within.

Terrified the miracle would turn, Alice focused on that vaginal flagellation. She knew it to be deliberate. Richard must have contemplated her sex. The thought of him studying her there ensured the next, aimed at the same place, would further sow the seed of gratification.

'Thirty-three,' she hummed. 'Thank you.'

Richard knew that something was amiss. 'Can it be?' he asked, placing a hand on those fired cheeks. 'That Satan permits you indulgence?'

'Sorry?' Alice frowned.

'That the devil turns your pain?' His hand descended, dipped between her legs and felt the soft folds. Alice closed her eyes, sickened by his touch.

'We shall see.' A finger parted her, delved just inside, checked for moisture. Finding none, disappointed he straightened. 'Put your legs together, Alice,' he said, determined to extricate a cry of pain.

He whipped her high on the thighs, those six stout rods flailing the limbs, the fine ones arcing about the far leg. Pain revisited briefly. 'Th-thirty-f-four,' she managed. 'Th-thank you.'

Driven by zealotry, the ulterior motive denied, Richard adhered to his promise. Heedless of the welter of painful marks provoked to that trim posterior, he persisted with the rigorous handout.

Richard slashed those lissom thighs a second time, the burn staggering, the whip from the ends destructive. Dragged from the brink of bliss Alice winced, the noise muted. 'Blimey!' the only acceptable expletive that came to mind in those seconds of torment. 'Thirty-five,' she hissed. 'Thank you.' No more to the legs, she mentally begged, her bottom having attained Kate's phenomenon.

Richard had perceived the difference in reaction, so those tortured thighs he concentrated on. 'Aaaah!' she cried to the next, openly sobbing. 'Th-thirty-six, and thank you.'

The tyrant leant to the successor, those resolute twigs scalding above the knees. 'Thirty-seven,' she submitted, her voice hoarse. 'Thank you.'

Steadying herself for another she was unprepared for a change in tactics. Her uncle aimed the next high up, slashing the meagre flesh above the buttocks, whipping the small of her back. Though unpleasant she found it preferable to her legs. 'Thirty-eight, thank you,' she uttered.

Richard coloured her there with the following two, before switching the birch for the last time. Alice provided the requisite count.

He had constructed the final wand in a cruel way. About a central stick of sturdy proportions he had bound six of half that thickness, but still stout and resilient. Surrounding those there were the usual pliable twigs; a dozen or so. Those travelled a good six inches beyond the reach of their more durable brethren.

'Lay flat on the desk, Alice,' he said, his voice as cold as the arctic wind. 'Push your bottom out.'

He raised that formidable rod, his fist barely able to cope with its girth. Alice gripped the edge tenaciously. She buried her face between tensed arms and grit her teeth in trepidation. Richard brought the wand to bear with ferocity. That central stick hit with the force of a rattan, those about it lashing with aggression. The fine tips wrapped about the hip to inflict fire upon the groin. Eyes flung wide Alice lifted her torso from the desk; the pain sickened and lingered, barely easing before the next detonation.

She straightened hands, clutching at the inferno in her behind. 'I don't deserve this,' she wailed. 'No one deserves this.' She eyed the rod in his fist. 'Why don't you just skin me alive? It would be quicker.'

A mad glint to his eyes, Richard snarled and reached out. Alice ducking didn't save her. He took her by the back of the neck and forced her over. 'You harlot. You deserve anything I give you. What you did is beyond Christian belief. I will ensure you never, ever indulge in such wanton, disgusting behaviour again.'

The girl thrown back over the desk, Richard delivered another furious cut, Alice screaming, the hurt beyond her. He lifted the rod once more, irrespective of her not counting, but another's hand prevented him from pursuing the vicious stroke. Trembling, Richard turned to see Jonathan holding his wrist.

'I think the girl has had enough, don't you, Mr Barker?'

'She is possessed of the devil,' he growled in answer. 'I must drive Satan from her.'

'I don't believe so. She has erred. You have dutifully corrected her. Leave it at that, unless you wish to place her in a hospital. Where, I might add, the doctors will have to tend her, and I don't think they will be in any doubt about the cause, do you?'

Jonathan released Richard. The man's hand slowly descended. The anger seemed to abate. 'Perhaps she has learned her lesson. But should she act the licentious tart again I will not hesitate to flog her without mercy.'

'Can I speak with you in private, Mr Barker?'

'I suppose so.'

Jonathan steered Richard from the study, saying to Kate who waited outside, 'See if Alice needs anything.'

Within the walls of a large living room Jonathan lit a cigar, offering one to Richard. The man declined. 'I understand Alice is attending Heptonstall next term.'

'That is correct.'

'Not cheap. Though I understand a very good school that provides excellent results.'

'I don't flinch from my responsibilities. And yes, they almost guarantee results.'

'Why pull her from Carters?'

'That is my business, sir.'

'Of course. It's just that I know the fees to be about the same. I understand you told Alice that you couldn't afford Carters.'

'No, not at all. I informed the girl that she would go to Heptonstall if she accepted my guardianship.'

'I see.' Jonathan pondered for a moment. 'I have a proposal. I can relieve you of those expenses.'

'Why would you want to do that?'

'Kate is an only daughter. She has no company here at the house. The village is too far away for her to make friends there. She adores Alice, and I believe that Alice has a fondness for Katy. I would like them to live here as sisters and would be quite willing to pay for the privilege.'

'I don't think I can agree to that.'

'That would be a great shame, Mr Barker. Katy would miss out on a worthwhile relationship. Alice would be settled. Your bank balance would be healthy. I wouldn't have to worry about my daughter, nor you about your niece. So may I ask what your objection is?'

'My sister and brother-in-law have left her in my hands, sir. I don't know you from Adam. How can you expect me to simply turn her over.'

'You can visit as often as you like. I will even send Harry to collect you. You may come unannounced. I have nothing to hide, sir.'

'I need to keep the girl under my wing.'

Jonathan withdrew a chequebook from the inside pocket of his jacket. Opened and with pen in hand, he asked, 'How much?'

'It is not a matter of money.'

'Then what?'

Richard licked dry lips. 'She would have to remain under my control. I would wish her to spend some time with me. She must attend Heptonstall. And I will brook no further interference from your good self.'

'Agreed. Shall we say a five hundred pound fee for Alice acting as chaperone to Katy? Considering your true relationship to Alice, I don't see how you can refuse such an offer, do you, Mr Barker?'

Richard nodded. 'That would be most agreeable. However, Alice must never hear of this little arrangement.'

With the terms mutually acceptable, Richard left. Alice would attend Heptonstall, and he could still direct her upbringing and carry on his insidious guidance without the cost. Richard took his seat in the Jaguar a happy man.

Jonathan returned to the study where Katy tried to console a sobbing Alice. 'You should see what the swine has done to Ali,' Kate snapped.

'Yes, I know,' Jonathan replied, expression grim. 'I wish I had intervened sooner. However, the decision was not an easy one.'

He approached the girl, and lifting her chin, gazed directly into tear-filled eyes. 'I do have some good news, however.'

'You've shot the bastard,' suggested Kate.

'Language, Katy. No, I haven't shot him. I have persuaded the man to relinquish part of his control.'

'What part?' Alice asked hopefully.

'The part where you stay during holidays.'

'You don't mean?'

'From now on you come here.'

'How much did that cost you, father?'

'Don't be so presumptuous, Kate.'

'Well he didn't listen to kind words and diplomacy, did he?'

'I chose the easiest path, that's all. I could have crucified the man, but I thought there would be little point in starting a war.'

'How much did you pay?' enquired Alice.

'That is irrelevant.'

'Not to Ali it isn't. Ali has scruples. Ali hates the thought of being in debt.'

'She's not in debt. She will have to repay me.'

'But I haven't any money until I'm twenty-one,' protested the girl.

'It's worse than that, Alice. You have to keep my mischievous daughter company. For that I would pay a small fortune.'

'For that I might demand one,' the girl replied, depression lifting.

Chapter Seven

Suave, sophisticated, handsome, paternal, kind, successful. All those attributes ran through Alice's mind. She wallowed in the strange feeling. Was she besotted? Her first love – and that demon usurped the kinky devil in her.

With all the rooms available Jonathan would not hear of the girls sharing. 'No need,' he said, Kate knowing not to argue. 'You both need your own space, your privacy.'

'Shame,' opined Katy, once out of earshot.

'You only wanted to resume where we left off,' Alice pointed out.

'I've read another article since then, Ali,' Kate replied, grin impish. 'Now I know even more.'

'I don't think I want to hear it. How long have your parents been married, Kate?'

'Forever. Why?'

'Just wondered. Are they very happy together?'

'Who knows. They don't bawl at one another, if that's what you mean.'

'Jonathan seems such a lovely man.'

'Father is. And mother is a wonderful woman. I'm a very lucky girl.'

'Has he ever wandered? You know, played around?'

'You think he would tell me if he had?'

'No, I suppose not.'

'I'll tell you one thing though, Ali. He looks upon you as a daughter, not a potential lover. You've got your head in the nimbus again. You're too young for him. He's forty-seven. The two will never meet in a loving embrace.'

'What about a lusting one?'

'You've got the hots for him, haven't you? You fancy my father.'

Alice looked at her feet, and nodded.

'It's only because he's dug you out of a hole, Ali. Don't confuse gratitude with love.'

'I expect you're right. He is the light at the end of the tunnel, except you of course, Kate. And without you none of this would have happened.'

'So you owe me one then?'

'Of course.'

'Whip me then, Ali. Tie me to a tree in the woods and whip me.'

'I couldn't. I wouldn't know how too. God forbid that I hurt you, Kate.'

'Then learn what to do. Look, I know where I can lay my hands on an old leather flogger. Oh, Ali, it's my ultimate fantasy, don't refuse me, please.'

'And what if we're discovered?'

'We won't be. I promise. Anyway, my family isn't like that sodding old shit of an uncle of yours. They'd probably look the other way.'

'If you're absolutely sure, Kate. Where do you want me to do it?'

'In the woods, of course. Tell you what, we'll go skinny-dipping first. Then feeling all tingly and fresh you can tie me to a tree. Naked, of course. And then you can give me a thorough flogging. You can whip me until I orgasm. That's my dream.'

'And you'll keep the marks hidden? Talking of which, what about that caning you took yesterday from Malcolm? Surely your bum is all sore and striped.'

'No one will see the welts. And I heal fantastically fast. Here, have a look.' The girl lifted her skirt and pulled down her knickers.

'I don't believe it,' Alice gasped. 'There's only a few faint lines there.'

'See. You whip me today and I'll be ready for another tomorrow.'

'There's something else I should tell you, Kate.'

'You fancy mother?'

'No, idiot. When Richard…'

'Pig. You call him pig in future.'

'When pig was birching me, before he got really brutal, well, I actually enjoyed it for a time. My bum went all icy. This strange lovely feeling penetrated to my, my you know what. I thought I was closing on an orgasm for a while.'

'Welcome to the world of masochism, Ali,' Kate beamed. 'See, you didn't believe me, did you? You can experience that as often as you want. I'll whip you, Ali. I'll take you to paradise. And I'll finish it off for you as well. I'll lick you, Ali. I'll tongue your vagina.'

'Is that what you read?'

'Hmmm. That or a cucumber.'

'A what?'

'Or marrow, if you fancy it.'

'I don't think so.'

'How about a milk bottle? Washed and sterilised, of course.'

'What sort of books are you reading, Kate?'

'Juicy ones.'

'Where's this whip kept then?'

'I'll show you.'

Kate ran off, Alice following on her heels. Jonathan watched them through the patio windows. 'One of my better decisions,' he whispered, smiling.

Kate led Alice to a cellar. Therein she showed her a range of implements and apparatus.

'Good grief, Kate, why are these kept here?'

'Props for photographic sessions. Kinky pictures wouldn't mean much if there was not the odd piece of torture furniture about, would they?'

'So are these photographs done here then?'

'Regularly.'

'Do you see any of it?'

Kate shook her head. 'All carried out behind locked doors.'

'Can I see some of these magazines, Kate?' Alice asked, curiosity getting the better of her.

'Ask father.'

'Maybe I will.'

They held each other's gaze. Ali's churlish. Kate's suspicious.

'So Kate, where's this leather flogger then?'

'Here.' The girl reached up and took a single tailed plaited whip from a hook on the wall. She offered it to Alice.

'Kate, this looks a nasty piece. It's going to hurt.'

'No Alice – glow. Just like your bum did with the birch. I'll be able to touch nirvana with that.'

Alice glanced about for a suitable receiver. A padded bench provided that. She raised the whip over a shoulder and brought it down with a crack on the tarnished hide. A small whirl of dust rose, a slight indentation left in its wake.

Alice frowned. 'Are you sure about this, Kate? You've always been slightly mad, but now I believe you're slipping into total insanity.'

'How can you say that after your admission? You know how nicely it can glow.'

'Only if it's not too hard.'

'Well it won't be, will it? You don't have to whip me with all your strength.'

'You'll be tied up, Kate. I might take advantage of that. The devil may well take over. I did tell you I have a problem with demons.'

'You're having me on, aren't you?' Kate asked, a touch concerned.

Alice grinned. 'Course I am, idiot.'

'We probably won't get it right straight off. It will take some practice. But unless we make a start we never will.'

'How many lashes, Kate?'

'One hundred.'

Alice gasped, incredulous. 'You won't do it. Not a hundred.'

'The rule, Ali, and you have to stick to this; once I'm tied to that tree you ask me if I want to proceed. If I say yes you carry out that punishment no matter what. I have to know you'll do it.'

'But what if it gets too much and you scream for me to stop? I couldn't continue, Kate. No way.'

'It's my fantasy, Ali. It has to seem like a real flogging. In real floggings they don't stop because it hurts. It's supposed to.'

'I don't know, Kate.'

'Please, Ali. Anyway, I'll be so turned on that it won't hurt. I'll love every minute of it.'

The whip dropped into a bag, the pair made their way back through the house, and once outside heading for the woods Alice breathed a sigh of relief.

'Rope Kate,' she suddenly said. 'You forgot the rope.'

'Coils and coils of it in the boatshed,' Kate told her, and then as they approached the lake she asked, 'Did you notice that old wooden pillory in the cellar?'

'Couldn't miss it, really,' Alice admitted.

'Now that I would love to experience.'

'Then why don't you?'

'Eh?'

'You've only got to slip your big head and hands in the holes.'

'No, I mean *experience*. You know, getting whapped in it.'

'Bit big to haul down to the woods, isn't it?'

'We'll wait until mother and father go out for the night.'

'If you say so.'

'I'll do you in it if you like. Bring your bum up to boiling point and then do things to you. In there you wouldn't be able to say no.'

'What things?'

'Try it and you'll see.'

Alice ignored the familiar sensation below and opened the door to the boatshed. She peered into the gloomy interior. A small rowing boat gently rocked at its mooring, the surrounding duckboards surprisingly clear of debris. All the associated paraphernalia lay at the back of the shed.

'I'm not rooting around in that, Kate,' she announced.

'What, frightened of spiders, Ali?'

'No, terrified.'

'I'll get the rope.' Unconcerned, the girl strolled to the rear and selected several coils of thick hemp. She held one up. 'It's coarse, Ali. I just love the feel on my naked skin.'

'So would I,' admitted Alice without thinking.

'Oooh, Ali! I could tie you up. I could bind you in such a fashion you'd orgasm.'

'It's stuffy in here.' Alice changed the subject. 'Let's go.'

Kate followed to the lake's edge, watching the roll of her friend's hips. 'How's the bum now, Ali?' she called out.

'Sore, Kate – bloody sore.'

'Want me to kiss it better?'

'Give it a rest, will you?' Alice surveyed the small lake. 'Is it deep?'

'No, about five feet at the most.'

'And you're sure no one will see us?'

'What does it matter? We'll only be swimming naked, more's the pity.'

'I've heard about women that can't get enough.'

'Nymphomaniacs.'

Alice nodded.

'Perhaps I am one,' Kate acknowledged. 'Or perhaps I just haven't got bored with it yet.'

'Do you think you ever will?' Alice took off her blouse.

'Yeah, probably – I'll get married, have kids and turn into the accepted fridge. What's up – I shall say to my doting hubby – you had it last year? You're not due again until nineteen sixty-eight.'

'Not you, Kate,' Alice mused. 'I'm sorry officer, I didn't know he had a weak heart. Can I ask you madam, did he always have a one inch red raw penis? No sir, when we wed it was virgin pink and nine inches. When did you marry, madam? A month ago, sir.'

Kate tossed her top into the grass, laughing. 'Oooh, officer, you have a remarkable bulge in your pants. Yes madam, nine inches and I'm keeping it that way.'

Alice slipped off her skirt. 'Is it true, madam, that this is your eighth husband? Yes sir. How old are you exactly? Twenty-two and three months, four days, nine hours, six

180

minutes and eighteen, nineteen, twenty seconds.'

Kate took off her skirt. 'Did they all die this way, madam? No sir, Johnny tripped in the bedroom and pole-vaulted through the window. That was on our honeymoon.'

'Here goes,' whispered Alice, removing her bra. 'And what occurred with the others? David suffocated during a loving embrace. Robert fell from the chandelier and Peter was impotent.'

Kate freed her generous bust too. 'Reginald suffered from Lickers Syndrome; he got tongue-tied at the wrong moment. Donald was a missionary and I like it anyway but that, buster. Roger fulfilled his name but used to arse about too much.'

In unison the girls dropped their knickers. 'Cold, is it?' asked Alice.

'Freezing, Ali… it is *freezing*.'

They leapt into the clear waters together. 'Jesus!' shrieked Alice. 'It's like the Arctic Ocean!'

'Stimulating, Ali,' Kate said, her teeth chattering. 'Stimulating.'

They swam and larked for some fifteen minutes before hauling their frozen bodies from the stark embrace of the lake. Together they lay on the grass, enjoying the hot sun.

'Kate?'

'Yes?'

'How would you tie me up? If I wanted it, that is.'

'So the ropes probed intimate places.'

'When Malcolm tied me to that chair – the second time – he placed the rope so that it parted my vagina. Jeez, was that some sensation!'

'You can't beat a thick, fleshy cock for that, Ali.'

'The bible says—'

'Oh, the bible!'

'Sex before marriage is a sin.'

'Only if you get caught. Or you beget a bastard.'

'What does it feel like, Kate? You know, being entered.'

'If you're lying there like a stranded codfish, pointless I would say. But if you're all worked up and gagging for

181

it, well I guess it's like a drink of water when you're parched; a tub of ice cream when you haven't eaten in three days; a whip on the bare bum when you're screaming for it. Bloody satisfying.'

Kate thought for a few moments. 'It's not just that warm, stiff prick gliding into your well-lubricated hole, or the feeling of your fanny stretching to accommodate it. No, it's the ultimate act; the unison of two lovers; the culmination of sexual horseplay; a crescendo of pure bloody bliss.'

'You mean that?'

'Not really, it's the poking that brings you off.'

'Are you ready for the woods?'

'Of course.'

Alice picked up her bra.

'No Ali, naked. We go naked.'

'What about our clothes?'

'Leave them here. No one will pinch them.'

'What if we're seen?'

'We won't be. Don't worry; mother and father aren't the walk in the woods type, and the servants are too busy.'

'And Harry?'

'Washing the cars.'

'No surprises then?'

'Now would I? Oh, best put your shoes on though. It gets a bit rough under foot in the woods.'

So they walked without a stitch on.

'How does it feel, Ali?' Kate asked. 'You know, being as nature intended?'

'Exciting,' Alice admitted. 'I feel so free. No school. No pig. No clothes.'

'Your bum's a bit of a mess. Shame about that. I could have whipped it for you otherwise.'

'Maybe some other time. We'll see.'

Alice carried the whip, Kate the coils of rope.

'Can you imagine what Jonathan would say if he were to see us now?' Alice mused.

'Probably, can I join you?'

'You don't mean it?'

'He's a very broadminded father.'

'What would he really say, if he knew what we're doing? Truth now.'

'He might be a bit shocked. But I think he'd understand.'

'Jenny?'

'She'd go stark raving bonkers.'

'But she knows what Jonathan does for a living?'

'Of course, but that's business.'

'Does Jonathan know of your bent?'

'I think so.'

'And Jenny?'

Kate shook her head. 'No.'

They walked into the copse, some ten acres of woodland, Katy leading. Two hundred yards further on and they broke into a small clearing, Kate announcing, 'This is it.'

'Pre-selected?' asked Alice.

'Didn't want to walk in circles wasting time, did we?'

'I wish we'd brought our clothes.'

'Why?'

'Because when we've finished it would be nice to get dressed and not have to risk bumping into someone on our way back.'

'I've already told you, we won't be. And besides, that's all part of the thrill of it, Alice – the possibility of being caught.'

Alice adjudged her friend's vexed expression. 'Oh, I'm sorry. I must be a right bore. It's just that I'm not so outgoing or as adventurous as you. I see the dark side of everything, whereas you are the incurable optimist. I'll shut up, Kate, I promise. Whatever happens I'll try to enjoy it. Okay?'

Kate put her arms about Alice, hugging her. 'And whatever, Ali, I love you. It's you that keeps my feet on the ground. God knows where I'd be if I didn't have you to drag me back from the fire. We make a good couple. We complement one another's idiosyncrasies. Friends for life, eh, Ali?'

'And lovers, Kate? And lovers?'

183

Kate pushed her to arms' length and stared, bemused. 'What, no men? No cocks? No bending over backward to please?'

'Broadminded lovers?'

'Bisexual is the word.'

'Maybe I am and maybe I'm not. Time will tell if I ever leave this confusion behind.'

'As I said before, decisive.'

'Which tree, Kate?'

She pointed. 'That one.'

Alice followed the finger. An oak had split early in its growth and formed two diverging trunks, each about a foot thick. Small branches sprouted, forming natural anchoring points.

'You mean, spread between the two?'

'Mmmm.'

The pair advanced on the favoured tree. Kate stood before it and raised her arms. 'See, perfect. Use those small branches to tie my hands to. And tie my feet to those stakes in the ground.'

'Where did they…? Oh, of course. You put them there, didn't you?'

Kate merely smiled, her eyes sparkling.

Alice wound a tether to each wrist and scrutinised the anchor points. 'I don't know if I can reach, Kate.'

'Of course you can. Stand in the V and shin up the trunk.'

Alice clambered between the trunks and reached up, her breasts inches from Kate's face. 'Nice tits, girl,' Kate remarked in a guttural tone.

Ignoring her, Alice secured first one and then the other wrist. Then she posed before Kate, her bust about face level. Smiling, she placed her hands on each side of a breast and pushed them together. 'You like?' she asked, coy.

Kate leaned as far as her bonds would permit and licked the cleavage. 'Oh, I like all right.'

Alice pulled her to those succulent fruits. 'Suck my nipples, wench,' she sighed huskily, and Kate obliged,

184

Alice indulging, head thrown back, mouth open.

'Play with me below, Ali,' Kate urged. 'Finger me.'

Alice slowly descended, licking from bosom to pubic coils, Kate sighing every inch of the way. She nibbled that curl-covered mound, fingers stroking the inner thighs.

'Oooh, Ali, be careful… you'll bring me off.'

'I thought that's what you wanted?' her lover rebuffed.

'Not yet. If I come that whip will hurt like fuck.' Alice's tongue darted, licking the moist slit. 'Ali, please don't.'

'Why will it hurt Kate?' Perfect teeth harassed, tugging at the pubic hair.

'Because you'll release all my emotion. There will be nothing to convert the pain. You'll spoil it.'

The devil in her, Alice ran a finger the length of those succulent lips. 'Perhaps I want that, Kate. Maybe I get my kicks from seeing someone writhing in agony.'

'Stop pissing about. I know you don't mean it.'

'How do you know, Kate?'

'Because you wouldn't hurt a fly.'

'So you don't want me to sink my tongue deep into your fanny?'

'Of course I do, stupid. But not now. Later, after you've whipped me.'

Alice moved away a little, and hands on hips she flaunted her luscious body. 'What do you think, prisoner? Do I meet with your approval?' She about-faced and waggled her backside at the captive.

'It's times like this that I wish I had a prick,' Kate said sincerely. 'I'd stuff you something wicked.'

Thrusting her chest out, Alice enquired, 'Do you think Harry would feel that way?'

'Harry would feel with both hands and then his cock.'

'What about Jonathan?'

'And what about Jennifer's cane on your bare backside?'

Alice batted her eyelids. 'Seriously Kate, do men find me attractive?'

The girl shook her head. 'They would kill each other to get their hands on you. Now for Christ's sake get on with it.'

Alice tied her legs apart, utilising the pre-positioned stakes. She picked up the whip and settled on a position to Kate's left. 'I'll give you a taster, and then you tell me if you want to continue.'

'Whip my bum first. Get me all aroused before you start on my back.'

The scourge Alice held measured four foot in length, from the five millimetre thin tip, to the butt of the inch thick stock. The leather old and tarnished had been plaited to within six inches of the end. A single piece of tough hide enhanced the conclusion.

With no idea how to swing a slipper let alone a snake whip, Alice had a lot to learn, and that would be at the expense of Kate's sensitive hide. 'How hard?' she asked.

'I don't know. Just whip me and we'll go from there.'

Alice brought the implement to bear, the tip slapping Kate's buttocks.

'Harder, Ali, a lot harder.'

She swung into action, powering that brute in an arc, the lash acutely smacking naked flesh. Kate gasped. She ground her teeth. 'Exquisite! Oh God, what a sting!'

'Is that hard enough?'

'That's about right. But if you want to use more strength, then I'm not in a position to argue, am I?'

'You want the ton then?'

'Yes, I do.'

'No backing out, Kate. One hundred lashes no matter what.'

'One hundred lashes, Ali. And no backing out.'

'Right.' Alice repeated the stroke, the exacting leather striping from cleft to hip. The girl thrust her hips forward, buttocks clenched, haunches dimpled, thighs tensed.

Alice didn't ask if it was too much. The deal had been set. She provided a third. Kate twisted on her bindings; teeth biting lower lip. 'Oooh God!' she hissed.

The next Alice watched in horror, as delivered with a touch more gusto the tail struck the target and continued its fatal path, but before she could stop that flight it circled completely, catching her with sickening impetus on the lower back. 'Fuck!' she squealed. 'Fuck. Fuck. Fuck.'

Hand rubbing the violence she hopped, Kate intrigued by the jostle of breasts. 'What's up?' she asked. 'Get jealous, did you?'

'Shit!' Alice wailed. 'I don't know how you can stand that. Jesus, it stings!'

'I must admit I never thought of that,' Kate said mischievously. 'We can both be flogged at the same time.'

'I can assure you there will be no repetition of that mistake.' With that Alice began practicing on a tree trunk. A quick learner, she readily mastered the art of snapping back on the length a split second before impact.

Kate watched in silence, finally unable to resist. 'Lucky tree.'

The next lash, the fifth in the tally, silenced Kate with respect to smart comments. Hands seized upon the ropes as she ascended to tiptoe. Knuckles protruding her head fell back, hair draped upon her shoulders. She growled, her mind bordering upon surrender.

'Not glowing yet then, Kate?' gibed Alice, with deadpan expression.

The bound girl relaxed. 'I'll get there, don't you worry. There's the pain barrier to transcend first.'

'Do you want me to back off a bit?'

'No.' She stared hard at Alice. 'I can take it. It has to be a proper flogging, not a half-hearted attempt.'

'Okay, Kate, no more miss nice girl.' She caught her with the sixth, a beautiful crack on the lower portions.

'Fuck!' Katy spat.

A round dozen having raised an equal number of livid welts, Alice scrutinised the cheeks. 'Look Kate, the left buttock is feeling left out. All the marks are on the right. I'll have to rectify that. How you doing, anyway?'

'Getting there. It's all this trial. If you didn't have to experiment then I'm sure I'd be glowing by now.'

'You want it real, Kate, you can have it real.' She stepped back and let fly, that backhander striping the opposite cheek. Kate sucked air.

Rhythmically Alice flogged, those copious hindquarters

shivering to the continuous onslaught. Each stroke cut within five or six seconds of its predecessor. Kate twisted this way and that, her body in constant tension. Scarlet stripes gathered, slowly smothering the overtaxed flesh.

Alice strode back to Kate's left. She glanced at the girl's face, posed in concentration. Not the time for idle banter, she decided. Adopting a more suitable position she cracked the whip, the tail snaking neatly across the cleft. She noted Kate's moan and proceeded with another dozen well-placed lashes.

Those ample flanks etched, the cheeks adopting a heated tint, Alice eyed the fleshy back and deep-laid spine. She aimed high, lashing the shoulders, ensuring the tail fell short of the side. Katy squealed. Her back arched. She twisted and writhed. Frightened she had exceeded her tolerance, Alice relaxed as Kate uttered, 'More...'

She flogged those shoulders a dozen times, Katy wriggling, yanking on her bonds, punctuating each hearty slap with a curse.

Alice paused to take stock. Katy wet with perspiration begged. 'Please, don't stop, don't break the magic.'

The girl's mid-back met with the shock of the whip, Kate seeming to writhe in ecstasy rather than purgatory. She was there, thought Alice. She had found paradise. How? How could anyone enjoy that?'

Unceasing, Alice dealt the following dozen to the girl's loins and lower back, her torso a mishmash of burgeoning stripes. Then Alice met with a dilemma; where to go next. Kate would not thank her for seeking advice. Kate so obviously in a sexual fever with six dozen meted out. A rapid decision required; least Kate lost the advantage Alice aimed at those spread legs. The tail slapped a thigh and curled to the inner, a branding left in its path. Kate, in euphoric state pursed her lips and sighed, 'Yes... s'beautiful.'

The reaction comforting, Alice laid another alongside, its hallmark vivid. Six she treated that limb to before providing its twin with the same. Sixteen lashes remained. Alice hesitated.

'Between my legs...' whispered Kate. 'Whip me there.'

Delirious, she barely responded as the leather wrapped her hip and sliced into her pubic mound. Deeply sucking air, eyes closed in rapture she begged, 'Again...'

An intense hiss signified the swift advance of leather, that first hitting mauled rump before executing an accelerated arc, biting into soft lower belly. Kate rose on tiptoe, a cry of exultation piercing the silence. 'And again,' she pleaded.

Alice duly obliged.

'Tits, Ali.' All reason had evaporated. 'Lash my tits.'

Seeing no point in arguing, Alice manoeuvred to Kate's left. Landing a stroke upon that whipped middle back she ensured the tail encircled the ribs, the last three inches cutting inexorably into unresisting breast, the supple tit surging with the force. 'Ah, sweet Jesus,' the girl hissed. 'That was fucking cruel. Again, Ali, again.'

Shaking her head in disbelief the girl reluctantly complied, that smarting breast reeling to another caustic slash. Back arched, chest thrown out, Kate seemed to offer herself in sacrifice to some invisible god. She uttered not a sound, her head gently lolling. Without warning Alice loosed another.

She noted the husky groan, the tension of muscle and tightening of buttocks, guessing Kate lay within a whisper of a glorious climax. She dealt her a fourth, that feeding the nipple, the girl bucking with the shock.

'The other titty's jealous, Ali,' she heard her friend murmur.

A few strides placed Alice to inflict sublime torment upon that. The first slashed indiscriminately, the heavy orb briefly indented. The second cut at an angle inducing a diagonal welt. The third extended to sting the already punished breast, and the fourth bit deep into the areola.

Eight lashes remained.

'Only one place left, Ali,' the girl intimated, and dumbfounded, Alice asked where. 'My legs are well parted.'

'You're not serious!'

'I'm mad. I'm delirious. Nothing can hurt, Ali. Nothing. I've never experienced anything like it in my life. Do it, Ali. Whip my fanny. I'll never forgive you if you don't.'

Expression grim, Alice took up position directly behind Kate. She judged the distance and swing, and brought the whip up, snapping the tail inches from Kate's vagina. The tip struck, licked the pubic mound and fell away.

Amazed, Alice watched Kate writhe. That belaboured body glistened with impassioned sweat, Alice unsure whether she twisted in agony or ecstasy.

'Perfect,' Kate sighed. 'Bloody perfect.'

Alice did not demur. She provided a repeat, that tail compounding the searing heat to Kate's sexual difference.

'Ah! Ah! Ah!' Kate stammered, mouth agape, head thrown back. 'Such consummate torture.'

Alice misjudged and drove the next into the buttock crease, scalding anus and vagina, the tip probing the portal of pleasure. Voice temporarily stolen, Kate swung on her bonds, lost in the confusion of pain and pleasure.

Composure regained she challenged. 'Bet you couldn't do that again, Ali.'

She tried, but the whip bit raw buttock and thigh before hitting the dirt. Her next attempt bit vaginal lips and pubic mound for the third time. Alice closed the distance and brought the whip over her shoulder. The tail slapped Kate's hip, curled, and striking diagonally chewed her sex. The girl leapt, the ropes snapping tight. Only a gurgle offered evidence of its success.

Alice repeated the stroke across the other hip, that extricating an oath.

The last she placed neatly between the legs, inducing a bloated welt alongside the vagina.

Alice coiled the whip and placed it back in the bag. She climbed into the V of the tree and looked Kate in the face. That countenance, flushed and wet with sweat, offered a self-satisfied smirk. 'Well, Katy, how was it?'

'Magnificent, Ali... fucking magnificent... next time we'll make it two hundred.'

'You're a mess, Kate,' Alice said soberly. 'Just look at

your tits; it'll take weeks for those stripes to go.'

Kate studied the infliction. 'Oh, orgasmic!' she sighed. 'I'll masturbate in front of a mirror for the next week on those. Is my back in the same state?'

'Yes, Kate.'

'I feel incredible, Ali. My whole body is humming. I'm stinging all over. Oh to have been officially whipped in public, to be left here on display. Now that would be something else.'

'We'd be arrested.'

'And flogged!'

'I hardly think so.'

'Dreams, Ali… dreams.'

'And if you were arrested in somewhere like Arabia and sentenced to a flogging you'd be shitting yourself, Kate. It's only because with me, you know you're safe.'

'That's just it, Ali. I don't want to be safe. This is probably as close as I'm going to get, but a real flogging is what my psyche demands.'

'Do you want releasing now?'

'How about that licking you promised me?'

Alice petted the flat of Kate's stomach. 'Might have changed my mind.'

'Tease.'

The hand descended, fingers stroking the flesh. Those digits played with pubic coils before sliding lower and dipping between the parted legs. Kate exhaled, the breath rapid, then winced. 'Sore?' enquired her friend.

'You could say that.'

'I'll be careful.'

'No need, Ali. No need.'

Alice cautiously caressed the vulva before falling to a knee and kissing that tender mound. Kate observed, ogling the lithe form, the narrow waist and pert behind.

Tongue thrust out, Alice licked the foremost part of those vaginal guardians. She parted the vulva and probed, the taste sharp and salty.

'Lost your objections then, Ali?'

'What the hell, Kate; you're right, life is for living.'

'That's my girl.'

'You're sopping down here.'

'I should be. I reckon I came a half dozen times.'

'That good, eh?'

'You'd better believe it.'

Alice persevered until she sensed the telltale shiver informing her of Kate's satisfaction.

Once released Kate rubbed her wrists and hands, bringing the circulation back. 'Do it again soon?'

'It's your body.'

'It could be yours.'

'I don't think so. I need to get control of whatever it is first. Just because it was nice for a while, that doesn't mean it will be next time.'

'Unless you try you'll never learn.'

'Let's get our clothes,' Alice suggested, changing the subject, 'I'm hungry. What's for lunch?'

'I don't know,' Kate said playfully. 'I might eat Harry.'

'You're insatiable.'

'I'm a nymphomaniac, remember?'

Chapter Eight

The pair reclined in the living room listening to seventy-eights played on a gramophone. 'How did that compare with what Stagnant gave you?' asked Alice, intrigued by Kate's complete masochism.

'Stagnant is a full grown woman with a practiced swing, who used a thick cane with all her strength. You are a slightly built and inexperienced angel who didn't want to hurt her best friend. But you were quick to learn, Ali. I really enjoyed your lathering. Who knows, in a few years you might be the queen of discipline. I certainly look forward to another round.'

'Did it hurt much to begin with?'

'Sickening is the word which springs to mind. With the cane you feel the length that hits. With the whip the tail hurts. All the force is in those last few inches. Mind you, once my chemistry met the challenge it proved pure bliss. I think it has something to do with the implement and the way one conceives it. The whip to me is very erotic. The divine or sublime implement of correction. The ultimate, if you like. The merest suggestion of having it used on my naked body turns me to jelly. Sexual jelly, that is. To be chastised out in the open accentuates that, and by a gorgeous female wearing nothing is the cream topping.'

'I thought you wanted a man?'

'I always want a man. But the woman is more illicit. The more frowned upon the act the more turned on I am. Complicated girl, ain't I?'

'No, Kate, I'm complicated. You've sorted yourself. You know what you want and you're not frightened to go after it, to seize it by the horns. Me? I'm an emotional mess.'

'You've been turned upside down. Give it time. As I've

said on numerous occasions, I'll do anything you want me to. I'll tell you anything you want to know.

'Now I have a question: did you get anything out of whipping me?'

'I think I would have if I hadn't been so frightened of hurting you,' Alice admitted frankly. 'I'm not appalled by the act. If I was I wouldn't do it. I have to admit, whipping you gave me a buzz. Seeing you tied and defenceless, stripped to your birthday suit, and that sound of leather on bare flesh. Yes Kate, I think I could get to like it a lot.'

'Do you still believe you need to see this head examiner?'

'He's a priest, Kate.'

'Same thing.'

'I ought to. If only to resolve the clash between what I am and my religious beliefs, and understanding of the doctrine. Anyway, I've made the appointment.'

'So cancel it.'

Alice shook her head. 'I'll see what he has to say.'

'What you going to tell him? That you like being tied up? That you get a kick out of whipping your best mate in the woods? That you have lesbian tendencies?'

'I'm not sure. It will depend on what he's like. I might just infer, not actually own up to particular instances.'

'Best of luck, Ali,' Kate derided. 'Don't let him turn you though. You've finally accepted life is for living. Be happy, Ali, not contrite.'

Alice later happened on Jonathan reading a sheaf of papers in the garden. 'Something interesting?' she asked, and the man looked up and greeted her with a warm smile. 'What are you reading?'

He took off his sunglasses. 'It's a manuscript, Alice, submitted by a new writer.'

'Any good?'

'It has its merits. I'm not so sure I'll publish it, though.'

'It's a kinky book, then?'

'A *dirty* book, yes.'

The phrase was not lost on Alice. 'I'm sorry about that; I didn't think. What sort of kinky?'

'Bondage. Discipline. Sex by the cartload.'

'Any story to it?'

'Not really. It does follow a loose path. Would you like to read it? Give me your opinion?'

'Would that make any difference?'

'It might.'

'Okay.' Alice took the manuscript. 'But what about Mrs Howell, won't she mind us discussing such things?'

'She might,' Jonathan said, 'but some things are worth the risk. Don't you think so?'

Alice didn't answer. She wandered off clasping the text to her bosom. What exactly did Jonathan mean, some things are worth the risk?'

The novel proved to be a tiresome work. It titillated at times, scenarios she had not given consideration to set off that buzz. But overall she decided the work to be beyond reason and trite. She returned it to Jonathan.

'So what is your concerted opinion, Ali?'

'Interesting in places,' she opined. 'But I found it generally boring.'

'My thoughts exactly,' he concurred. 'Maybe I'll ask you to read others. There will be a fee, of course.'

'I don't have any money.'

He chuckled. 'No, Ali, I pay you.

'But you said interesting in places. Which sections in particular, may I ask?'

'I thought his descriptions—'

'Her descriptions,' the man corrected.

'Oh… well, I thought *her* descriptions of bondage profound. She really had you there. Some of the whackings were quite sensual as well.'

'You have a particular interest in bondage, I understand.'

'Richard told you?' She felt her face colour.

'I'm afraid so.'

'And you still want me here? Oh, I feel so embarrassed.'

'Yes, I still want you here. And there's no need to be embarrassed. You would be surprised by the amount of interest there is in bondage.'

'Really?'

'Quite so. One of my more profitable fields. Of course it varies from the odd pair of handcuffs to intricate equipment. From simply being tied to the bed for sex to incarceration for a lengthy flogging. But there are many that practice the art.'

'Art?'

'Yes, art, Ali. An expert could make you feel as if you were wrapped in sensuality. A novice might do the opposite.' He pondered for a moment or two. 'Sensual whackings? I got the impression you found a whacking abhorrent.'

'Richard and the birch, you mean?'

Jonathan nodded.

'It's different reading about it and receiving it.'

'Of course it is. However, a spanking can be very erotic, delivered by the right hand. If you really fancy someone, Ali, it makes all the difference.'

'Yes, I can see that. But at the end of the day you either like pain or you don't.'

'You're years ahead of yourself, aren't you?'

'How do you mean?'

'An old head on young shoulders.'

'You see me as mature?'

'Yes, with the… no, I shouldn't say that. It might give the wrong impression.'

'No, please,' she wanted to hear it, whatever it was. 'What were you going to say?'

'I was going to say, a mature head with the body of Aphrodite.'

Thrilled, Alice didn't know how to react.

'See, I've given you the wrong impression now, haven't I?'

'No,' she stammered, 'not at all. It's a lovely thing to say. A real compliment.'

'The truth.'

There the conversation dried up.

Jonathan dropped the manuscript into a bin. He reached inside his jacket and took out a wallet. Thirty pounds he withdrew and handed it to Alice.

196

'What's that for?'

'Your fee. I understand your wardrobe is lacking some finery. Ask Harry to take you into Buxton. You'll find a good boutique on the high street.'

Alice shook her head and offered the money back. 'I couldn't take this,' she insisted. 'I only read part of the book.'

'Do as you're told, young lady.'

'Tomorrow?'

'If you wish.'

The next day Alice returned with several bags, Kate having accompanied and assisted in the choosing.

'Are you going to model them for me, Ali?' the girl asked excitedly.

'I've never had such expensive clothes before,' Alice beamed. 'I can't wait to try them on.'

Kate followed Alice into her room and took up residence on the bed. Alice began stripping. 'Are you going to sit and watch me undress, Kate?'

'Of course.'

'The idea was I put on a fashion show for you. You're not supposed to see me undress and dress.'

'But I want to. I like to look at your body.'

'You're about as deep as a film of dust, aren't you, Kate?'

'Up front, that's me. I say what I mean.'

Alice lifted her jumper to her bust, and catching the hem she pulled it up, covering her face, arms contorted.

'Hold it!'

'What is it, Kate? Is something caught?'

'Yes, Ali, hold it there.' Kate crawled over the bed, and putting her arms around the girl, licked the hospitable contours of her stomach.

'Eugh! What are you doing?'

'You caught me,' Kate said between licks. 'Caught me off guard. Gorgeous belly, Ali. All lovely and soft and flat. I wish mine was.' She pulled back the trouser waistband. 'And look where it leads.' Kate sank a hand into the dark.

Alice whipped off the jumper. 'Kate! For goodness sake!'

'No, Ali, for my sake.'

'Get your mitt out of my knickers, Kate,' Alice said determinedly. 'I want to try these clothes on.'

Sulkily, Kate pulled a face, and her hand out.

'Thank you.'

When naked, Kate embarrassing Alice with her insatiable scrutiny as the shy girl held up a light green lacy bra and matching panties. 'Just look at these,' Alice enthused. 'No Kate, the underwear, not my tits. I never thought I'd have anything like these.'

'All you need now is a man to take them off.' Alice's face warmed, and Kate smirked. 'Have I touched a raw nerve?'

'No, not at all; I should be used to you by now.'

Alice tried on the bra. 'What do you think, Kate?' She held her arms out.

'Does something for your tits, doesn't it? Your cleavage would send a man crazy.'

'You reckon?'

'I know.'

Alice slid into the matching panties – nothing more than a skimpy back and front sewn to a circle of lace-covered elastic. She twirled, and Kate leapt from the bed and sank her teeth into Alice's buttock, the girl squealing.

'Sorry Ali, I couldn't resist it. That bum is so perfect. And with the knicks on even perfecter.'

'More perfect,' corrected Alice. 'I think I'm too fat in the lower reaches.'

'Trust me, Ali, that butt is strawberries and cream. In fact, I think your body gets closer to perfection very day. I think you're there, and it gets even better.'

'You sure you haven't got a fellow hiding inside you, Kate?'

Kate chuckled her dirty chuckle. 'If there was I'd shag him.'

Alice reached back into the bag and withdrew a

198

suspender belt. 'My first,' she announced gleeful.

'Whoever the lucky bloke is, Ali, you're going to send him to an early grave.'

'There is no man, Kate. Why won't you listen?'

'Them clothes is for a man, Ali.' Kate nodded sagely, impressed with her own perception. 'Girls wear a shirt and jeans otherwise.'

'I wanted to be feminine,' Alice argued indignantly. 'That's all. If only for five minutes. Thirty pounds is a fortune, Kate. I'll probably never see the like again. I just had to buy some finery with it.'

'Course you did. I told you father's generous.'

'He is very kind.'

'Especially when he wants something.'

'What's that supposed to mean?'

'Just remember Jenny's revenge...' Kate warned, 'that's all.'

'I have no fear of your mother,' Alice said stoutly. 'There is no need to.'

'If you say so.'

'Kate!' Alice snapped, emerald eyes blazing.

'Guilty conscience, or what?'

'Katy, I'm warning you.'

'Only teasing, Ali.'

Alice glared at her best friend for a few seconds, and then slipped on a skirt; a flowing piece of pastel pink that reached to the knee. She sought assurance. 'Not too short, is it?'

'No, it's fine. Knees are in.'

An expensive satin blouse followed, the colour matching. 'Oh, this feels like absolute heaven!' she squealed happily.

'It looks it.' Kate lazily examined her fingernails. 'Especially on you.'

Alice held up a pair of black stockings. 'Shall I put these on?'

'If you want, Ali. But I won't be held responsible for my actions if you do.'

'How do you mean?'

'It's that little bit of white thigh above the black stocking,

199

Ali. It drives us guys mad.'

'Why?'

'Don't ask me, but it do.'

Alice sat on a chair and eased a stocking over a foot. Cautiously she stroked the black nylon the length of a calf, and lifting her skirt, drew it to its conclusion. Kate lay back and sighed. She sank a hand inside her panties and played with the soft curls there. Idly she watched Alice clip the stocking in place and dress the other leg. 'I wish I had a cock, Ali,' she said with crude frankness. 'I'd fuck you till sunset.'

'Only until sunset?' Alice teased.

'Okay, until my balls ran dry.'

Alice thought of Jonathan. Of him fucking her until his balls expired. She closed her eyes and imagined his privates – his thick stem of a cock and hanging sac. She sighed and delved into the last bag.

From that she plucked a bolero manufactured from a light Italian cherry leather. She slipped it on. 'Just the shoes now, Kate,' she said.

'You look a million dollars, Ali. No more the waif and stray. Now we have the immaculate woman. Better take the tags off before you go parading before father.'

'He paid for it all. It's the least I can do.'

'What about make-up?'

'I didn't buy any. Do I need it?'

'Not really. But most women do.'

'I wouldn't know how to.'

'Mother will show you.'

'Oh, I don't know, Kate.'

'Course she will. Mother's a dear, really.'

Alice felt her bottom squirm. 'No, I think I'll leave it.'

Kate shrugged, her hand moving idly inside her panties. 'Up to you, but father likes a bit of war paint.'

'You sure she won't mind?'

'As long as you don't tell her why.'

'Oh, all right Kate,' Alice said, rising to her friend's constant digs. 'I like Jonathan. I like him a lot. He's really sweet. I've never met anyone like him before. He paid for these clothes and I want him to see me at my best. I know he wouldn't be interested in me. As I said before, he's too old, I'm too young, he's married to your mother, and I'm his daughter's best friend.

'But if my dad were still alive I'd run to him and show off.'

'A replacement dad, then?'

'Well, yes...' Alice said quietly, 'I suppose he is.'

'Good.' Kate sat up brightly. 'That's that sorted. Now let's go and see mother.'

Jennifer Howell, an attractive blonde in her late thirties to early forties, greeted Alice with a beaming smile. 'Good gracious, Alice, you look divine,' she said. 'What a transformation from teenager to woman.'

'I needed some new clothes,' Alice admitted. 'Pig, er, I mean Richard, wouldn't let me have anything decent.'

'Pig?' Jenny looked amused. 'I like that. It suits, doesn't it? I can just see Richard snuffling about in the swill and maggot-ridden apples.'

She fixed her sharp blue eyes on Alice. 'Have you come for my opinion?'

Alice noted the expert make-up Jenny had applied to her own face. 'What advice would you give?'

'Don't go near any men dressed like that.'

Taken aback, the girl asked, 'Why?'

'Because they will eat you alive,' Jenny stated with conviction. 'Maybe only with their eyes, but they will devour you. And who could blame them? You are beautiful.'

'Thank you, Mrs Howell.' Alice blushed under the unfamiliar compliments. 'It's okay then? It all goes together?'

'Total harmony.'

'So, um, could you show me how to apply make-up?'

'With a fresh and gorgeous face like that?' Jenny said. 'You don't need it.'

'You don't think so?'

'Well, maybe just a touch of mascara to highlight your eyes, a dab of pink to show off those wonderful lips, and maybe a hint of rouge to deepen those cheeks. And then, young lady, you will be absolutely stunning.'

'Completely shagable,' whispered Kate.

'You think so, Kate?' enquired her mother, not amused.

'Sorry mother.'

'I suspect you will be.'

Jenny applied the make-up, explaining every move. Job complete, she gave Alice her own make-up tray, telling her, 'Practice makes perfect, my dear.'

Still unsure in step, the maroon high-heel shoes upsetting her stride, Alice made for the study, Kate in hot pursuit. She stood outside and took a deep breath. 'Kate,' she whispered, 'can you do me a favour?'

'Leave you to it, you mean?'

'Please.'

'Okay. Just leave some for mother.'

'How many more times, Katy?'

'Joking, Ali, just joking.' The girl ran off.

Alice knocked lightly, and heard Jonathan's dulcet tone. 'Come in.'

Opening the door she tried to stroll in with an air of nonchalance, but as the man swung in his swivel chair so her ankle turned. Alice stumbled forward and fell headlong in his lap, and Jonathan caught and steadied the young woman. 'I've heard of girls throwing themselves at men,' he chuckled, 'but this is ridiculous, Ali.'

'Damn, I've ruined it!' she wailed.

'Ruined what?' He checked her attire.

'I wanted to look suave and sophisticated,' she explained. 'And what happens? I end up a heap in your lap.'

'And a deliciously attractive heap, might I say.'

She stared into his eyes. 'You think so?'

'My breath is gone. A stunning vision rests on my lap. A transformation, Ali. A beautiful girl has escaped her chrysalis. She's grown her wings. The most desirable butterfly alights to drink of life's nectar.'

'Oh.'

'Ah that I was twenty years younger. I would chase you to the ends of the earth.'

'Your age doesn't matter.'

'It doesn't?'

'No.'

'Stand up. Let me drink of this vision.'

Alice struggled to her feet. She posed before Jonathan.

'You look like a sack of potatoes, Ali,' he scolded lightly. 'Relax. Swing your hips to one side. Bend your leg slightly at the knee. Put your hands on those divine hips. That's it. Now smoulder.

'Smoulder, yes. Think of the man you'd most like to bed. Laurence Olivier, perhaps. Now lust him with those beautiful eyes. Offer your curvaceous body to him. That's better.'

Jonathan leant back. 'Admirable. Give me a twirl. Let me feast my eyes upon that delicious rear.'

Alice turned.

'Words fail me. It is with the greatest restraint I keep my hands to myself.'

'You... um... you don't have to,' she ventured, amazed at her own boldness.

'Temptation!' he said, his tone playful, Alice wondering for a moment if he was patronising her. 'How can I resist such seductive temptation...?'

And then he reached out and gently stroked a shapely buttock – a shapely buttock emphasised by the tight fitting skirt. Alice gasped softly and shivered. Her tummy turned somersaults; electric fire filling it.

'Exquisite,' the man murmured. 'The most desirable bottom I've ever seen. I am a bottom man, Ali, and I'm in awe of yours.'

'You make me feel wanted, Mr Howell,' she said truthfully. 'I've missed that.'

'Of course you're wanted, Ali. We all love you here. Kate, Jenny and I. You are the second daughter I could never have. And you are an absolute delight. You brighten the day.'

She faced him. 'Is that how you see me? Truthfully?

As a daughter?'

He smiled. 'Lust is a tricky road, Ali. Beset by mires and quicksand. A man could lose himself. He could lose his loved ones. He could even lose his fortune.'

'And if the path was marked so there was no chance of losing your way?'

'How could that be guaranteed?'

'Absolute secrecy,' she dared to say. 'No one would share the secret. All manoeuvres guarded.'

'Clandestine meetings tend to end in tears,' he said seriously. 'Are you prepared for that?'

'I seek an identity, Mr Howell. I search for fulfilment. I will snatch at happiness if only for a moment.'

'Infatuation burns like a candle. It flutters and snuffs with the wind. Even if relit it will surely end when the wax is used.'

'I understand what you say, Jonathan. I don't wish to be a burden. I am intrigued. Maturity draws me as a moth to the flame. I am prepared to be burned.'

Hands placed together, he pressed them to pursed lips. 'You're young, Ali. You have your whole life ahead of you. You'll find your flame. You'll discover love and passion. And I envy the man that finally fulfils you. Maturity may entice now. But as you broaden your horizons and grow in confidence you'll look to your own age. Older men are set in there ways. They are tiresome. Some try to relive their youth, but none can turn back the clock. We've had our day.'

'You are so sweet, Jonathan.' Alice leaned over and kissed him on the forehead. The top three buttons of her blouse unfastened, she inadvertently provided an option to witness the smooth compressed breasts within. Jonathan did not miss the opportunity.

Alice turned, and as she walked to the door he remarked, 'You know something, Ali?' She paused, her back still facing him. 'Those hips were made for French knickers. You should try them. I'm told they are very comfortable.'

'French knickers?'

'Yes. You might find a camisole equally sensual.'

'Sensual?'

'A particular liking of mine, I'm afraid.'

'I'll bear it in mind.'

Kate awaited her in the living room. 'Well?' she gushed. 'What did father say?'

'He thought I looked nice.'

Head to one side, Kate studied Alice. 'Was that it? You look *nice?*'

Avoiding eye contact, Alice confirmed the half-truth. 'Yes.'

'It took nearly ten minutes to say you look nice?'

'Not entirely. I fell on top of him.'

'You what?'

'Bloody shoes. I strode with all my feminine charm towards him, intent on impressing, then my ankle went over and I ended up on his lap.'

Kate put a hand to her mouth and giggled. 'I bet he enjoyed that.'

'He was very sweet about it.'

'So, no eloquent charm? No persuasive rhetoric? No wandering hands? A total disappointment, in fact.'

'You don't have a very high regard for your father, Kate, considering how he loves his little girl,' Alice said stiffly.

'Of course I do,' Kate countered. 'I love him dearly. But I know what he's like. I've seen women fall head over heels for him. I've seen the way he wallows in it. I love him, Ali, and I love you. That's why I won't begrudge you both a little bit of hanky-panky. Who knows, it might be just what you need.'

'You're serious, aren't you?'

'Absolutely.'

'But Jonathan would be committing adultery. He would be unfaithful, to your mother.'

'Only if he gave his heart, and he won't.'

'So in your book, a quickie is okay.'

'It's only sex.'

'Would Jenny see it that way?'

'Nope.'

'Well she has nothing to worry about,' Alice said resolutely. 'I'm not interested in that, and neither is your father.'

Kate smiled, as if she didn't believe a word.

The following day, their marks on the mend, Kate asked Alice if she would be interested in seeing a play.

'What is it?' asked Alice.

'Some sleuth thing at the Hippodrome in Buxton.'

'When are you going?'

'Tonight.'

'I'm not really into dramas, Kate.'

'You could wear your posh gear. Hook yourself a young beau.'

'I've got a bit of a headache. I might have an early night.'

'What is it?' Kate pressed. 'You don't have to worry about paying. That's all taken care of.'

'No, it's not that. I really could do with an early night.'

'Shame. Father can't make it either, so there's a ticket going spare.'

'Is that why you asked me?'

'No, silly. We'd have got you one at the foyer anyway.'

'Thanks for the invite, Kate, but I can't sit still that long. And the smoky atmosphere will only make my head worse.'

'Just me and mother, then...' Kate gave Alice a scrutinising look, 'and you and father left alone at home...'

'Don't start.'

Jenny and Kate left at six, shortly after tea. Jonathan retired to his office in the study. Alice wandered upstairs to lie on the bed. There she discovered a parcel wrapped in pink tissue paper and ribbon. Somewhat perplexed she opened it, and a pair of white silk French knickers and a matching camisole set her mind reeling.

Was it merely a gift, or did the gesture carry undertones? Jonathan had neither received nor repelled her clumsy advances. If she put on the gorgeous underwear and offered herself would she be making a fool of herself? Or did the handsome man wait for her at that very moment?

The tantalising opportunity beckoned. If she remained in her room then Jonathan may conclude a disinterest. The chance might never arise again. Alice stripped and tried the garments on. She studied her reflection in the bedroom mirror. The underclothes felt sensual, lustrous against her naked skin. They exaggerated her figure, the knickers clinging to her buttocks, emphasising the fullness of those cheeks. They plunged into the V of her groin, the dark coils beneath a mere shadow. The material delved her vaginal folds, the sensation arousing.

The camisole outlined her naturally firm breasts without pressing them together, the protrusion of nipples undeniable. The buttons left unfastened offered a glimpse of sleek flesh, the divide tempting. She turned sideways, noting the prominence of bosom and bottom alike, the curvaceous legs and creamy slim thighs. Would Jonathan be aroused by her? Would he find her irresistible?

She covered those teasing enhancements with the recently acquired skirt and blouse, slipped on high heels and made her way downstairs. She stopped in the hallway to examine her appearance. She lacked make-up. Men like war paint. Jonathan likes war paint

Back upstairs she sat at the dressing table and opened the box Jenny had supplied, surprised to find added a tiny bottle of *Chanel*. Painstakingly she applied mascara, lipstick and rouge, and a dab of perfume behind each ear and between her breasts. She caught her hair and clipped it up. Satisfied, she again descended the stairs.

Alice hesitated at the study door, then turned and fled, running to the living room. There she sat, elbows resting on knees, hands supporting jaw. Nerves had taken her. Did she really want to go through with it? She chanced making a complete idiot of herself. She risked alienating the whole Howell family. Kind people, who had taken her in, offered a home and protection from the sadistic Richard.

Jonathan, a mature man, would not settle for kissing

and petting. Jonathan would want her. He would demand the whole hog. Was she prepared to lose her virginity? What if she fell pregnant?

Alice inhaled deeply, steadying her nerves. Pouting, she tried to analyse the compulsion, but that proved impossible. All she knew was she wanted Jonathan. She yearned to be with him. For him to make unconditional love to her. To lay naked with him. To feel him inside her.

She noticed a whiskey bottle perched on the sideboard. Although liquor had never passed her lips she thought it might settle her nerves. She half filled a spirits glass and sipped the contents. The corners of her mouth turned down, the drink burning throat and stomach alike. She gulped the remains and poured herself another.

Alice raised the glass. 'Here's to living, and goodbye hymen.' She downed the lot. Coughing, near to choking, her stomach in revolt, Alice smoothed the creases in her skirt, and arming herself with a copy of *Unchained Melody*, headed for the study.

She didn't knock. She waltzed straight in. Jonathan, working on a set of figures, glanced up to concentrate on hers. 'Alice,' he smiled, 'have you come to keep me company?'

'Oh, most definitely.' She felt the first influence of the drink. Her bum didn't glow but her belly did. 'I've got a record here. Can I put it on?'

'Yes, of course. I could do with a little distraction.'

'That's what I had in mind. Thank you for the underwear, by the way.'

He smiled. 'I couldn't resist it. I was in Buxton this morning and well, as I said, I couldn't resist it. I hope it fits. I guessed your size.'

'They are perfect, as you will see.'

Alice placed the record on the turntable and flicked the automatic play switch. She took a deep breath and waited for the music to commence.

As the strains of the love song began, so Alice danced. Jonathan settled back to watch. Fully aware she had only three minutes in which to complete her act, she didn't dally. Within seconds she began unfastening the blouse. Legs marking time, hips rolling to the rhythm, she methodically worked her way to the last one.

Contriving her own composition, she pulled the blouse apart and slipped it from lean shoulders, it descending her back in a series of sideways jerks.

Presenting her back, she let the blouse fall. Fingers settled on the skirt waistband and flicked the button loose. Similarly she freed the remaining three. Hips swaying she inched the garment down, those rich silk knickers provocatively revealed.

She stepped from the skirt, Jonathan lightly applauding, believing that to be the end. Alice aware she only had a minute or so remaining, evocatively lifted the camisole, Jonathan's expression changing to one of astonishment.

Body in motion. Hips gyrating. Legs slightly parted, head rolling, she manoeuvred the garment clear of her breasts. She held that position for several seconds, Jonathan riveted. Then she removed it entirely, the camisole sliding down her arms. Alice tossed it, the man catching that and the undeniable fragrance of *Chanel*.

The desirable female paraded towards him, her easy footfalls enhancing the quiver of breasts. She stopped inches away then pirouetted, her naked back and well-filled knickers gripping his attention. Thumbs finding the elastic she eased them down over rolling hips, Jonathan entranced. She flirted with the partial revelation of that striped and bruised rump, thrusting it out on the conclusion of each rotation. Edging them down until the record finished.

As the music faded so Alice let the knickers fall. Kicking them clear she faced him, her stance as he had advised. Flushed, her head swimming with the combination of alcohol and adrenaline, she smiled, anticipating his reaction.

Mouth slightly open, Jonathan seemed lost for words. His eyes roamed her nakedness, admiring every inch of her breathtaking womanhood. 'Incredible,' he at last managed. 'You've turned me inside out.'

'Not all of you, I trust,' she heard herself say.

Jonathan laughed. 'What happened to that naïve friend of my daughter's? I, I don't know what to say. Jonathan Howell lost for words. Good lord, Ali, you are *beautiful*. Every inch of you. Such perfection…'

'Do you want to feel that perfection?' she whispered, eyes sparkling.

'Dare I? Dare I touch you? Do you even begin to realise what you do to me? Ali, don't ever do this with a man you hardly know. You evoke a passion that so easily could run out of control. It is with the greatest effort I control myself.'

'Then don't.'

'What do you want?'

'You.'

'Good grief! I thought we played a game. I thought it was an enjoyable flirtation. I didn't realise you wanted to…'

'Make love?'

'You're the same age as my daughter, Alice. How can we?'

'You don't want me, then?' she pouted, not realising she incited his passion even more in doing so. 'I've made a complete fool of myself.' The world began to move. Her head swam. She felt nauseous.

'No, not at all,' he said quickly. 'I'm flattered. Honoured. I wouldn't have missed it for the world.'

'Oh, I don't feel too good.' Alice leant forward, seeking the desk for support, Jonathan sighing at the suspended breasts so close.

'What is it?' Frightened her legs wouldn't support, she chose Jonathan's lap to bolster her. The man placed an arm about her shoulders. 'What is it?' he repeated.

'At least kiss me,' she protested sulkily, so he bowed to her face and pecked her on the forehead. 'No, on the lips. I am wearing lipstick. Kate said you like lipstick.'

'I shouldn't be doing this,' he warned, finding her lips. She hugged his neck and held him, their mouths entwined, Jonathan half-hearted, Alice positive. She delved him with her tongue, seeking his. His free hand moved up her ribs and cupped a breast. A swarm of butterflies invaded, mixing with the nausea.

He pulled away sharply. 'You've been drinking,' he accused.

'I needed some Dutch courage,' she admitted.

'That explains a lot. You're not used to it, are you?'

'First time,' Alice giggled. 'First time for many things tonight.'

'And tomorrow? You'll wake and regret what you've done.'

She frantically shook her head, furthering the dizziness. 'No, no I won't.'

The man whirled in a dilemma. Every ounce of him wanted to fulfil Alice's wish, but her innocence and his marital bondage held him back.

'Please,' she whispered. 'Please take me.'

'You should be courted, cosseted, wooed and spoilt before you give yourself. You should make your man work very hard to win your body. It is the ultimate gift, Ali. Not something to toss into the frying pan because it suits the ingredients.'

'Everything you say makes me want you all the more, Jonathan.' The drink took its toll, and Alice began to lose control of her mouth and inhibitions.

'And if I shun you tonight, you'll hate me?'

'With all my being.'

Not breaking eye contact his hand fell to her thighs. He stroked them apart and settled fingers between her legs. There he fondled, petted and finally delved. Alice lifted her torso, offering a nipple. Jonathan readily suckled, despite his reservations. Heart thumping, Alice was in euphoric state. Breathing erratic, she wallowed in the hard won attention, the sensations racking her body incredible. Everything Kate had said about sex was true. So why not her testimony on masochism?

'Jonashun,' she whispered, blinking slowly.

'Hmmm?' he uttered absently.

'Perhaps I'm in need of paternal correction.'

'How's that?' he asked, bemused.

'I did steal the whiskey. And I think I'm a bit typshy now. And I have taken all my clothes off.'

'You think you're in need of a spanking. Is that it?'

'Yesh.'

'Don't you think your poor bottom has had enough?'

'It doesn't have to be hard.'

'I won't lie. That would give me the utmost pleasure. But I do like my victim to wriggle and writhe a little bit. Besides the obvious, animation is the turn on.'

'Then spank me harder. If I can take the birch then I can takes anything.'

'You do seem anaesthetised.'

'I'll tell you a secret. I glowed with that birch. For a while I did. I wanna see if I can glow again.'

'Perhaps a little drunk is the time to try.'

'I'm not drunk. I'm tipsy.'

Jonathan helped her up and over his lap. That inviting rump stimulated. The cheeks not yielding to gravity stiffened him. He placed a hand on a smooth flank, the skin cool, resilient. He stroked to the thigh and cupped the rise of buttock. Squeezing, fingers probed the resisting flesh. 'Such a beautiful…'

'Arse,' Alice completed.

'I could kiss and lick it all over.'

'Be, hic, my guest.'

'How many drinks have you had, Ali?'

'Just the two.'

'You really aren't used to it, are you?'

'I only 'ad a 'alf, hic, glass each time.'

'You are going to have one hell of a head on you in the morning. You're only supposed to pour a quarter inch.'

'Why, hic, have such big gla-hic-sses then?'

Jonathan continued petting those mouth-watering cheeks, stroking and squeezing. He ran a finger the length of the cleft, lifting it away before touching her vagina.

'I'm enjoyin' thish.'

'So am I, Ali. So am I.'

He lifted his hand and struck, a light slap, the buttock

212

trembling.

Eyes closed, world revolving, Alice moaned. 'Ummm… nice.'

Jonathan smacked the other cheek, then caressed the sting.

'Jonathan.'

'Yes Ali?'

'Can we do this, hic, over the desk. Hic-my head keeps on spinning. Hic.'

'That isn't half as much fun. Tell you what, let's retire to the living room and use the settee.'

'Sounds good. Hic. Bloody hiccups. Hic.'

Jonathan helped the girl to the lounge, and settling himself, he took hold of her hand. 'Why don't yer, hic, takes yer pants off?' asked Alice, all inhibitions eradicated.

'Ah, I hadn't thought about it.'

'I wanna, hic… bloody soddin' hiccupsh… I wanna see yer, hic, bits. I wanna feel yer bits. Hic. I wanna feel yer, hic, cock in me stomach.'

'It doesn't go there, Ali. Vagina, yes. Mouth, very nice. Bottom, sometimes. But never belly.'

'Bottom? That's different, hic.' Alice wrinkled her nose. 'Hic-don't knows I fancy that.'

Jonathan pulled her over his lap. Arm placed on the small of her back he slapped her gorgeous bottom, the flesh shuddering tightly. 'You may not,' he whispered inaudibly, 'but I certainly do.'

'Eh?' she mumbled.

'Not too hard, is it Ali?'

'Nah, s'lovely.'

Jonathan checked the time by the clock over the fireplace. He estimated they had another three hours before the family returned.

He smacked her bottom steadily, indulging in the feel and quiver of nubile flesh. Alice rested her head on her forearms, regaling in the continued smart. Gradually her butt warmed, coloured to a carmine hue. Intolerable it wasn't.

It glowed, as Kate would say, and those embers inspired

and nourished another fire. An energy that licked at and captivated the hub of satisfaction. Her delicate features creased in rapture, she dwelt on that lustful act.

But her thoughts were snapped back to reality. 'You're not writhing, Ali. You're enjoying it too much. No animation.'

'Then spank me 'arder,' she retorted.

So Jonathan upped the ante, Alice immediately reacting to the increased assault. 'Ow!' she squealed. 'Ow! Ouch! Hic-ow! Ow! Ouch!' She kicked her legs and clawed at the cushion, feigning protestation. She felt his cock rise, the shaft pressing to her belly. She tried to imagine its size, settling on sufficient.

Her backside stung. It closed on sore. But still the storm assailed her crotch. She closed on a climax still loosing the expletives. Jonathan struck even harder, her buttocks fair jostled. Alice yelped and tried to avoid the smarting missiles. The bubble within still expanded.

Carried to fever pitch, backside burning, those fires as fierce as her desire, she experienced the first titanic waves of orgasm. The bubble burst. A tide of energy flooded, affecting groin and belly alike. It even seemed to ascend the throat. The sensations overwhelmed. The uninitiated Alice staggered by its enormity. She tensed, gasped, then squealed in delight, Jonathan guessing the reason. He kissed the scarlet sphere, then licked, saliva cool, the touch inciting further passion, adding to the girl's euphoria.

'Thatsh nice,' Alice slurred.

'I could frame this bottom and hang it on the study wall. Then every day I would admire it.'

'Just me arse?'

Jonathan slid his tongue the length of the cleft. Alice shuddered. 'I bet you photograph well, Ali.'

'Only ever 'ad a few snaps done.'

'I know a professional. Perhaps we should commission a portrait.'

'With or without my clothes?'

'We'll discuss it tomorrow. How do you feel?'

'With me 'ands,' and she giggled at her own feeble

joke.

'Your head, Ali.'

'S'goin' round an' round.'

'Feel sick?'

'A little bit.'

'Best lay on the couch.'

'I am, aren't I?'

'On your back. I'll take your mind off it.'

Alice rolled, Jonathan wriggling out from beneath. 'I can't do it to music like you, but...' He unfastened his shirt and tossed it aside. Shoes kicked off he dropped his trousers. Alice watched, fascinated.

'Are you ready for this?' he asked.

'Depends if it's a maggot or a torpedo.'

'Ali! Where did you learn to talk like that?'

'Katy,' she revealed without thinking.

'I might have guessed. I'll have to have words with that one.'

'Just words? No stick, or whip?'

He laughed. 'And you really think that would have any effect?'

'Probably not.'

'Like father like daughter.'

'I done Katy.'

'Katy? How did you "done" Katy?'

'Whipsed her in the woods.'

'I see.'

'Whipsed her good, I did.'

'And she asked you to?'

'Insisted, she did.'

'Hiccups gone?'

'Don't remind me.'

Eyes fixed on the prolific bulge in Jonathan's pants she gasped as he unveiled his piece. 'Oooh, Jay,' she gasped, 'that's one to be proud of.'

'I've had no complaints.' He climbed between her legs and knelt, Alice reaching out, grasping the rigid member. 'So meaty.' She caught his testicles with the other hand. 'So full.'

215

'Have you been with a man before, Ali?'

'Only Malcolm, but he don't count. We just played.'

'So you are still intact?'

'S'gotta go sooner or later.'

'A treat, first.' He descended, parted her vaginal lips and probed with his tongue.

Alice's back arched. She grabbed Jonathan's hair. 'Ah…!' she hissed, the stimulus almost too much. Jonathan persisted, his tongue settling on the clitoris. Alice squirmed and twisted, and sucked air as the climax rapidly approached. Unwittingly she tugged his hair, pulling the man this way and that. 'Oooh, Jay, that's out of this world!'

He answered not, her scent and taste an irresistible aphrodisiac. Alice yelped, and writhing in ecstasy she let him go, hands clawing at air instead. 'S'unbelievable… s'wonderful… oooh, Jonathan, I don't want it to ever stop.'

He rose and settled on the couch. Alice recovered. She eyed the mast rising from his crotch and pulled herself up. Crawling forward she seized his cock and smoothed back the foreskin. Jonathan watched, intrigued. Slowly she closed on that glistening head, mouth slightly open. He closed his eyes as her lips peeled wider apart and it slipped in, the orifice wet and comforting.

He stroked her hair as she suckled, astounded that she knew of such erotic pleasures, staggered that such an inexperienced virgin would. But he said nothing and revelled in the practice.

'Use your tongue, Ali,' he guided after a while. 'Lick all round the head.' He tensed. 'That's it… ah, what a siren you are.'

His hand traversed her back and settled on those voluptuous buttocks. He caressed them, imbibing of the invasive waves of pure pleasure. Alice slid her free hand to cup the drawn testis. She played with them, unrelenting in her carnal task.

Jonathan felt the first tide of orgasm. Should he warn the girl? Should he say what was on the way? He decided no. She should know. And to warn may put her off permanently.

'Suck me harder, Ali,' he demanded instead. 'I'm close... so close. That's it. *Jesus*, you're good.'

Both felt his balls spasm, Alice by hand, and the subsequent jerk of penis warned of the seed's approach. Alice remained stoic, cock firmly embedded in mouth, lips tight about the shaft, and she accepted the warm slimy sperm, filling her mouth, the taste peculiar. She released him, refusing to swallow. Her cheeks full she sought somewhere to eject the foreign matter. Jonathan offered cupped hands and Alice spat the fluid out, relieved to be rid.

'You didn't like the taste, I take it?' he asked, amused.

'It isn't that. I don't want to get pregnant.'

'Oh, Ali!' Jonathan exclaimed, laughing. 'A girl that can suck cock and thinks she'll get pregnant by it. What a contradiction!'

'You mean I can't?'

'No, Ali, you can only get pregnant by unprotected vaginal intercourse.'

'Oh, I feel an idiot now.'

'Do you want to do it?'

'What, get pregnant?' she gasped, shaking her head emphatically. 'No.'

'No, have proper sex,' he clarified patiently.

She checked his penis. 'But you're all limp.'

'Ten minutes, that's all I'll need.'

'I'd like to.'

'Perhaps we could pass the time with a length of rope. Seeing as how you and I both find that appealing.'

'Tie me up, you mean?' Alice's head was gradually clearing a little.

'Or down.'

'What a night this is turning out to be.'

'I keep a room downstairs in the basement. I suggest we retire to that; throwing on your clothes is one thing if we're disturbed, removing fifty foot of rope is quite another.'

217

'What is this room? A dungeon?'

'No, Ali, it's where a lot of the photographs for my magazines are taken.'

'You could take some of me.'

'I could indeed.'

Jonathan collected up the clothes ensuring no evidence of their tryst remained. He led Alice below and unlocked the door to that room.

The girl expected the cold stone cellar that she and Katy had investigated, but that turned out to be a storeroom. The one Jonathan invited her into proved completely different.

Well lit and large it suited a studio. Each corner embraced a different effect. From the proverbial dungeon to a backdrop of woodland, complete with tree stump. It entertained a low platform mounted with post, the wall behind a mural of mediaeval houses. An ancient pillory stood stark against an impressively painted stone wall. Two devious sets of stocks lay either side.

Sight refusing focus, Alice gazed in awe at the contents. 'Coo,' she applauded, 'what a room.'

'We have numerous backdrops painted on canvas. We simply unroll and hang them to suit. Anything you fancy, Ali?'

'Gosh, I fancy them all.'

'I'll give you a tour.' He led her by the hand and up the three steps to the post. 'Try this for size.'

Unsteady, she gazed at the upright. 'What is it?'

'A whipping post. The victim, if you like, is held by these steel manacles. She is then soundly flogged. The camera is set up so it captures the houses behind. No one would know it wasn't for real.'

'And the victim. Is she for real?'

'We tried various means of cheating. At the end of the day nothing will suffice like real whip marks.'

'Do they enjoy it?'

'Some do, yes. Others are quite happy with the payment.'

'They suffer for money.'

'I suppose so.'

'How much, Jay? How mush to be whipsed?'

'That would depend on the particular scenario.'

'Say, a hundred lashes.'

'Fifty pounds or thereabouts.'

'That's an absolute fortune!'

'They can only work now and then. We have to vary the women to keep the interest. So I have to make it worth their while. Want to see how it feels?'

Alice tottered up to the post and raised her arms. Jonathan fastened the black painted manacles about her wrists. 'Well?'

'Oooh, I feel so vuln... vuln... helpless.'

'You are. I could do whatever I pleased now.'

'Like?'

He embraced her from behind. Cupping her breasts he squeezed them. One hand descended to toy with the curls of her pubic mound. 'See, whatever I like.'

'What whips would you use?'

'You want to feel it?'

She hesitated a moment, and then nodded.

A rack at the side of the platform held a dozen or so implements. He selected a light single-tailed scourge. 'Ten strokes, Ali. For seducing your host.'

He dwelt on that posterior for a while, the whip's tail trailing on the boards. Giving excited him. Of all the bottoms he had seen proffered at the post, Alice's had to be the closest to his ideal. He provided a taste of leather on rump, the girl wincing apprehensive, the smart absorbed into that pot-pourri of lust and excess.

She glanced at Jonathan, the man still naked, his second lash igniting further passionate reaction. Alice took the ten as if child's play. That posterior nicely stoked, Jonathan released her.

'It's back, Jay.' Alice fondled his cock. 'Up and running.'

'I don't want to pour cold water on our evening, Ali, but I think that would be best left until you are sober. It's a big step and I don't want you to have regrets.'

'But I…'

'No buts, Ali. You're beyond caring, and I think you should care.'

'So gallant.' She doubled up, slapping a hand to her mouth.

'What is it, Ali?'

'Sick!'

'Hang on.' Jonathan grabbed a bucket and held it before the girl. She heaved and then vomited, stomach in spasm for some time after.

Jonathan shook his head. He lifted Alice in his arms and carried her upstairs, putting her to bed. Bucket placed by her, he returned to the basement to dress and collect her clothes.

Outfit in hand, he found Alice leaning out of the bed retching, her fists clutching at the bucket rim. Unable to leave her, he hung up her blouse and skirt and sat on the edge of the bed. Hands placed as support on her shoulders he waited for her to finish.

Eventually she pushed up, Jonathan aiding. She lay back, face flushed, sweat dotting her forehead. 'I feel like shit,' she divulged.

'I'm afraid tomorrow morning won't offer much relief either.'

'Never again.'

'We all say that until the next time.'

'I'm so sorry, Jay. I didn't mean to mess the evening up.'

'You didn't. There'll be other times. You're a beautiful woman, Ali. You won't be long in receiving another offer.'

'But you will, won't you? I want you to.'

'We'll see. Sober up first. Get shot of the hangover and we'll see what happens.'

He sat stroking her head for some time, the lover paternal. Deciding her stomach had settled for the time being he emptied the bucket. Placing the pail back should she require it, he heard Jenny and Kate noisily enter the house.

He met Kate on the stairs. 'Where's Ali?' she immediately asked.

'In bed.'

'Ooooh,' she cooed.

'She's in bed sick,' Jonathan said without humour.

Kate's smile disappeared. 'What's wrong with her?'

'I don't know. A bug, I presume.'

'I'll go see her.'

Jonathan made to grab her but missed. 'Kate! Leave her. See her in the morning.'

'No father, I'll see her now. She might need me.'

Kate ran into the room, Alice throwing up again. The reek assailing her nostrils, the shrewd girl recognised the smell immediately. She landed heavily on the bed, putting an arm about Alice. 'You bugger!' she scolded. 'You've been drinking.'

Alice retched in reply.

'Does father know why you're throwing up? Why Ali? Why get drunk?'

'Didn't mean to,' Alice whispered.

'No, I don't suppose you did.' Kate helped the girl lay down. She didn't want to leave, so not knowing quite what to do or what to say she studied the room. She espied the underwear Jonathan had bought, thrown on the bottom of the bed. Picking them up she remarked, 'I haven't seen these before.'

Alice opened an eye. 'They're new.'

'Really? So when did you buy these, then? I wouldn't have thought they were your style.'

'Pressie.'

'Who from?'

'Jay.'

'Jay?'

'Jonathan.'

'What's been going on, Ali?' Kate asked pointedly. 'You drunk, father buying you sexy undies.'

'Nothing Kate, honestly.'

'He hasn't taken advantage of you, has he?'

'No! Course he hasn't.'

'Something's going on. I'll grill you in the morning.'

Alice awoke with a thumper. Shards of glass seemed to probe the eyes, those feeling as if they had been abraded with emery. She rolled over to check the time, stomach reminding she hadn't been forgiven. Blurry memories drifted back. Stripping for Jay. The spanking. What he did with his tongue. Alice smiled and shivered. What she did with her mouth. She grimaced. Still the man seemed to enjoy it. The basement. What then? A fog fell upon the rest of the night, Alice uncertain what might have transpired.

Holding her head she rummaged through a limited wardrobe, finally donning jeans and shirt. Barefoot she padded downstairs. Kate awaited, arms folded.

'How you feeling, Ali?'

'Terrible.'

'Want a hair of the dog?'

'A what?'

Kate picked up the whiskey bottle. 'It was this you were drinking, wasn't it?'

Alice nodded.

'Why Ali? Why did you get drunk?'

'I felt ill and shivery. I'd heard a tot could make you feel better.'

'A tot maybe, but not half a bottle.'

'I didn't drink half a bottle, Kate,' Alice protested. 'I had two small glasses. I'm not used to it, that's all.'

'Why did father buy you French knickers and a camisole?'

'Who told you that?'

'You did. Last night. In between ringing your guts.'

'I was drunk. You can't take any notice of a drunk.'

'All right, so who bought them for you?'

'Do you have to Kate?' Alice grimaced. 'I've got a splitting headache.'

'I won't tell. I'm your mate. I just don't want to see you used, that's all.'

'Jonathan was in Buxton yesterday,' Alice owned up. 'He bought them. He said I would find them more comfortable than normal underwear.'

'Do you?'

'I haven't had a chance to try them on yet.'

'So why do they smell of Chanel?'

'You're a right little Sherlock, aren't you?'

'I get the picture. "I bought these for you, Ali. They'll look real sexy on you. Why don't you wear them for me tonight while the wife's away?" Been spliced, have you Ali?'

'No I have not!' Alice retorted adamantly. 'I might have tried them on while I was drunk. I don't recall.'

'You aren't going to tell me what happened, are you?'

'Nothing happened!'

'I'd tell you every lurid detail.'

'Okay Kate, do you want the fucking truth?'

Kate stared dumbfounded.

'I made a right ass of myself. I came onto Jonathan in a big way and he rejected me. Oh nicely, but still he told me he wasn't interested.'

'For the best,' Kate nodded sagely. 'You want a young stud. Not a middle-aged married man.'

'I don't want anybody, Kate,' Alice said petulantly. 'All I want is to finish my schooling and rid myself of that bloody debt.'

Kate grinned, mischief written all over her face. 'If you had got father into bed, he probably would have paid your fees.'

'It's not going to happen,' Alice maintained. 'And now I've got to face living here, with that embarrassment hanging over me.' Then a memory flashed through Alice's mind, and she felt herself blush. 'Kate...' she said tentatively.

'Yes Ali?'

'I think I may have dropped you in it last night.'

'How?'

'I might have told Jay that I whipped you.'

'Why the hell would you do that?'

'It slipped out while I was drunk.'

'Thanks, Ali! Thanks a bundle.'

'He knows what you are, doesn't he?'

'He guesses. He doesn't know.'

'You said he was broadminded.'

'He is, Ali. He's also devious. Oh, he loves me all right in his own way. And he'll do anything for me, within reason. But money is his main objective in life. He runs this dirty book racket, as you know. It's all right for women to be flogged and photographed for financial gain, but he'll draw the line at his daughter doing it. He doesn't know what I am. He just thinks I'm impervious to discipline. He thinks I'm headstrong.'

'Still, what can he do, Kate? You like the cane.'

'Ali, remember when I got kicked out of Carters?'

'I can hardly forget, can I?'

'I lied. That caning hurt like fuck. As soon as the marks were gone father had me visit the study. I cost him, you see. Fees paid and me sacked. I'd had sex. Father keeps a rod in his study that makes Stagnant's look like a twig. He flogged me until I screamed for mercy. And then he flogged me some more. I had to lay on my face to sleep for days after.'

'But when pig birched me Jonathan stopped him.'

'He didn't think you deserved it. Also, he wanted you here. He's not one to whip you for nothing. And I suppose I did deserve a whacking for what I did.'

'Why does he want me here?'

'Work that one out for yourself. The French knickers?'

'So what's he likely to do?'

'I don't know, Ali. But never tell him anything like that again.'

'If he canes you, then he should cane me as well. I mean, I was part of it, wasn't I?'

'Would that make you feel better?'

'I'd hate to see you get it because of my big mouth.'

'Ali, if he canes me then he will cane you, be rest assured. You'll have the choice. Whacked or Richard.'

'He never said anything last night.'

'You were drunk. What would the point have been?'

'I find it hard to believe, Kate. He's so sweet.'

'You see the side he wants you to see. If I'm right

224

you'll see another side soon.'

Alice put her head in her hands. 'Out of the frying pan into the fire. I think my bum was put on this earth purely for flogging.'

'No, you're not into the fire, Ali. Father won't whack you on a whim. He has to have a very good reason. It all depends whether my sexual perversion is good enough reason. He looks after you, doesn't he? He treats you. He'll see you right.'

'I suppose so.'

'So Ali, just learn not to get drunk and keep that big mouth shut.'

Chapter Nine

They spent the rest of the day with a cloud over them. Jonathan, though, remained closeted in the study. After tea Alice went to lie down and Kate ran a bath. There in the steam and suds she wallowed, thanking God for the reprieve.

Then the door swung open and Jonathan strolled in. Kate covered her breasts with suds and hands. 'Father!' she squealed. 'I'm taking a bath!'

'I know,' he said, smiling. 'Isn't father allowed to see his little cherub in the buff now she has grown up?'

Not really knowing what to say, she replied, 'Well I suppose you can't see much, can you?'

'You're my daughter, Kate. I see you as such. I have no interest in you other than for your welfare.'

'I fare well, father. No complaints.'

'Where's Ali?'

'Still not fully recovered. She's lying down.'

'Has she told you why she is feeling unwell?' Jonathan sat on the bathroom stool.

'You said it was a bug, didn't you?'

'She got herself drunk last night.'

'I see.'

'No games, Kate. You know, don't you?'

The girl nodded. 'She thought it would help her. She felt feverish.'

'I suspect she did. What else has she told you?'

'That she made a play for you and you turned her down.'

'The drink, I assume.'

'Oh, Ali's got a crush on you, father. She thinks the sun shines out of your porthole.'

'It will pass. And you, Kate, have you managed to avoid further physical involvement?'

'I said after Carters that I would toe the line, didn't I?'

'Yes you did. But have you kept your word?'

'I haven't been with any boys, father. Cross my heart.'

A smile flickered. Jonathan leaned forward, face serious again. 'Evasive Katy. I don't suppose you've been with any men?' The smile returned. 'Or maybe even girls.'

'I don't understand what you're driving at.'

'You are wayward and headstrong. Maybe it's my fault to some degree. Perhaps I should have spent less time working and more with you. I'm probably wrong for spoiling you. But I'll not give up on you. I'll do my best to see you grow into a responsible woman with morals.'

'No two people are the same, father.'

'What are you trying to tell me?'

'That different people have different ideas, or wants.'

'Accepted. But I would not condone a murderer because he sees killing as right. There are rights and wrongs.'

'I made a mistake. Women have urges as well as men, you know. It didn't seem wrong at the time. It seemed exciting.'

'And now?'

'I won't defy you.'

'So you still can't see any harm in it?'

'It was only a bit of loving. I was on my own at school away from my family. That boy offered me something I felt I needed. Oh, father, it was only sex.'

'And from casual sex comes bastards, syphilis, gonorrhoea and crabs. No one has any time for a slut, Kate. No one respects a tart. If a man can have you that easily, then he will do so, and then find himself a decent girl for a wife.'

'I hear you! I promise I won't play around.'

Jonathan dipped a hand in the bathwater. 'It's cold, Kate. Stand up and I'll towel you down.'

'I can dry myself, thank you.'

'I know. But Katy, I want to dry you.'

'Why?' The question sounded more a whine.

'Because I think you are hiding something.'

'What could I hide? I'm naked.'

'Stand up if you have nothing to fear.'

'I have a right to some privacy. I'm a fully formed woman.'

'What's this? Suddenly shy? You don't mind strangers seeing you, but your own father?'

'I'm not standing up and that is that!'

Jonathan pulled the plug.

'You sod!'

The water draining, suds covering some, she tried to shroud the remaining nudity.

'Now, no more games,' Jonathan said firmly. 'Stand up or I'll ask the butler to help me.'

Knowing the game lost, Katy grudgingly rose.

'Turn around, girl.'

She obeyed, not sure what would happen next. Jonathan reached out and stroked the foam from her backside. Kate screwed her face in anticipation.

'What have we here?' Jonathan asked.

She took a deep breath. 'Whip marks.'

'All over your back and legs as well. Turn around, Katy.' He stared at her chest. Removal of the suds revealed others. 'Who, Katy?'

'You know who.'

'Then why?'

'Because I bloody well like it.'

He shook his head in dismay. 'What have I fathered? Have you no inhibitions? No control?'

'You can talk. What about all those girls in the basement? I suppose that's natural.'

'That is business. I don't give a damn what they do for money. I don't care what trollops get up to. But I do care what you do.'

'So what's it to be? A repeat of my sacking?'

'I'll have to think about it.'

'If you stripe me, you'll have to stripe Ali as well.'

'She's not my daughter. You are.'

'That's not bloody fair. She was just as much a part of it as me.'

'Alice is a guest. What would you like me to do, send

228

her packing?'

'No!' Kate climbed from the bath. She flung her arms about Jonathan. 'Please father, don't cane me like before.'

'What are you worried about? You like it, don't you?'

'I could never make you understand.'

'No Kate, I don't suppose you could.'

'He's thinking about it.'

'I'm so sorry, Kate. If I hadn't of thought he knew, I would never have said anything.'

'Well he knows now. That's for sure.'

'The fact I get off scot-free makes me feel even worse.'

'No Ali, getting that cane on your bare backside would make you feel worse.'

'Perhaps I should go.'

'No, that would make it even worse for me. Look, he hasn't decided yet. Perhaps he might let me off.'

'I really hope so, Kate.'

Alice escaped from the anxious Kate, and ensuring nobody saw, knocked on Jonathan's door.

'Come,' he called.

Alice entered; Jonathan seated with his back to her. 'What is it?'

'Jay.'

He swung in his seat. 'Ah, Ali, I thought it was Kate.'

'Um, I wondered if I could have a word about her,' Alice ventured.

'No good you pleading her case,' he said. 'I haven't quite decided what to do yet.'

'You know what I am, Jay. You don't seem to mind. But with Kate you see it with intolerance. She is what she is, and as I know, nothing can change that.'

'You think I'm wrong then?'

'Yes. Double standards. Not because you run the business you do, but because you got a sexual kick out of spanking me last night. Kate is just the same except a receiver.'

'Let me ask you a question. If you hadn't been drunk

last night, would you have obliged me?'

'I had made up my mind to try and seduce you.'

'Really?'

She nodded.

'Why, for heaven's sake? I'm a middle-aged old bore. You are a gorgeous, youthful girl. What on earth do you see in me?'

'Maturity,' Alice stated without having to think. 'Charm. Eloquence. Good looks. Want me to go on?'

He smiled. 'I could listen to compliments like that all day. Now, how far would you have gone sober?'

She shrugged. 'I don't honestly know.'

'It took drink to loosen your resolve. You, Alice, are a responsible young woman. Even without the whiskey, and I know you didn't mean to overindulge, you still may have well tried it on. But I doubt you would have asked me to spank you. Control, Ali. Control. Something my daughter lacks.

'She took you into the woods. She pressured you into carrying out an act which, although you might have been inclined to, you wouldn't have succumbed to normally. An act also in the open, where anyone could have seen. Deny it.'

'I can't.'

'See, you're not a liar either. Kate will dodge the truth for as long as possible. And then she will lie to save her skin.

'As for my participation in last night's performance, I am a grown man, able to make my own decisions, rightly or wrongly. You are a guest in my house. I condoned your actions by co-operation. I can hardly chastise you for them, can I?'

'I feel terrible about getting Kate into trouble. It was me that told you. You wouldn't have known otherwise.'

'You did us all a favour. Kate has to learn discretion. I have to instil that in her, or else she is on the road to ruin.'

'It sounds like you are going to cane her.'

'I am.'

'Poor Katy. I can't stand by and see her thrashed for

something I was involved in. It was me that whipped her. I tied her to the tree. I'm just as much to blame.'

'What can you do about it, Ali?'

'Nothing, I suppose. I think I might leave. Go back to Uncle Richard. There's only a few weeks to term.'

'What would you have me do, Ali?'

'I accept what you have said. But if Kate has to be punished, then so should I.'

'How noble. Do you think that would make Kate's caning more tolerable?'

'Not for her.'

Jonathan thought for a while. 'I'll tell you what, Ali,' he said. 'Have a look at the rod. See what you think.'

He took the cane from a shelf and handed it to Alice. She held it, the length gleaming. 'It's ever so thick,' she whispered, her eyes wide.

'Yes, Ali.' He took it from her hands and flexed it. 'See, quite a bend for such a thick cane, eh? Heavy, too.' He raised it and struck the back of an armchair. A hefty thud indented the cloth, sending the dust drifting. 'Fancy that on your backside, Ali? Not sensuous, is it? It is a deterrent. Once felt always avoided. Or at least, one would hope so.'

'Would you allow me to take half of Kate's punishment?' she asked.

'You really are loyal, aren't you? Another prime quality. If I halve Kate's punishment then I send the wrong message. But if this is so important to you then I will give you the same. But you must promise you will stay with us.'

'Will Kate see me get it?'

'Proof, you mean? No, I don't operate that way. Privacy. Exactly the opposite of what Kate desires. So I will cane her in here and she can wait outside while I cane you. She will hear it, Ali. And there is no mistaking this rod on a bare bottom.'

'Bare?'

'Of course. What other way is there?'

The suggestion, the manner in which Jonathan

announced his intention, weakened Alice's knees. Sensual pins and needles played havoc below.

'The pair of you are both marked at the present. I shouldn't really let that make a difference. However, as I am attached to you both I will defer it for another few days. Say, Saturday evening. Jenny goes out then. At least we can keep it from her.'

'Thank you, Jay.'

'Don't thank me. It's your bottom.'

'I've spoken with Jay, Kate.'

'Twisted him around your little finger, have you, Ali? Tell him I'm fucking Harry, did you? Got me extras?'

'He is going to cane you, I'm afraid.'

'Oh, wonderful! Did he show you that brute of a thing?' Alice nodded.

'What, have a gloat did you? God! I think I might run away. Get a job on the streets. I am a tart, after all.'

'He's going to thrash me as well.'

'You what? Why? He said you were a guest, and hosts don't whack guests.'

'Because I told him I was equally responsible. And if he didn't I'd leave.'

'But why, for Christ's sake?'

'Because I am. I landed you in it, Kate. I couldn't see you go it alone and me get away with it. I have to take my share. I wanted to trade, get yours halved, but Jonathan wouldn't wear it. So I get the same.'

'You bloody idiot! You stupid lovely fool.' Kate threw her arms about Alice. 'You shouldn't have. You really shouldn't have.'

Alice held Kate to her. 'And if I hadn't, you would have hated me forever more.'

'No I wouldn't. Oh, I blow steam, but I wouldn't hate you forever, Ali. Maybe a week or a month, but not forever. You do realise you won't be able to sit for ages?'

Alice pulled a face of anguish. 'I accept that, Kate,' she said bravely. 'Jay demonstrated that rod on the armchair. It will be the worst whacking I've ever had.'

'Did he say how many?'

'No. And I didn't ask.'

'Bums in the fridge Saturday night, gel.'

'That might not be a bad idea.'

Alice slept fitfully. She peered at the clock in the early hours. A quarter to three. Every time she dozed off she recalled that rod biting into the chair, and imagined it beating her backside. Her stomach lurched. Her vagina seemed to climb to her throat.

The door opened and a half dressed Jonathan crept in. Wearing only pyjama bottoms, he stood by the bed.

'What is it, Jay?' asked a tired Alice.

'I couldn't sleep, Ali,' he whispered. 'I didn't wake you, did I?'

'No. I can't sleep either.'

He squatted on the edge of the mattress. 'Anything to do with Saturday?'

'A lot to do with Saturday.'

'Me too. You don't have to go through with it you know.'

'Are you going to let Katy off?'

'I can't.'

'Then I do have to.'

'Obstinate.'

'No Jay, fair is the word.'

Jonathan pulled back the covers and rested a hand on her nearest breast. 'You do something to me, Ali. I've never met anyone quite like you.'

She placed her hand on his and pressed it to that breast. 'I still want you, Jay, no matter what.'

He sighed heavily, wearily. 'What a mess,' he murmured.

'It could be worse.'

'I suppose so, but right now I can't see how.'

'Jenny could have come back early and caught us.'

'Yeah, that's worse.'

'In a way I'm glad it's you punishing me and not Jenny. I think I can take it from you.'

Her free hand wandered to the gap in his pyjamas. It slipped through the opening and grasped the limp phallus within.

'I really don't want to hurt you, Ali,' he said. 'Play is one thing, but that rod will punish. It will hurt like hell.'

'Don't you hold back, Jay. I want the same as Kate. Exactly the same. She'll be outside listening. She's shrewd. She'll know if you're using less strength. She already suspects us. If she sees you offering favouritism then she'll know there's something between us.' His penis rose to the comfort, Alice's fondling effective. 'Don't you worry about me. If I'd still been with Richard then I'm sure I would have received worse by now.'

She crawled from beneath the covers, her hand encouraging the erection from hiding. Foreskin withdrawn she sank on that tool, her lips spread, mouth filled. Pretty butt in the air she pleased Jonathan, the man taking advantage of her suspended breasts.

One eye warily on the open door he risked discovery, Alice's manipulations too agreeable to decline. For the second time she carried the man to climax, Jonathan cupping his hands for the rejection, but Alice shook her head, smiling. 'No need, Jay,' she said sweetly.

'You mean, you've swallowed it?'

'I wouldn't do it for just anyone, you know.'

'I wish I had time to do something for you. But I'd best get back.'

'Saturday night, Jay.'

'Like I said…'

'No, after I mean. What time is Jenny due back?'

'Not until about eleven. But Katy will be here.'

'What if you were to commute her caning to something like lines? You know, I must behave responsibly at all times and keep my imperfections from the public eye, two hundred times. She'd have no time to…'

'Nice try, temptress,' he smiled. 'Much as I want you, Ali, I'm not willing to ease up on Katy. She's intelligent and has the makings of a first class businesswoman. She's shrewd, cunning and decisive. All I have to do is provide guidance. She has to learn to be conservative.'

'Successor to the Howell empire?'

'I don't see why not. Do you?'

'Knowing Katy, she'll probably be as much in front of the camera as behind the scenes.'

'And that is exactly what I have to teach her not to do.'

'With the cane?'

'If necessary.'

'And when will she be too old for that?'

'I hope by then she will have changed.'

'And if she hasn't?'

'That bridge I will cross when I get there. Goodnight, Ali.'

'Night Jay.'

Alice lay back. Leaving the covers off she quietly stroked herself. 'Soon,' she whispered. 'Soon.'

Saturday galloped toward the pair, the day arriving all too soon. Both fraught with nerves they accompanied Jenny on a shopping expedition. That they thought to be preferable to sitting about waiting.

'While we're here,' announced the woman, 'we might as well get your school uniforms sorted.'

'I've already got one,' Alice imparted.

'Cheap?' questioned Jenny.

'He spent as little as possible, yes.'

'You will need two blazers, four skirts, five blouses and at least a dozen pairs of pants and socks. Then there's the PE kit.'

'That's a lot of money, Jenny,' Alice protested.

'You're one of the family now, Alice. And so we'll treat you like one.'

A tear welled in the girl's eye, Jenny quick to spot it. 'What's up, Alice, did I say something wrong?'

'No,' she whispered. 'No, it's just that I'm so bloody happy at the moment. I couldn't have hoped for things to turn out so well.'

'You could go back to Carters if you wanted to, you know.'

She shook her head. 'No, I want to be with Kate.'

'And I thought you had sense.'

Harry overwhelmed with bags, Jenny held up two five-pound notes. 'Look what I have left. No sense in taking them home. Pick yourselves a nice dress each.'

Even when with her own parents, Alice had never been treated so often or so well. She felt a touch guilty about her liaison with Jonathan. Jenny really didn't deserve that. In a couple of weeks, she thought, she'd be back at school. Maybe things would cool then.

Alice rummaged through the conventional winter warmers. Katy tapped her on the shoulder. 'No, Ali, a party dress.'

'What for?'

'A party, idiot.'

'What party, numskull?'

'The money is for a dress for the end of holiday party, that mum and dad will throw for us.'

A smile lit Alice's face. 'Really? Who else comes?'

'Invite who you want, Ali. But for Christ's sake pick something raunchy, and I'll guarantee you'll have the pick of the men.'

'I do hope you're going to keep your legs firmly together, Kate.'

'Can't dance like that.'

'You know what I mean.'

'You just stay off the booze and we'll both be all right.'

'Point taken. I'm sorry, Kate…'

'I know. Just be careful in future.'

Alice chose a tight fitting evening dress that hugged every curve and flared at the knees. A low back and deeply cut front permitted a generous view of her torso.

Kate slobbered over it in the fitting room. 'Oh, if only I could get away with something like that! I'd have every man in Lancashire on their knees.'

'You exaggerate, Kate.'

'Okay. Every man except Richard.'

'That's more like it. Honestly, do you think it suits?'

'I think it was made for you.'

Alice adopted the pose Jonathan had suggested. 'Do you fancy me, Kate?'

Kate grinned mischievous. 'Fancy you? I could eat you!' She grabbed Alice and buried her face in the girl's cleavage, licking alternately the upper slopes of each partially exposed breast. Alice giggled and fell back against the partition wall, Kate pinning her there.

'And when I'm done with your gorgeous titties I'm going to nibble your pussy,' promised the incorrigible Katy.

'Are you indeed?' came a voice from behind. Kate spun. Alice straightened. Jenny glared.

'Just horseplay, mother,' Kate said defensively.

'Horseplay? Not very ladylike, is it? Downright disgusting, I would say. Horseplay that warrants the horsewhip, I believe.' She took a handkerchief from her handbag and dabbed away the saliva from Alice's breasts. 'And I'm disappointed in you as well, girl. I thought you were more responsible.'

'I'm sorry, Jenny,' Alice apologised. 'I really am. We were just messing about, honest.'

'There's acceptable play, Ali, and there is unacceptable mischief. What you two were doing was distasteful to say the least.'

Harry packed the bags in the boot aware of an unfavourable air. He winked at Kate, the girl pulling a face. Jenny sat in front with the chauffeur, the girls taking to the back seat in silence.

Alice bent to Kate's ear and whispered. 'What happens now?'

Kate answered in the same fashion. 'Horsewhipped, me thinks.'

'But we're seeing Jonathan this evening.'

'Do you want to tell Jenny?'

'No. Do you think Jay will put it off again?'

'No. Do you?'

Alice stared out of the window and cursed. 'Oh Christ!'

'He won't help you, Alice,' Jenny remarked without turning.

The woman wasted no time. She ushered the girls into one of the three reception rooms and then went to collect the implement.

'She whacks really hard, does she?' asked Alice, her stomach executing somersaults.

'And how, Ali. That horsewhip has a six inch tail on it, and that bugger stings like hell.'

'So much for my big mouth, Kate.'

'So I owe you one now. I call that quits.'

'Are you going to glow with this?'

'Who knows?' Kate shrugged. 'Maybe.'

Jenny returned, three foot whip in hand. 'I haven't time to waste,' she stated. 'I have to bath, change and go out. What you two were doing was disgusting. I just hope and pray it was due to youthful exuberance, and you will grow out of it. But I am not prepared to have it going on under my roof. I don't know which of you is the perpetrator, or if you are both equally culpable. Whatever, it will cease. I do not wish to witness that sort of filth again. Am I understood?'

They nodded as one.

'Very well. Kate, you first. Skirt up. Pants down. Kneel on that chair and bend over the back of it.'

Feeling beneath her skirt, Kate lowered her panties. Kneeling, she reached for the leg brace, her butt thrust up and exceedingly stretched.

Harry, sensing a punishment session imminent, peeped through a window. Quietly smoking a cigarette, he lurked in a position able to witness everything.

Jenny lifted the skirt then pressed the horsewhip into Kate's lower buttocks, the flesh so tight it made little impression. She adjusted her stance, then brought the piece up and dealt a forceful cut. Kate gripped the chair brace tenaciously, waiting on the next.

Alice winced as that flexible brute whipped again, the flesh hurled from its path, the smack gut wrenching. She noted with trepidation the stripe the first incited, the mark on Kate's hip extreme. She studied her feet, unable to watch as the third lashed, Kate releasing a squeal. How did she manage it? All those years of blissful avoidance of corporal punishment dissolved with a fusillade of belt, cane, birch, and finally horsewhip. Perhaps the death of her parents had unearthed a deep resentment; a recalcitrance she failed to see.

Jenny applied the sixth stinger to Kate's rapidly warming bum, the stripes negotiating those broad buttocks hip to hip. Each volatile slice extricated a murmur of muted protest, Kate either providing a performance or genuinely suffering.

A mixture of fear and arousal nagged. Whilst an element dreaded her turn on the chair, another quickened to the formidable drubbing that Kate was being subjected to. Those old demons haunted, Alice still not able to accept or comprehend her bias.

Nine slashed discriminately, Kate beseeching. 'Please mummy, I'm sorry! How many more?'

Mummy? The name sounded incongruous under the circumstances, especially from the worldly Kate.

'As many as I deem fit, young lady,' came Jenny's sharp retort.

'Oh, bugger,' Kate growled as her mother struck again.

'For swearing,' Jenny admonished, slashing the girl's thighs three times in quick succession, checked her watch, then two more she added before saying, 'Think yourself lucky I haven't the time for a proper session. Alice, as an informally adopted daughter of this family, do you accept the discipline that goes with it?'

'Of course I do,' she replied as Kate carefully pulled up her panties.

'Then you will have no objection to accepting the same as Kate?'

'No objections, Jenny,' Alice said stoically. 'And for what it's worth, I think I deserve it.'

'Creep!' hissed Kate, and her mother rounded on her.

'What was that, Kate?' she demanded.

'Nothing, mother.'

Dropping her panties, Alice knelt on the chair. She flicked up her skirt and lay over the back.

Harry lit another cigarette. All eyes, he had seen Katy on many occasions. Alice kindled a new interest.

Jenny lashed Alice's rump with an impressive stroke, the tip whipping to the cleft, the tail slicing beyond. Face contorted the girl uttered no sound, the sting in her bottom unimaginable.

Entranced, Kate indisputably enjoyed the part of witness as much as participant. Blind to how torturous to the uninitiated corporal punishment could be, she feasted on the swish, smack, and movement of naked buttocks. Her own behind fired she indulged in the warming of Alice's to further that stimulation.

Alice's acquaintance with correction limited, she failed to comprehend the full benefits of masochism. Certain circumstances, she accepted, brought about that wonderful prodigy. But they were influences beyond her ken. She had not the acumen to control it, whatever it was. She simply begged it to visit, to linger and to transform.

Jenny's whip hurt like the tortures of hell. An explosion of misery that lingered until re-ignited by another sprinting incendiary. The whip ploughing her left buttock, the demonic attachment ripped into the right. Although determined to remain silent, the seventh proved too much as it slashed joint of buttocks and thighs. Alice squealed as that connection shocked, the smart remaining, burning, refusing to ease.

'The strap, Kate,' directed Jenny. 'The thick one. And be quick about it.'

As Kate returned, broad leather in hand, Alice climbed from the chair, a dozen fine welts embroidered on her petite backside.

Harry rubbed his crotch.

Jenny took the strap. Seizing Kate by the back of the neck she frogmarched her to the table. She pushed her down, hitched up the skirt and yanked down the pants. That striped and coloured bottom wobbling, Jenny raised the strap. She cracked it with gusto on those shivering cheeks. Kate yelped.

Without pause or compassion Jenny brought the leather in an arc and lashed her again, only two seconds between detonations. Alice followed the flight of strap with horror as it rose and swooped, the devastation appalling.

Jenny permitted no time for composure. She welted those buxom dunes without respite, the strength and rapidity of strokes too much even for Katy. The girl wriggled, writhed and squirmed. She kicked and attempted evasion. She yelled, cussed, and pleaded. All to no avail. Jenny, determined to quell her rebellious nature, kept that leather in motion, that backside taking on the deepest hue of crimson.

Sympathy exuded from Alice. She recognised the fearsome capability of that dense hide. Having been there she knew only too well the purgatory it instilled. She gazed paralysed at those buttocks in constant motion, the stain of discipline mottled and coating her rump from back to thigh.

It glowed all right, but Alice surmised Kate didn't enjoy it; each hearty slap Kate acknowledged with a howl, that trounced posterior and Kate at the end of their tether.

Jenny, still angry, tossed the leather aside. She hauled Kate to a standing position and snarled in her face, finger wagging. 'Any more out of you and I'll whip you in front of all the servants. And I'll do it on your bare backside. Do you hear me?'

Kate nodded, sullen. 'Yes mother.'

'Right. I'm going to get changed. I will expect you, both of you, to be on your best behaviour for the rest of the holidays. One indiscretion, and I mean *one* indiscretion, and I'll thrash you without compunction.'

'Yes mother,' replied a humbled Kate, her hands tentatively rubbing that sore behind.

'And that goes for you as well, Alice.'

'Of course, Jenny.'

Head purposely held high, Jenny left them to it.

'How's your bum, Kate?' Alice asked. 'Does it glow?'

Kate scowled at the open door. 'Get changed? Into what, a human being?' Alice's voice seemed to penetrate. 'You could fry your breakfast on it, Ali. How the hell am I going to take father's cane now?'

'More to the point, how are we going to explain the marks?'

'Easy. Lie.'

'And what happens when we get found out?'

'Depends on the fib.'

'I think we should tell the truth.'

'Oh you would, wouldn't you Ali? What do you think will happen? Father, mother caught us in a lesbian clinch and striped us for it. That is, if you recall, exactly why we are seeing father tonight. Oh we've learned our lesson, haven't we? He'll give us both extras. Don't forget, Ali, you get exactly what I do. That's what you wanted. Of course, you could always part your legs for him and get us both off the hook.'

'I don't think that would work, do you Kate?' Alice countered. 'Jay's not interested in me that way.'

'Of course he is, dolt. The only thing stopping him is your virginity and your age.'

'What do you mean?'

'If you were a little older and experienced he'd have been in there by now.'

'What's my age got to do with anything?'

'Simple, Ali. You're the same age as me so he'd feel like he was shagging his own daughter. That wouldn't suit his few morals. So Ali, Jay has to keep his dick in his pants for the time being.'

'Like I said, he's not interested,' Alice argued. 'He does see me as a daughter.'

Kate laughed.

'You have such a low opinion of him, don't you?'

'He's a man, and men are governed by their cocks.'

'So what do you want me to say to Jay? Regarding the stripes, I mean.'

'Own up, I suppose. You're right; he'll only ask mother and it'll be a repeat performance if we lie.'

At seven-thirty Alice crept up to her bedroom. She stripped, and replaced the conventional underwear with Jay's gift; the least she could do would be to electrify him.

They decided to face Jonathan together, to explain the reason for Jenny's lathering.

Kate knocked. Jonathan opened the door and beckoned her in. Both girls walked past him.

'What's this?' he asked. 'A deputation? There is no negotiation possible, I'm afraid.'

Alice spoke. 'We have something to tell you first,' she said.

'A confession? You want other offences to be taken into consideration. Caned for them now rather than later?'

'In a way, yes.'

'Now that is Alice Hussey, but I doubt it is Kate Howell. What did you do, Ali, cleanse her soul?'

'Unfair father.'

Jonathan smiled. 'Okay, own up then.'

'We were both punished by Jenny earlier this evening Jay,' Alice confessed.

'I see. What for and how?'

'While we were shopping this afternoon, Kate and I, er, we were excited, Jay, thrilled by our new party gowns, delighted by our uniforms. We were carried away.' Alice studied her feet, too embarrassed to continue.

'So what happened to warrant a punishment?'

'We did exactly what you are whacking us for tonight, father,' Kate told him.

'You've lost me.' Jonathan envisaged them naked and whipping each other in the shop.

'Just tomfoolery, father. I did something to Ali which I am totally ashamed of.'

'What did you do, Kate?'

'I licked her breasts.'

'In the shop?'

'In the changing booth. She had on this gorgeous gown. Her bosom was partially exposed. Ali joked whether I fancied her. I leapt on her. My fault entirely.'

Jonathan rubbed his jaw and shook his head. 'What am I going to do with you, Kate? How the hell am I going to curb that wild streak?'

'The jolly old stick, I suppose.'

'Don't be flippant.'

'Sorry. Nerves, father.'

'I don't think you've got any, Kate. None in your head and certainly none in your backside. How did your mother punish you?'

'A dozen stripes with the horsewhip. Oh, and an extra three for swearing. Oh, and a thoroughly good thrashing with the strap for flippancy.'

'And how's your bum now?'

'Sore,' she said, pouting. 'Very sore.'

'So the cane is going to be blue murder then.'

'It is anyway.'

'Well, I'm impressed by your honesty. Both of you. As far as I'm concerned you've been suitably punished for your extremes.' He paced slowly to the side, and then back again. 'In future keep that enthusiasm for one another within the confines of this house, and out of your mother's sight. I dare say you will get it out of your system eventually.'

'Are you condoning us, father?' Kate said hopefully.

'No Kate, but you will do what you want to. I'm not stupid enough to believe I can stop you. What I am saying, and keep on saying, is keep it private. Learn control, Kate. Learn to appear saintly even if you can't manage it in practice.'

'So are you still going to cane us?' she asked.

Jonathan lifted the rod from its shelf. He flexed it. 'Yes, Kate, I am.'

'Oh bother.'

'Wait outside please, Alice.'

The girl shut the door and pressed an ear to the wood. She heard Jonathan's voice. 'Bend over, Kate. Touch your toes. That's it, right over.'

Several seconds passed, Alice assuming Jay bared the target. She heard the dreaded slice of air and the awful

244

smack of rod on bum. Kate squealed. Alice swallowed hard.

How many was the question that hovered in both minds, Kate's backside fired and Alice absently rubbing hers in anticipation.

Ten seconds passed before the second thwacked noisily, the victim crying out, the howl almost a scream. Second thoughts tempted Alice. She could walk away. She didn't have to yield to the Howell method of discipline. She knew Jay would let her off.

How could she, though? Shirk her responsibilities? What sort of message would that send? Irksome as it seemed, she would have to go through with it.

Six had reduced Katy to a sobbing wretch – the girl who could joke about Stagnant's trouncing. Alice couldn't even begin to imagine how cruel that cane must be. She listened intently to the continuation of hostilities, poor Kate pleading for Jay to cease, the man seemingly impervious to those heartfelt cries.

The twelfth bit, Kate crying out amidst the tears and sniffles. Was that it? Ten seconds passed, Alice with heart in her mouth. *Whack!* The thirteenth. 'Aaaaaah!' seemed to pierce the door.

Alice clung to her own buttocks like a limpet, drawing the skirt up, fingers delving the flesh. How on earth was she going to take that?

Fourteen ripped into battered haunches, the wail mortifying.

She listened, hoping and praying the session would soon end. Fifteen slashed. 'Aaaah!'

Another traumatic pause. Sixteen. 'Aaaah!'

Heart pounding, Alice trembled. Seventeen. 'Pleeeeease, no more!'

Alice wiped her mouth. Her legs shook. Eighteen. Kate wailed.

Silence fell.

Jonathan's voice interrupted the quiet. 'Send Alice in please, Kate.'

She stepped back from the door, wanting to bolt. Mouth

dry she watched as Kate came out. Eyes bloodshot, tear tracks glistening, one hand clutching her rear, she quietly said, 'Your turn, Ali.'

Legs of jelly, barely feeling the floor beneath, Alice closed the door behind her. Ashen she faced Jonathan.

'You don't have to do this, Ali,' he said. 'You know that.'

'I do,' she heard herself reply.

'And you want exactly the same as Kate?'

'Of course.'

'As I said before, it's your bottom. Okay, bend over there please.' He pointed at the floor.

Alice touched shoes. Jonathan lifted the skirt and laid it over her back. He placed a hand on those sleek knickers. Gently he stroked her bottom. 'For me?' he asked.

Alice nodded.

'Thank you.' He slipped fingers inside the elastic and eased them over her flanks. 'Exquisite, Ali. Exquisite.' The drawers fell to the floor.

'One last chance.'

She shook her head.

'Very well.'

The cane rose, hovered for a split second and then accelerated towards her seat. Alice squeezed her eyelids shut and gripped her ankles. The cane struck with awesome power. For all its thickness and density it bent to blast her haunch, the pain defying description.

She straightened, fingers clawing at the furnace mauling her behind. Jaw tight, no utterance forthcoming, she gazed stricken at the ceiling.

'Changed your mind?' asked Jonathan.

'N-no,' Alice replied. 'N-not at all.'

'Then you had best return to your position, hadn't you? I don't want to have to start again.'

'Y-yes, sorry.' Buttocks tensing apprehensively, she noted with utter dread the shrill slice of air. That irresistible rod met with delicate yielding fleshy lower cheeks, instantly burrowing, jarring, pulverising all in its path. Alice could not contain the unadulterated agony. The jolt to her mind sickening, she spewed an abject yelp. The world at that moment seemed a hopeless place.

The inferno still raging, that interminable ten seconds suddenly seemed totally inadequate. The cane homed in, located unspoilt territory and devastated. Alice shrieked, her backside blazed, the horsewhip seeming like a tease in comparison.

Compassion rated second in Jonathan's preferences. Not a sadist as such, not a man to revel in another human being's misery, simply a man that revelled in cane on bare backside. Not one to seek excuse, but a draconian when reasons pressed. Jonathan would sooner have refrained from disciplining Alice. He would sooner have planted his cock, but Alice had insisted and the man dutifully obliged.

Cane livened lower rump, struck with the speed of a tornado, torched those flanks as if seared by lightning. Alice clenched fists, her teeth ground together so hard they hurt. The lower half of her posterior boiled. She uttered no sound, the vocal chords paralysed.

Jonathan regarded the result. Two broad red stripes rose from the pale cheeks, another etched, the fourth filled with colour.

He added a fifth mid-buttock, the scalded meat scurrying from the impact. Lungs in spasm Alice let loose a stifled cry. 'Uh, uh, uh!'

No smile lit the martinet's face. Grim, he pursued his business. The cane left its mark on upper quarters, the discomfort there grossly untenable.

Struggling to remain doubled, wishing she had kept her mouth shut, Alice quailed at the next. The rod slammed into taut upper reaches, the scorch amplified beyond all reason. All control decimated she rent the air with a squeal before spontaneously bursting into tears.

'Do you wish to continue, Ali?' enquired Jonathan.

'No,' she sobbed, 'of course I don't want to bloody continue. But I have to, don't I? Kate's wearing eighteen of your stripes, so I have to.'

'As you get older, Ali, you'll see matters in a different light. You'll come down off that high horse and step away from the moral field. Survival's what counts. You don't have to suffer this.'

'Who knows, Jay, it might even glow.'

In reply Jonathan caned her for the eighth time. 'Did that glow, Ali?' he pressed.

'N-n-no, J-Jay.' She shook her head, the hair tossed.

'How about this then?' He performed a downward slice of the rod, whipping the apex.

'Aaaah!' Alice straightened, hands clamped to those tormented cheeks. She staggered, tears cascading. 'Ah... oooh.' Face twisted in agony she stammered, 'Bu-bu-bugger. It won't stop st-stinging.'

Entertained by her frenetic dance, Jonathan idly flexed the rod. 'Do you know, Ali, you look as beautiful in hell as you do in heaven.'

'I w-wish compliments could ease the pain.'

Jonathan placed the rod on the desk, and turning Alice, placed a cool hand on that burning rump. Thoughtfully he rubbed, the welts thick and bloated beneath his fingertips. Alice sighed.

'Better?' he asked.

'Your touch is always welcomed,' she panted. 'I think it would take an iceberg to cool this fire, though.'

He stroked her thigh, then moved his fingers between her legs. There he fondled her sex. 'Is that better?'

'It's taking my mind off it.'

'Pity you're only halfway through.'

'How's it looking?'

'Your bum? Corrugated.'

'It feels skinned.'

'No, it's not that bad. Bad, but not that bad.'

'I know it's a punishment, but do you have to whack me quite so hard?'

'It is meant as a punishment and a deterrent. The idea is you behave rather than face this again. I firmly believe in the deterrent. If one is in the wrong then one should be prepared to face the music. I leave you in no doubt as to what to expect.

'Do you think me an ogre?'

'No Jay, I would agree with everything you say if it wasn't my bum on the receiving end.'

'So, what do you want to do?'

Alice bent over and touched her toes. 'It's not what I want, Jay, it's what I think is right.'

Her right haunch heavily embossed, Jonathan switched sides. Left-handed he provided an expert lesson in obedience. Kate, trying to construe the meaning of the lengthy silence, heard the emphatic slap of cane on naked butt. She noted Alice's anguished yelp, and with mixed feelings delved into her panties.

The cane slashed about the cleft and wrapped to the left haunch, fresh nerves assailed, gruelling torment dispensed. Alice sank deeper into the abyss of despair. The familiar and ominous hiss heralded the conclusion of those interim ten seconds. She nearly gagged as the rod bit, the slash of flesh disturbing.

Twelve down, six to go, ran through her distraught mind, but the next dislodged all concept of an end in sight. It chewed the sensitivity of buttock and thigh joint, already tormented by the whip. Alice heaved and choked, the torture exceeding her fears. Tears ran freely. She tossed her head in despair, hands wrung in distress.

Jonathan cut even lower, that considerable rod slicing trembling thighs, the smack formidable. Fingers groped at the hurt, grappling with the offensive trial laid there.

The man held that cane aloft. As those limbs returned to dangle ineffectually he urged it through an arc, to sweep into those poor cheeks mid-flank. Alice teetered, stumbled forward, one hand clawing at the grim furore raging in her haunch.

She breathed rapidly, her guts in turmoil, vision blurred by tears. Although the punishment crucified she still idolised the man. She would have done nigh on anything for him. Alice would have accepted fifty of those strokes had he said she deserved them. Such was her upbringing, her disposition, her loyalty. Jonathan had stolen her heart but had not fully realised the fact.

The cane raided mauled flesh, an end in sight. Mind

numbing it drove deep into scarlet rump, the thump solid and debilitating.

No glow. Pure hell.

She filled her lungs for the penultimate, a vile spoiling of upper haunches, the deep breath dispelled in a strained rasp.

She had to wait for the ultimate. The final blast of heat. The last stroke of retribution.

Jonathan examined, scrutinised the ladders of welts. He touched and smoothed the hot flesh. Finally he decided on a morsel that had not been marred.

He stepped back, Alice bracing herself. An American would have called it a humdinger, the English a scorcher. Whatever, the cut lifted Alice onto tiptoe, a branding iron slammed into her flesh. She rose with speed executing a frenetic dance, hands beneath her skirt, madly massaging, trying to assuage the fire.

She wriggled, face contorted whilst Jonathan placed the cane back on the shelf. 'Heptonstall,' he said, 'is a faculty with high results. They attain those by strict discipline. What you have just endured is a taste of what to expect should you not meet their expectations. And I'm afraid, Alice, what you will probably experience there anyway. Katy chose that hell on earth because you said you were attending next term. I agreed because the place may just sort her out. My advice, work hard and keep your head down. You might escape the worst that way.'

He faced the girl, Alice still rubbing the smart from the last stroke. 'I don't want to have to do that again, Alice. I really don't. If you can't resist carnal exploration with my daughter then ensure I don't see or hear of it.'

Countenance tearstained, Alice bent to retrieve her knickers, the movement causing further aggravation. She winced.

'Don't put those back on for a moment, Alice.'

He walked to the door, opened it and said to a waiting Kate, 'You can go. I wish to have words with Alice and I don't want you eavesdropping.'

He closed the door again and locked it. A warm smile

replacing the austerity Jonathan advanced, the girl puzzled. 'Now to tend your injuries, Ali. A dog licks his wounds, this one is going to lick yours.'

She shivered. Electricity buzzed through her groin. She forced a smile, teardrops glinting in those green pools.

Jonathan knelt before her and raised her skirt. He nibbled the curls of her pubic mound. 'Let's have that lovely arse, Ali. Permit me to ease your discomfort.'

Alice turned and tendered the whipped bottom, Jonathan's tongue cool and comforting. He traced the puffy stripes, licking from end to end. Alice settled to his attentions, happy that the lover had resurfaced, the disciplinarian usurped. She did not understand how a person could whip her so deplorably one minute, and make love to her the next. But she readily accepted the reversal.

'You've never been…?' he began.

'Never,' she answered, foreseeing the question.

'I wish Kate hadn't. I have a suspicion that she may be at it with one of my staff.'

'She hasn't said anything to me, Jay.'

'Watch that chauffeur. He's a Jack the lad. Thinks he's God's gift to the female race. The trouble is, the girls think he is as well.'

Alice picked that moment to confront him. 'Are you resisting me because of my age?' she asked.

'That does come into the equation, yes.'

'You don't have to, it would be perfectly legal,' she said hopefully, stating the obvious.

'I know it would, Ali,' he said patiently, 'just like what we've already done together is perfectly legal. But these matters have a habit of blowing up in your face.'

'So you're just fencing? You've no intention of going all the way.'

'I haven't said that. There was the other night when you were sick, but otherwise there always seems to be someone around.'

'We won't be disturbed now, will we? Jenny's out and Kate is sulking somewhere.'

'Just like that?'

'Spontaneity.'

'It'll hurt first time.'

Alice laughed.

'What's so funny?' demanded Jonathan.

'You,' she giggled, 'you idiot.' She showed him her backside. 'Hurt as much as that?'

'How about meeting me halfway?'

'What, just stick it in a little bit you mean?' she teased.

He shook his head, smiling. 'No,' he said carefully. 'I mean, you started with fellatio. So how about buggery as a next step?'

'You want my bottom?' she gasped. 'Shame on you, Jay. What do I get out of that?'

Jonathan licked his lips suggestively, Alice understanding his meaning.

'Oh, but it's still not the same as a wedge of flesh, is it?'

'Is that Ali speaking or Katy?'

'Ali of course.'

'Vulgarities do not maketh the woman, Ali.'

'Don't you like the tart? I thought all men coveted the tart.'

'Not this one.'

'So if I wore heavy mascara, and a short skirt and stockings with high heels, you wouldn't be interested?'

'I didn't say that.'

'Would you like that, Jay? Should I dress to kill?'

Jonathan unbuttoned her blouse. He lifted the bras over her breasts and filled his hands. 'How about *undressing* to kill?'

'It seems like you have that in hand, sir,' she sighed. 'They are in a very delicate position.'

'So they are. Now how about my proposal? Would you?'

'A deal, sir. You must know all about those. If I consent then I will expect a good and proper shafting come the end of hols party. I've procured a lovely dress for the loss of my virginity.'

'If the occasion permits, Ali.'

'Oh it must, sir. A deal's a deal.'

252

'Very well.'

She offered a hand. 'Shake on it, sir.'

Jonathan accepted.

'Good. Now how would the honourable Jay Howell like his bum served?' she asked cheekily.

'First a rubber and a dollop of Vaseline,' he said matter-of-factly.

Jonathan left the study and headed for the kitchen. There in a cupboard he found his grease.

'Finished?' asked Katy, Alice having had the foresight to cover herself.

'Not quite,' replied Alice.

'Bum sore?'

Alice nodded. 'Yours?'

'We'll compare marks later. Where's father gone?'

'To get a drink of water, I think,' Alice fibbed.

'What's he chatting about?'

'This and that. School, you know. That sort of thing.'

'Will you be much longer?'

'I don't know, Katy.'

She glanced to her right. 'He's coming back. See you later.'

No sooner had she flitted away again than Jonathan returned. 'Okay,' he said, his voice a little tight, the thought of what delights lay in store getting to him, 'turn around, young miss, I have something for you.'

Alice undid her blouse and slipping it off, tossed it onto the desk. She disposed of the bra and bent over the desk, legs parted.

Jonathan lifted the skirt. Top of the jar removed he greased a finger. Pulling her cheeks apart he spread the jelly, and as a final touch inserted the finger. Dropping trousers and pants he pulled back the foreskin of his willing erection, before dextrously sliding on the thick rubber shield.

He inspected the severely striped rump, erection jerking, scrotum tight about the balls. 'I won't deny it, Ali,' he whispered, 'a rigorously caned bottom does turn me on.'

'Perhaps I'll let you do it again then.'

'I couldn't do that to you for pleasure.'

'Not even if I wanted you to?'

'But the pain; you said yourself it crucified.'

'I'd go through it for you, Jay. Who knows, if it were done in a sexual way I might even enjoy it.'

'Glow, you mean?'

'Yes Jay. I've been there. I know it to be possible. I just have to work out how to control it.'

She felt his stiffness press to her anus, then grimaced as the puckered little entrance gave. Alice dug her nails into the desktop leather as he penetrated, broken glass seeming to lacerate.

A knock on the door terminated their dream. 'What!' bellowed Jonathan.

'It's me, father, Katy. Mother's on the phone.'

'What does she want, Kate?' he yelled, discarding the rubber and hauling up his pants and trousers.

'I don't know, do I? I didn't give her the third degree you know.'

'Well go and bloody ask.' He addressed Alice. 'Sorry about this, Ali. Best get your togs on. Some other time, I'm afraid.'

'I won't hold my breath, Jay.'

'Dad!'

'Coming!'

'Mum has broken down. Well she hasn't personally, the car has. Can you pick her up?'

Jonathan opened the door. 'Is she still on the phone?'

'Yes.'

He stomped past.

'He looks all hot and bothered, Ali,' Kate said. 'What you two been up to in here?'

'Very little.' Alice had difficulty in concealing the disappointment.

'Oh, did I spoil something? Had you finally got father to take an interest in you? Sorry, Ali.'

Alice pushed her aside. 'Grow up, Kate!' she snapped.

Kate trotted after the strutting redhead. She followed her up to Alice's bedroom where the girl rounded on her.

'What do you want now?'

'Oooh, we are in a mood, aren't we? All hot and horny, were you? Had it in, did he? Have you joined the ranks of the initiated now?'

'No I haven't, Kate.'

'So that's it – he didn't get that far. How far did he get, Ali?'

'Can't you think of anything else?'

'Seems you can't.'

'Kate, we weren't doing anything. Now piss off!'

'Wanna see your marks, Ali. Katy wanna compare notes. You said you would.'

'If I do, will you leave me alone?'

'Of course, if that's what you really want.'

'It is.'

Katy pushed by. 'Shut the door then, Ali. Best lock it too. We don't want another whacking, do we?'

Alice complied, then lay facedown on the bed. Carefully Kate lifted the skirt and eased down the French knickers. 'Wear these for father, did you?'

'They're comfortable.'

'Ooooh… I think your welts are bigger than mine. What a state. Fancy volunteering for that. I bet that really hurt.'

'It did.'

'So Jay doesn't love his Ali after all.'

'I never said he did.'

Kate ran a finger the length of a particularly thick stripe, the discoloration closing on purple. Alice winced. 'Sore?'

'Of course it's bloody sore, Kate. I've been whipped, haven't I?'

'I hope you've learned a lesson here, Ali. Never put your hand up for anything.'

Kate traced the buttock division. 'What's this, Ali?'

'What's what?'

'It's greasy.'

Alice's stomach lurched. 'What is, Kate?'

Kate put the finger to her nose. 'You dirty cow!' she squealed.

Rolling onto her back, Alice glared.

'No good you giving me dirty looks. He's had it up your arse, hasn't he?'

Alice frantically tried to conjure an excuse. Nothing would come to mind.

'The Fifth Amendment won't help, either,' Kate went on exuberantly. 'Dear father has buggered you, hasn't he?'

'As it happens, miss know it all, he hasn't actually,' Alice denied haughtily.

Kate held up the finger. 'What's this for then, got trouble shitting, have you?'

'Don't be so coarse.'

'Ah!' The bulb lit in Kate's mind. 'That explains "What!" doesn't it? Foiled at the final hurdle. Poor father. Poor Ali. Did Katy interrupt a good old anal rogering?'

Alice mumbled inaudibly.

'What was that, Ali?'

'Yes!' she spat.

'I don't know why you're so secretive about it. I told you I don't mind.'

'How can you not mind? He's your father, for Christ's sake. He's your mother's husband.'

'So if you feel so guilty, why do it?'

'Because, Katy, I can't help myself. I know it's wrong, but I want him so bad. Katy, I'm prepared to let him do anything if it means I can be with him.'

'Oh dear.' Kate shook her head doubtfully. 'Anything?'

'Yes,' Alice insisted. 'I even said he could cane me again if he wanted to.'

'Oh, you have got it bad, haven't you? Sorry I had to interrupt you. If mother hadn't rung I would have left you to it. So what did father say about a repeat of hostilities to your bum, then?'

'He objected. Said he couldn't get pleasure out of hurting me.'

'And you believe him?'

'Of course I do.'

'It's your bum, Ali. If Harry wanted to do that to me I'd tell him to take a short walk off a long pier.'

'And you like it.'

'Not that, I don't. Look.' She lifted her skirt. No panties beneath, Alice winced at the punishment dished out.

'Oh, they look sore.'

'Yours are worse.'

'I won't be sitting today, that's for sure.'

'Or tomorrow, either.'

'What am I going to do, Kate?'

'Ignore your head, Ali. Do what your heart says.'

'And you really don't mind?'

'I don't. Just don't let mother catch you. She's quite capable of inflicting worse than that.'

'Oh Kate, I need to sort my feelings out. Being here has helped. Perhaps I was looking for a miracle. It isn't going to be that easy. Maybe things will cool after this holiday period. Maybe I'll get over Jay.'

'Absence makes the heart grow fonder, Ali.'

'I hope not. For all our sakes, I hope not.'

Opportunity did not occasion itself again. The day of the party arrived, Katy and Jenny having spent days organising the event.

'So who is coming then?' enquired Alice, fascinated.

'A house full, Ali,' Kate told her. 'Family. Friends. Half the village and even some old faces from Carters.'

'Not Uncle Richard, I hope.'

'We sent him a special invitation. Even offered Harry to collect him. But it would seem the prospect of enjoying himself was too much. He declined.'

'You didn't really ask him, did you?'

'What do you think, idiot?'

'Who from Carters?'

'Stagnant. Attila the Hun. Geriatric Jenkins and Yankee do your flies up.'

'Stop pissing about Kate.'

'Jane. Kathy. Er, Pauline. Janet. Oh, loads.'

'Boys?'

'Do I detect an interest there?'

'Course I'm interested. I bet I end up the wallflower

though.'

'I'll take you up on that. What stake do you want to wager?'

'What can you afford, Kate?'

'I'll tell you what. If I'm right you get six strokes. If I'm wrong the reverse.'

'Jay's cane?'

'If you can take it.'

'You'll be taking it, Kate. Not me.'

'We'll see.'

The party set for eight, the girls began preparation at five-thirty. Katy bathed while Alice attended and then they switched.

Alice stepped naked into the tub. 'That bum was made for whacking, Ali,' Kate mused.

'I'll happily trade it for one that wasn't.'

Kate reached out and stroked a cheek. 'So soft. So luxurious.' She prodded. 'So firm. Lucky bitch.'

'The way you're headed, Kate, yours will end up all calloused and scarred.'

'Yeah, I know. And I'll end up with a hole a builder can mix his cement in. I've heard it all before.'

She watched Alice settle beneath the foam. 'You'll knock 'em dead tonight, gel. They'll be queuing to dance, salivating over your every move.'

'To be wanted, Kate, that would be nice.' Alice raised a hand. 'I know you want me, and I know I'm part of the family. But to be in demand, that would be something else.'

'Don't you go giving it away tonight,' Kate warned. 'You make them earn it.'

'Them? This is Alice Hussey, not Kate Howell, you know.'

'Sod!'

Jenny applied their make-up, two girls partially transformed into alluring women. The gowns completed the conversion. Kate in a gold dress with plunging neckline and billowing skirt, Ali in her black number. Together they received the arrivals.

Comments abounded with regard to their outstanding beauty. Both heads grew steadily.

In continual demand they danced, the partners changing constantly. Eyes initially for Jonathan, Alice parried the many requests for her company and primal offers for her body. She quickly learned diplomacy and how to rebuff with tact and humour.

Then from the crowd stepped a young man she could not ignore. Tall, strapping and intriguingly handsome, he took her hand and kissed the back of it.

'Would you do me the great honour of allowing me this dance?' he asked, voice husky.

Alice melted. 'That would be lovely.'

The music switched at that point from rapid beat to waltz. He took her in his arms and swept her off her feet.

'Coincidence,' she remarked, as they drifted about the floor.

'You have the better of me,' he replied, accent strong.

'The music. Suddenly it's a waltz.'

'Ah yes. I'm afraid I am not proficient with the new music. I am the old fashioned man, if you like.'

'Is that the only reason?'

'You have, how you say? sussed me. A beautiful woman such as yourself should be held close. Can you blame me for contriving that?'

'So how did you contrive that?'

'I paid the band, of course.'

'Am I really worth that?'

'Five shillings? But of course.' The smile warned of the untruth.

'You're not English, are you?'

'No. Italian. I come from the vineyards of the north. Tuscany. I have been fermented like a good wine. Rich, tasteful and full bodied'

'I'm more like a stout, myself. Dark, strong headed, with a bite.'

'I have tried this drink. Guinness, I believe. It has hidden depths.'

'Are you rich?'

'Everything is relative. I have sufficient means. I could retire tomorrow.'

'How old are you then?'

'Twenty-six. And yourself?'

'What do you think?'

'Nineteen. Twenty, perhaps.'

'You are very observant.'

The waltz finished. 'Champagne. You must share a bottle with me.'

'That's French, surely.'

'I come from the Tuscany region, that doesn't mean I have to drink the wine.'

'I don't think we have any.'

'I have.'

He walked her to a table, arm about her waist, a young man from the village stepping in front of them. 'Can I have this dance, Alice?' he asked awkwardly.

'Sorry, I need a break,' she answered politely. 'I've been dancing solid for nearly two hours now.'

'Later perhaps?'

'Of course.'

'Thank you,' the Italian tendered.

'Why?'

'Having found you I don't wish to lose you quite so quickly.'

'You promised me champagne.'

'And there it is.' He waved an arm indicating a table, complete with magnum.

Two glasses poured, he offered one to Alice. 'My name is Giulio,' he told her. 'Giulio Di Stasio.'

'And if you didn't know, I'm Alice Hussey.'

'Drink, Alice Hussey, enjoy the fragrance of Southern France.'

'It sounds like you've been there.'

'I have. And you?'

'No further than Blackpool, I'm afraid. What brings you to England, Giulio?'

'Some business. Some pleasure. I have found both.'

He topped up their glasses.

'What business are you in?'

'Publishing.'

Alice drew a conclusion. 'You are an associate of Jonathan?'

'I am.' Expression inquisitive, he asked, 'Do you know what he prints?'

'I haven't actually seen any as yet.'

'But you do know of his subject?'

Alice nodded.

'Have you ever been tempted to pose?'

'I haven't been asked.'

'You would make a wonderful model.' Giulio plucked a card from his breast pocket and offered it to Alice. 'Should you ever decide to, then please allow me first refusal.'

'You'd refuse me?'

'A phrase, that is all.'

'Tell me, Giulio, how much would that pay?'

'That would depend.'

'Depend on what?'

'On what you would be prepared to do.'

The drink already affecting her, Alice leaned forward. 'What if I was to model cane stripes in the pillory without a stitch on?'

Giulio lifted an eyebrow. 'That, with a figure like yours and your youth and beauty, would be worth a princely sum.'

'What's a princely sum?'

He smiled, oozing charm. 'If I was the one to impress your delectable rear, then I think we could be looking at as much as a hundred pounds.'

Alice beamed. 'That's an absolute fortune.'

He took her hand in his and stared into those green eyes. 'If you wished to spend a weekend with me then perhaps I could increase that further.'

'What are you suggesting, Giulio?'

'Nothing improper, I assure you. Your company alone would merit cosseting.'

Just then Kate interrupted the dalliance. She plonked

her behind heavily in a chair. 'Who's this then, Ali?' she demanded. 'Who's this gorgeous hunk of, if I'm not mistaken, European manhood?'

'Sod off, Kate.'

'Charming. It's one thing hooking him, Ali. Now you've got to land him.'

'This is my friend Kate, Giulio. Commonly known as the pain.'

The man offered a hand. 'I was told the English woman is outrageously beautiful. You, Kate, are both. Outrageous and beautiful.'

'Aren't I always, Giulio. How's the wife these days?'

The man laughed. 'Katy, you are as always the supreme bitch.'

Incredulous, Alice asked. 'You know each other?'

'Giulio has been defrauding father for years. He went to charm school and passed with credits. In fact, they offered him a job. How near to your bed have you managed to draw Alice, Giulio?'

'You pierce my heart with your accusations, Katy. You know I am not like that. I come from an honourable family. I only speak what is in my heart.'

Kate leaned forward and whispered to Alice. 'Ask him about that mole on his left buttock.'

'I do not have the mole on my buttock – left or right,' assured Giulio.

'Ask him if he's circumcised,' Kate went on, unperturbed, 'he is.'

'Take no notice of Kate. She only seeks to annoy me as usual.'

'Have you told him how old you are, Ali?'

Alice shot Kate a warning glance. 'I have told Giulio,' she said adamantly, 'I'm nineteen.'

'Nineteen? Good grief, Ali. How can you tell such fibs?'

'Katy!'

'She's twenty-two if she's a day, Giulio. Eternal youth, eh?'

'Two years older than you, Katy?' Giulio grinned.

'Have to go, got guests to see to.' Kate left, a trifle

flushed.

'That one has been trying to seduce me since coming out of nappies,' Giulio mused. 'She tells me she is twenty but I check. She is not. Now, Alice, where were we?'

'At your house, I believe.'

'Think it over. Ring me if you want to pose. We'll arrange something. Now, more to drink?' He lifted the bottle and refilled Alice's glass.

Well on the way to inebriation, Alice enquired, 'That mole, does it exist?'

'Would you like me to prove it?'

She giggled. 'Drop your trousers here, you mean?'

'If I remember correctly, there is a gazebo in the garden. I could demonstrate my innocence there.'

'Oh, I don't know Giulio, I might get carried away.'

'And you think that would upset me?'

'Shall we see?'

Giulio took her by the hand, the pair leaving the party via the French windows. The night air humid they strolled to the gazebo, some hundred yards from the house.

There he cupped Alice's face, and gazing into her eyes, he asked, 'The truth Alice, how old are you?'

'Twenty next month, Giulio,' she answered. 'I became friends with Kate through her father. I know she's young but she is good company.'

'That I wouldn't disagree with.' He kissed her. No tentative exploration; his lips pressed to hers, Alice readily responding. Enraptured she gave herself fully for the first time.

'Your lips are like the cherry blossom, Alice,' he praised, drawing breath. 'Exquisitely soft. Beautifully presented. Full of promise for the coming summer.'

'And yours, Giulio, are experienced.'

He resumed the clinch, then lowered those attentive lips to kiss her jaw, neck and shoulder. She held him, her arms about his neck as he investigated even lower. She felt his hot breath between her breasts and those warm lips teasing her there.

His hands eased the straps from her shoulders, Alice

not resisting. Slowly he peeled the fabric from her bosom, those shapely orbs exposed.

'Perfect,' he sighed, he fondled. 'So firm. Such a delectable shape.' He bent to her, nuzzling into the gap, and kissed one then the other. Alice ruffled his dark curls, indulging in every second.

His mouth alighted on a nipple. He toyed, licked and nibbled. Alice sighed.

Their lovemaking more animated, Giulio sought her shapely bottom, fondling those pronounced cheeks through the flimsy material. All the while he remained heedful of her breasts.

Rising from those succulent fruits he asked sensuously, 'Would you not care to explore too?'

Snatched from self-gratification Alice unbuttoned his shirt, fingers trembling. A tanned and muscular chest met with the first foray. Hands stroking, she touched that with her lips, the taste of man sweet.

A gentle pressure applied, Giulio guided her down, Alice caressing, petting to the trouser waistband. Gazing longingly up at him she knelt, her body naked to the waist.

Nervous, tense, elated, she released the belt and then the fly. The trousers fell, revealing the skimpiest underpants she could imagine. She breathed deeply, and expelled it hesitantly.

'It is keen,' Giulio declared, to explain the prominence lurking behind the lustrous pouch. 'And who can blame it?' he added.

Unsure through the haze of alcohol, Alice froze.

'It begs release, Alice,' he quietly coaxed. 'It craves your touch, your passionate affection.'

Hands rose. Fingers curled within the elastic. Alice urged the pants down, those gliding over narrow hips, the totem slowly revealed.

'See Alice, my penis salutes your beauty.'

'It is impressive, Giulio.' Her mouth felt dry with tension. 'I've never seen one so thick.'

'Once experienced, never forgotten.'

She grasped the stem, feasting on its girth. Closing the

gap she kissed the tip, Giulio surprised, enthralled. Circumcised, she encompassed it without forethought, lips stretched. She heard the man's grunt of appreciation and began the manipulation Jonathan had taught her.

'Oh, Alice,' Giulio managed. 'I never expected you to… I never in my wildest dreams thought you would please me in such a manner.'

Alice did not reply. She suckled and licked. The member lodged firmly, her mouth barely capable.

She fondled his testis, feeling the drawn sac, investigating the pods within. Giulio hovered in a world of his own, a blissful province.

She drew him to the edge; his balls prepared to express their gratitude, she released the inflamed erection. Giulio staggered. He gripped his piece, prepared to finish the job, but Alice deterred him. She took his hand and pulled him to a slatted bench. There she wriggled the dress over inspiring hips, to offer her near naked form.

Giulio shook his head. 'Staggering,' he opined. 'Simply staggering.'

He knelt. Savouring the plunging green laced panties, the mist of pubis tantalising, he reached about those hips, fingers sampling the resistance of nubile bottom.

Digits aroused her before locating the lace and facilitating the removal of that guardian cloth. He fell urgently upon the soft curls and nibbled the mound, teeth biting, tongue caressing, Alice enraptured.

Guided, she lay on the bench, legs wide, feet resting on Giulio's shoulders. Having descended the mound, not losing contact, he raked her vulva, the tongue teasing, inciting, throwing her into euphoric convulsions. He sank that probe, warm and wet, parting the pussy lips, stirring an onslaught of lubricating juices, Alice high on adrenaline.

She tugged her hair. She clawed the air. Back arched she clutched at her breasts, fingers gouging, squeezing. Expression concentrated, she pulled at the nipples. Finger and thumb tweaked, those teats attaining a supreme erection.

The well dipped and tasted, Giulio applied pressure to

the clitoris, Alice rapidly responding to the persuasion. Her body heaved. She grasped his head and holding him there to the last throw of orgasm, cried out her jubilation.

Both beyond recall, Giulio rose. Holding her calves he pressed his erection to the vaginal entrance. Alice unsure, hesitated on the admission of her true condition. She eyed that formidable length, and then closed her eyes, deciding on silence.

'Part yourself,' she heard him whisper. Only wishing to feel a man within, she reached down and pulled aside her lips. His hungry cock poised at the gates, tucked between her fingers.

He pressed, the burrow giving. Alice's expectant expression turned to anguish. Pain ripped through her vagina. She cried out, a hand frantically waved, hoping to stop him. Giulio didn't notice. He pressed home, the hymen tearing. Alice screamed.

'What is it?' the man asked, perplexed.

'You fucking swine!' roared in his ear, and thrown clear he received a jarring blow to the cheek, sending him sprawling. Stunned, Giulio shook his head, the moonlit shadow of Jonathan washing over him.

'What?' he begged, arms spread in supplication.

'What sort of trash are you, Giulio?' Jonathan demanded furiously. 'What sort of gutter rubbish seduces a virgin of her age?'

'Virgin? She never said she was a virgin. And what age? Alice is twenty.'

'And you believe that?' Jonathan's tone derided. 'Isn't it bad enough that I found you with my daughter? I should have killed you then.'

The man shook, overcome with terror. 'What are you going to do, Jonathan?'

'You have five seconds to get your Latin arse out of here,' Jonathan fumed.

'But my clothes!'

'Four seconds.'

Giulio grabbed what he could and ran, Jonathan planting a footprint on his bare backside as he sprinted past. Alice noted the mole on his left buttock.

Sitting, Jonathan put an arm around her and hugged the girl tight. 'What a way to lose your virginity.'

'I'm sorry, Jay. I could blame the drink. I could blame Giulio for leading me on. But the simple truth of the matter is, I'm a tart. Ever since mother and father died I've been engrossed with sex. It was only a matter of time before this happened.'

'Perhaps you are still reeling from the loss. Missing that love and attention.'

'Don't make excuses for me Jay. I know what I am.'

'I'll get you a blanket.'

'No Jay, don't leave me, please. Cuddle me.'

Jonathan collected her up and sat her on his lap. There he held her, a paternal replacement.

'What happened with Giulio and Katy?'

'I wouldn't say he seduced her. More likely Kate seduced him. I found them together. Naked. Whether he did or didn't I will never know for sure. I gave him a thorough hiding and threw him out. His father rang me a week later begging me to forgive him. I've known Flavio for years. We are good friends. For his sake I did forgive Giulio. I guess I knew he wasn't a hundred percent to blame, and I couldn't afford to lose the business. Wrong reasons.'

'And what about Katy?'

'I gave her such a thrashing. The poor cow couldn't sit for a week after.'

'Perhaps that's what I deserve.'

'Do you honestly think it would hurt more than what's happened?'

'Probably not.'

'Let it go, then.'

Jonathan held her so for nigh on an hour, before helping her dress and seeing her back to the house. And by that time if anything, Alice had fallen further beneath his spell.

To be continued...

More exciting titles available from Chimera

All **Chimera** titles are available from your local bookshop or newsagent, or direct from our mail order department. Please send your order with your credit card details, a cheque or postal order (made payable to *Chimera Publishing Ltd*) to: **Chimera Publishing Ltd., Readers' Services, PO Box 152, Waterlooville, Hants, PO8 9FS**. Or call our **24 hour telephone/fax credit card hotline: +44 (0)23 92 783037** (Visa, Mastercard, Switch, JCB and Solo only).

To order, send: Title, author, ISBN number and price for each book ordered, your full name and address, cheque or postal order for the total amount, and include the following for postage and packing:
UK and BFPO: £1.00 for the first book, and 50p for each additional book to a maximum of £3.50.
Overseas and Eire: £2.00 for the first book, £1.00 for the second and 50p for each additional book.

*Titles £5.99. **All others (latest releases) £6.99**

For a copy of our free catalogue please write to:

Chimera Publishing Ltd
Readers' Services
PO Box 152
Waterlooville
Hants
PO8 9FS

or email us at:
sales@chimerabooks.co.uk

or purchase from our range of superb titles at:
www.chimerabooks.co.uk

Sales and Distribution in the USA and Canada

Client Distribution Services, Inc
193 Edwards Drive
Jackson
TN 38301
USA
(800) 343 4499

Sales and Distribution in Australia

Dennis Jones & Associates Pty Ltd
19a Michellan Ct
Bayswater
Victoria
Australia 3153